Praise for *The Tangleroot Palace*

A *Publishers Weekly* Top-10 SF, Fantasy & Horror
2021 Upcoming Title

★ "Liu (the Monstress series) charms with this spellbinding collection of six short stories and one novella. The standouts are 'The Briar and the Rose,' a darkly fascinating retelling of 'Sleeping Beauty,' in which a female duelist discovers her witch employer is living in the stolen body of Princess Rose, and helps Rose to regain it; and 'Call Her Savage,' a steampunk western set during the Opium Wars and following half-Chinese antiheroine Lady Marshal as she struggles to be the hero others need her to be. Also of note are the haunting and eerie, 'Sympathy for the Bones'; 'The Last Dignity of Man,' about a would-be supervillain who realizes he must be his own superman; and two stories set in the world of Liu's Dirk & Steele paranormal romance series: the atmospheric historical fantasy, 'Where the Heart Lives,' which serves as a prequel to the series, and the dystopian 'After the Blood,' about Amish vampires, set in the series's future. The title novella offers a more standard secondary world fantasy, about a runaway princess drawn to an enchanted forest, but uses this familiar plot to probe the character's feelings of being trapped. Liu's mastery of so many different subgenres astounds, and her ear for language carries each story forward on gorgeously crafted sentences. This is a must-read."
—*Publishers Weekly*, starred review

★ "A collection of short stories exploring the emotional complexity, diverse physicality, and layered sexuality of resourceful women. . . . The only drawback to these seven stories is that readers will want far more time in each world."
—*Kirkus*, starred review

"*The Tangleroot Palace* is charming and ruthless. Tales that feel new yet grounded in the infinitely ancient, a mythology for the coming age."
—Angela Slatter, author of *The Bitterwood Bible*

"This is a superb collection from start to finish. Mysterious, beautiful and strange, harsh and charming, it fires the emotional palate."
—Charles de Lint, author of the Newford series

"Vivid writing that lights up my brain. Evocative settings. Memorable characters engaged in dark struggles. When I read Marjorie Liu's stories, I know I'm in the hands of a master."
—Carrie Vaughn, author of the Kitty Norville series

"Ferociously inventive, deliciously eerie, *The Tangleroot Palace* both chills and enchants. Don't be afraid: Liu's elegantly artful stories will coil around you, devour you, and you won't even mind being consumed."
 —Shana Abé, *New York Times*, *USA Today*, and *Wall Street Journal* bestselling author

"Some authors excel at one thing; others can do it all. Whether it's fairy tales or superheroes or the post-apocalypse, Liu always delivers, and with her own unique spin."
 —Marie Brennan, author of the Memoirs of Lady Trent series

"Rich and evocative tales with just the right amount of bite."
 —Kelley Armstrong, author of *Bitten*

5/5 Stars. "Each tale brought something beautiful and totally original to the table and I truly felt completely immersed in every sentence Liu wrote."
—*A Series of Various Events*

"Readers who love urban fantasies like those of Charlaine Harris or Kim Harrison will relish Marjorie M. Liu."
—*Midwest Book Review*

"Liu's books are kick-ass reads."
—Kelley Armstrong, *New York Times* bestselling author of *Bitten*

"Superlative."
—*The Miami Herald*

THE TANGLEROOT PALACE
MARJORIE LIU

Also by Marjorie Liu

A Taste of Crimson (2006)
X-Men: Dark Mirror (2005)

The Dirk & Steele series
Tiger Eye (2005)
Within the Flames (2005)
Shadow Touch (2006)
Red Heart Jade (2006)
Eye of Heaven (2006)
Soul Song (2007)
The Last Twilight (2008)
The Wild Road (2008)
The Fire King (2009)
The Dark of Dreams (2010)

Hunter Kiss series
The Iron Hunt (2008)
Darkness Calls (2009)
Inked (2010)
A Wild Light (2010)
The Silver Voice (2011)
The Mortal Bone (2011)
The Labyrinth of Stars (2014)

The Monstress graphic novel series with Sana Takeda
Vol. 1: Awakening (2016)
Vol. 2: The Blood (2017)
Vol. 3: Haven (2018)
Vol. 4: The Chosen (2019)
Vol. 5: Warchild (2020)

THE TANGLEROOT PALACE

MARJORIE LIU

TACHYON

SAN FRANCISCO

Introduction copyright © 2021 by Marjorie Liu
Cover art and illustrations copyright © 2020 by Sana Takeda
Interior and cover design by Elizabeth Story
Author photo copyright © 2020 by Nina Subin

Tachyon Publications LLC
1459 18th Street #139
San Francisco, CA 94107
415.285.5615
www.tachyonpublications.com
tachyon@tachyonpublications.com

Series Editor: Jacob Weisman
Project Editor: Jaymee Goh

Print ISBN 13: 978-1-61696-352-1
Digital ISBN: 978-1-61696-353-8

Printed in the United States by Versa Press, Inc.
First Edition: 2021
9 8 7 6 5 4 3 2 1

CONTENTS

INTRODUCTION

Greetings, friends.

I started writing this introduction when the COVID-19 pandemic was just beginning to unfold. An early adopter of its seriousness, I was living in Japan, close to the epicenter—and it was strange and surreal watching the societal threads, what we take for granted, pull apart bit by bit. Now, months later, I've returned to finish this introduction—and while I'd like to say the intervening time has given me a new perspective around my work, the only shift for me has been a deeper understanding of the limits of human imagination—including mine.

That said, here we are, together—and here, before you, are fragments of my imagination, sometimes limited, sometimes not. I've never been someone who lingers over my past work. I am very much a creature of the present. When I write, I live for the moment, passing through a story, inhabiting the skin of the characters—and when that story is done, so am I.

But I mean, **done**. With some rare exceptions, I have almost no recall over the content of my previous work, whether it's a novel, short story, or comic. Broad strokes, yes. I can say, "There's a merman! A gargoyle! A tiger shape-shifter!" But after that, my memory skids right off the road.

Even now, as I write this, I keep trying to test myself by looking at the titles of my novels, and it's dire, folks. I honestly don't know what the hell I've done these past seventeen years, except that apparently, I wrote a lot of words.

This amnesia was not some surprise. For years I've thought about why this happens, why the wall goes up after I write "the end." I asked a friend once, and she commented offhand that perhaps writing is like channeling a spirit in a prolonged séance—the spirit moves through me—but it's not as if I want it hanging around when I'm done talking. I send away that which no longer serves me—and move on to the next conversation.

Which is a nice and tidy way of thinking about it, but one could just as easily argue that I'm phobic when it comes to introspection. Remembering my work would require remembering *me*—and unfortunately, that's its own challenge.

But, anyway, that's a long way of saying that when I was approached regarding this collection, I had a hard time remembering what short fiction I had written that could actually fill a book. The answer, I realized in short order, was quite a lot. Nor is this collection entirely complete—there are a small handful of stories still floating around in other anthologies—but this an excellent overview of what happens when one never says no to offers of work.

With one exception, all the stories contained herein were written over an eight-year period or so, while I was pounding out paranormal romance novels and urban fantasies—and working for Marvel Comics, as perhaps the first woman of color writing for them. These are the stories of my twenties and very early thirties, slices of prose from a formative decade when I was still figuring things out (an ongoing process, I assure you), produced between crushing deadlines, driven less by ideas and more by emotions. They're time capsules, each one capturing a different stage of me, who I was, who I was becoming. Those are also the years when I was living in the Midwest, in the center of a forest—an impenetrable, tangled forest where every night the coyotes would howl, a forest where I never set foot because I never felt invited. But I had forgotten that, too—and I'm somewhat amused that it took me reading these stories to remember what it felt like to live in the middle of that forest—and to see how persistently those trees entered (and still enter) my work.

These seven stories are not presented in the order they were written, and some of them have been lightly (and not so lightly) edited. I know, I know . . . but I couldn't help myself! Don't ever let a writer, after more than a decade away from a story, have access to it again—they'll compulsively bring their new selves to the page and start renovating. Still, these are more or less the same as they were, tales about warrior women and runaway princesses; ordinary girls battling faery queens; a post-pandemic apocalyptic tale of an Amish vampire and the young woman who loves him; a teen who uses dolls to kill; even a depressed tech billionaire with some superhero identity issues. I look over them now and see the common threads—a longing for home, friendship, love—characters often driven by a weary hope in the possibility of something good.

Hope in the possibility of something good—even the tiniest, most wee little good—is sometimes all we've got. And that hope is never unavailable to us, even if seems far away or lost entirely. Hope is the driving force of these stories before you.

By the time you read this, who knows where we'll be—hopefully healthy, hopefully safe with our loved ones, hopefully figuring out our lives and making what we can of them, as always. Under the best and worst of circumstances, that's the aspirational baseline—to hope for a better tomorrow, to wake up each day with a little resolve, a little resilience, and simply try for *something*.

Easier said than done, right?

But I have this simple philosophy that's always served me well: "If you don't ask, the answer is always *no*."

It applies to everything in life, really—whether it's a job opportunity or something as nebulous as a dream. If you don't ask life for a possibility, if you don't dwell in possibilities, if you don't *hope*, the answer is always no.

And so I say, if you're reading this and going through hard times, try to dwell in the possibility of a better tomorrow, no matter how impossible it seems.

Ask the universe a question, see what happens. I hope—see, there it is again—I hope your adventure is beautiful.

—Marjorie Liu
August 2020

SYMPATHY FOR THE BONES

THE FUNERAL WAS IN A BAD PLACE, but Martha Bromes never did much care about such things, and so she put her husband into a hole at Cutter's, and we as her family had to march up the long stone track into the hills to find the damn spot, because the only decent bits of earth in all that place were far deep in the forest, high into the darkness. Rock, everywhere else, and cairns were no good for the dead. The animals were too smart. Might find a piece of human flesh in the yard by the pump with sloppiness like that. I'd seen it myself, years past. No good at all.

The leaves had gone yellow and the air bit cold, whining shrill like the brats left behind the dead, trudging slow beside their weeping mother. Little turds, little nothings. Just blood and bone, passed on from a father who was a cutter, a stone lover, mixing his juice inside a womb that was cold and sly. I did not like Martha. I did not like her husband, either. Edward Bromes was a hard man to enjoy, in any fashion. I cried no tears that he died.

Later that night, I burned the doll that killed him.

1

Next morning, frost: first kiss of winter. I added layers of wool, and laced my feet and legs into boots lined with rabbit, gathered my satchels, took up a tin can I hung from the hook at my belt, and marched from the rotten timber shack into a silver forest, glittering, spiked with light and a chill.

Persimmons had fallen overnight and the deer had not got to them. Quick business, but careful; those thin orange skins split open at the hint of a tense finger, and I ruined more than I cared to admit. Popped them in my mouth to hide the evidence. Spit out the seeds into my palm and tucked them into the satchel where I kept the needle and thread. The rest, what was perfect and frostbit, I carried in the can for old Ruth.

She was knitting when I came upon her, sitting on her slanting porch as though the cold was nothing to withered flesh. Crooked broken teeth, crooked smile that might have been pretty but for the long scar pulling her bottom lip.

"Clora, you brought me sweets," she cooed, setting aside her yarn. "Enough for pudding?"

I placed the tin can into her hands, which were scarred with needle pricks. "Not yet. Maybe tomorrow."

She caught my wrist before I could pull away. "And the ashes?"

I knew better than to hesitate. No good to pretend I was happy, either. Obedience was enough. Obedience was the same as falling on knees, like the Sunday regulars the preacher took down to the river to pray at the cross and handle the Lucifer snake he kept in a pine box.

I dug into the satchel and pulled out a small packet of folded calico, sewn shut with my finest black thread stitches. Ruth's smile widened, and she snatched it from my hand—holding it up to her nose and closing her eyes with pleasure.

"Good," she said, finally. "Edward had it coming for what he did to you."

I grunted, walking past Ruth into the cabin, unable to look into her eyes.

"Clean your needles," Ruth called after me. "Time for lessons, Clora."

I lit the fire, and while the flames leapt and scrambled within the stove, I relieved the burden of needle and thread: slender bone daggers punched with holes; and rough spools, collapsed with lichen-dyed browns and a rich burgundy soaked from sumac bobs, thin as a strangler's wire and finely made—by my own hands—hours spent at the fixing of such binding threads.

The needles still had blood on them. I sat down at the table, wet the bone with a dash of apple vinegar poured from a flask in my satchel, and scrubbed hard with the pad of my thumb. Skin to bone, trying to summon the proper devotion. I was still scrubbing, whispering, when Ruth limped into her home.

Her own needles gleamed white as snow, hung around her neck like a fan of quick fingers.

"Not saying their names right," she said, leaning so close the great bulk of her breasts touched my back. "Need to show your kin the proper respect, Clora. All my teachings to no account, otherwise."

And then her hand fell upon my hair, warm as the fire burning, sinking into my skull behind my eyes, and she said, "Try again tomorrow. Right now we got a poppet to make. Some Buck Creek girl set her eye on a cutter man from the quarry, and her mother wants him gone."

I spread the needles over the table. "Maybe he loves her."

Ruth snorted, and drew away. "Her mother brought a cutting of his hair."

Nothing more needed saying.

The ground was still soft over Edward's grave.

His brothers were too lazy to pack him down hard, or even lay stone on top, which was what he would have wanted, being a cutter at the quarry for most of his adult life. I took a stroll past Martha's cabin on the way to the hill, making sure she was home.

Wives were odd sometimes. Over the years, I'd seen a few who couldn't pull themselves from the graves of lost men, sitting up all through the day and night with Bibles, crosses, or nothing to hold but their skirts and faces, weeping and praying like God would give them a resurrection, like maybe their men were as good as Jesus and would be risen. Seemed to me that was arrogance bordering on sin, but not one that was any worse than murder.

Martha was home. I stood at the edge of the forest, staring at her lit windows, watching her make circles all around her kitchen. I could have gone closer, but the old coonhound was tied to the porch, and even though he knew me, there was no sense in sparking the possibility of him making an unattractive sound.

The forest sang at night, trills and clicks, and whispers of the wind in the naked rubbing branches. Coyotes yipped and somewhere close a fox screamed like a woman, making my skin crawl cold even though it was nothing to fear.

The shovel was heavy on my shoulder. So was the ax.

I found the grave before moonrise and started digging. Took hours. I didn't focus as I should. Kept thinking about Edward Bromes, and my last view of his body before his brothers slid him into the pine box: pale, stiff, eyes sewn shut.

I thought about other men, too.

I had to jump down into the hole, standing waist-high in loose dirt as I used the ax to pry apart the soft, cheap wood. Martha had insisted on something finer than a muslin shroud, but each groan of those splitting planks made my heart beat harder until I was breathless, expecting to hear shouts, dogs barking. The night was all as it should be, though: empty, quiet, crisp with frost.

Edward smelled a little, but no worse than other corpses. I looked down at him with nothing but a small tallow candle to enhance my sight, but that was more than enough. I had sewn the stitches myself to close his eyes, prepared the body for burial under the watchful, too watchful, gaze of his wife, and now we were met again and he was still dead, but with a purpose.

I cut off his right hand, wrapped it in oilskin, and reburied him.

By sunrise I was home, and had just enough time to wash up before I went for another day of lessons with old Ruth.

Think what you will, but I had no real family. Mother dead from the influenza, father run off with a woman who clerked for the big boss at the quarry. Gone ten years, and maybe he'd thought a six-year-old daughter would be cared for by relations, but a good hunting dog would have been more welcome, and was: old Tick, a bloodhound come down from Kentucky as a puppy, brought to heel by an uncle after my father run off, and I still recall Martha and Edward and another aunt being angry about the inconvenient burden of me.

I was another mouth to feed. By the time Ruth found me, I had no shoes, no coat, and my hair had to be shorn to the scalp because of lice and fleas. I still remember the sores on my legs and arms: insect bites scratched to infection, and the vinegar baths and salt scrubs, and willow bark tea forced down my throat for weeks, weeks, after Ruth took me in and clothed me like a doll in soft dresses.

"Clora, my sweet," she'd say, and I loved her for it. Decided, in that pure childlike naivety kin to wishing on a star that I would do anything for her, I'd care for her, I'd be hers in body and soul.

It was the soul part I hadn't realized would be a problem.

The poppet for the mother of the Buck Creek girl took three days to make.

I cut cloth from one of the old burlap bags folded by the fireplace, and took up a smaller, sharper finger-blade to shear out the shape of a man. Twice I did this, using the first as a pattern that I traced with a stick of coal. Ruth had taught me to do the same with twisted roots and vines, formed to take a human shape; or dried corncobs, or clay; but cloth had advantages that Ruth had spelled into me, such as it could be sewn into a vessel filled with all the sundry items a good hoodoo needed: blood and bones, and cuttings of hair, dried fluids from a man's loving, trapped on cloth, mushrooms, feathers, shell and stone. Little bits of power in the right hands with the right intent and desire, making a sympathetic echo that might correspond to a living human body.

"Need to fix that red stitch," Ruth told me, as I sewed. "Fix it or start over."

I pulled the bone needle back through the hole as Ruth turned away to her own sewing: a doll as long as my forearm, with a real face embroidered in her finest threads—black hair, blue thread dyed from woad for his eyes, a strong nose identified by a crooked line.

"Haven't told me who that's for," I said, quiet.

"Hush." Ruth put a fat persimmon in her mouth and began sucking on it. "You'll make another mistake. All my teaching will be for naught if you keep up this way."

I gave her a small smile, but with my eyes averted. I only made mistakes when I had a mind to do so. Ruth might say she wanted me strong and I'd tried to please her in that way before I realized better—before I seen a look she couldn't hide on the day I sewed a hoodoo that made a man burst his brain with apoplexy before I finished the last stitch. Us at the spring market in the valley, sitting under a tree, and all it was supposed to be was a lesson in seeing the hoodoo make a man itch. Not die.

So, I made mistakes after that. Small ones. Enough to make me look weak.

Not from guilt.

I wanted to survive.

I walked the poppet down to Buck Creek on the fourth day. It was cold and bright, and the closer I got to the bottom of the valley, the more houses I saw deep in the woods—and in the distance, the winding track of the dirt road that somewhere bled north into a larger road, and larger, beyond which I'd never seen.

I didn't need Ruth's directions to find the right home, built into the side of a rocky hill cleared of trees. I could hear the creek, but the chickens were louder, scratching in a large pen guarded by a hound gone gray at the muzzle. The mother was out in the yard splitting firewood, cheeks red from exertion and the chill, her bare hands the same color. Her smile was tight-lipped when she saw me, but I didn't take it hard. Asking for a bad act was the same as committing it, and didn't matter how it was done: God would be all for the remembering, when the final day was come.

"Didn't expect you so soon," she said.

"Soon as done," I replied, looking around. "Is your daughter here?"

Her gaze hardened. "Off to the quarry. She brings that man his lunch. Won't be reasoned with, no matter how hard I come at her."

"Shame," I said, wondering at how much I sounded like Ruth. "Terrible she won't believe you. About his way with women, I mean."

"I only want what's best for her. Plenty of fine men, without Betty making eyes at a no-good. If he gets her with child. . . ." The mother made a disgusted sound and leaned the ax against the cutting block. "God's work that Margaret down at the Bend heard of his wandering eye before I let it go too far."

God's work, maybe. My work, certainly. Rumors could cast a spell just as powerful as needle and thread.

I began to pull the poppet from my satchel, but the mother stiffened and took a step back.

"Not out here," she said, looking around as if a crowd from church had gathered in the trees. "Not here."

We went inside. Her cabin was dark, but it smelled like warm bread and coffee. She offered me none of that, except a handful of crumpled bills that looked like the right amount, though it was hard to tell. I didn't count them. Ruth knew how to handle a cheater well and good, which this woman surely knew.

I lay the poppet on the table. "You sure you want to do this yourself?"

The mother hesitated. "What does it take?"

"Burn it," I said. "Or stab it. Twist its head to break his neck. Anything you do will kill him, slow or fast."

She went pale. "That's the Devil's work."

I offered back her money. "You said you wanted him gone."

The mother stared at the doll and took a long, deep breath. I waited, already knowing the answer.

When I left her home, I carried the poppet in my satchel—and the money, too.

I walked toward the quarry.

The man was easy to find, as he was lunching with a girl no older than me, sixteen at best, pretty as morning with long blond hair and a face that might have been her mother's, if her mother had ever been young and happy.

I watched them from the edge of the woods and ate my own lunch: a soft-boiled egg, a bit of bacon between some bread. Tapped my feet and rubbed my hands, trying to stay warm, watching the man and girl smile and laugh and make lovey-dovey with their eyes—and me, wondering all the while what that would feel like, wishing and afraid, but mostly wishing.

The girl left with a laugh and kiss. The man watched her go. His eyes, for her only. If he had ever wandered, I was certain he would never wander on her.

I started walking before he did, making my way through the woods so that I was waiting for him on the trail down to the quarry. He took his time, and was whistling when he saw me—though that stopped when he said, "Miss?"

Nothing hard in his face. Nothing bad, as was believed. The girl was right to love him. I had known it for weeks now, from the first time I seen them together.

I put my hand in the satchel, on the rough skin of the burlap doll. "I've come to warn you, mister."

He frowned. "Who are you?"

"Someone who knows old Ruth," I said, and something cold and small entered his eyes, natural as the ill, bone-chilling breeze passing around us on the trail. Ruth was like that breeze in these parts, known and accepted, and respected out of fear. Most granny-women were, like as in the blood, born from the old country that was still rich in the veins of those who had settled these hills and valleys. Fear of a hoodoo woman was natural. Fear was how it had to be.

"Ruth has her eye on you," I said. "When it comes, it'll be her doing."

He paled. "Done nothing wrong. Don't even *know* her."

I stepped back into the woods. "Remember what I told you. It was Ruth who ordered it."

"Wait," he began, reaching for me. I slipped away, but he did not try to follow. Instead he ran up the trail, away from the quarry. Chasing the girl, I thought. She was something he wanted to live for.

I pulled out the poppet, and twisted its head clear 'round.

The man was buried two days later, and the night after I slithered into that proper cemetery and dug for him. If he was watching from on high, I didn't mind. I sawed off his hand and wrapped it up tight.

I was good at digging for the dead. Ruth started me at the age of twelve, from necessity. It was time. I'd become a woman, my first bleed, and needles couldn't be made from any old bone. So my own mother was first, and my grandmother after her—followed by *her* mother. Nothing less would do, Ruth said, and I believed her, though it made me cry. Took a long while, too, and lucky for me, my relatives were buried in the family plot, out in the hills where no one ever came.

All for sympathy, was something else Ruth taught me. Bones had to be sympathetic to make a hoodoo stitch work its wiles, and nothing was more in sympathy than a line of women, from mother to daughter and backward to beyond. Never mind any strife that might have pressed between generations. Who was left living mattered most to the dead. According to Ruth, that was me.

Though it seemed, as it had for some time, that it wasn't just the bones of those come before that might matter in the stitching. Any bone, from a body with desire, might have a say in the power of a hoodoo.

Any bone at all.

Now, there were stories come down from the hills that I remembered being told even as a child, and the telling of them was still rich on the tongues of the people who settled in the valley and high country, away from the quarry. Tales of the banshee and hag-riders, and the little folk who Ruth thought she could consort with, though I'd never seen anything but a raccoon sip the milk she left out, nights. I don't know if I believed in such tales, though I respected the possibility, given the power of the needle and stitch, which had to come from somewhere—and if not the world of the spirit, then maybe God, though I did not think He would approve the use for which His gift had been put.

It certainly was not for God that I was a conspirator to murder. And I had no confidence that He had a greater hold of my soul than Ruth.

Took me four years to realize something might be shifty, and by then I was ten. I got it in my head to go raiding some jar of sweets that Ruth kept just for herself, and it wasn't a minute after my first bite of peppermint that the pain started in, right in my stomach. I doubled over thinking I'd been stabbed, sure to find blood, but nothing was there but the certainty that my insides were going to spill outsides.

Calling for Ruth did no good. She was standing right there, watching. Holding a doll made of pale cloth, large as a swaddled babe and cradled in her arms, with a fork jabbed into its belly.

Ruth's eyes, satisfied and cold. "Been soft on you. And now you try to steal from me. After everything I done to keep you whole."

Well, it took me a week to walk after that.

But it gave me time to think.

That new doll, with the blue eyes and crooked nose, remained a silent presence. Ruth worked on it with a steadiness I'd not seen in years, taking care with every stitch, mumbling devotionals over her needles before she'd even thread them. I watched her clean those bone daggers each morning, and when it came time to fill that doll with the hoodoo, she made me go outside in the cold and practice my embroidery, claiming a need to concentrate in peace. It was no consequence to me. I knew what she was doing. Capturing a soul was no secret, even though she'd never taught me the way of it.

"Power makes you greedy," Ruth said, seven days after needling that first stitch. "I'm no innocent in that regard, as you well know."

I was standing beside the fireplace, bent over a tin pail that held a mixture of cow urine, fermented these last three weeks, and the smashed hulls of black walnuts. Preparing dye for the thread, spun with my own hands from wool shorn from the sheep that Ruth kept in a pen on the hill.

"Look at me," she said.

The doll was in front of her on the table, soft limbs stretched out, soft body embroidered with runes and blooms and glimpses of eyes peering from behind twisting vines. I looked for only a moment and then settled on Ruth, who was eyeing me all speculative. I kept still.

"You have never been greedy," she said, finally. "Never saw a sign of it in your eyes, and I been looking for years, since I showed you that first stitch."

"I don't want what you have," I said truthfully.

Ruth grunted, and pushed herself off the chair. "Good girl."

I hesitated. "Never asked who taught *you*."

Oh, the smile that flitted across her mouth. Made me cold.

"My teacher," Ruth murmured, stroking the bone needles laid out on the table. "My own Granny, with her wiles. My mother had no gift for the stitch, but there was something in me, from the beginning."

Her gaze met mine. "Same as I saw in you."

My cheeks warmed. "No use for it, except killing. That's no life, Ruth."

"Better life than what you were headed for." Her fat fingers flicked through the air above the blue-eyed poppet. "Would have been in a grave. Nothing to show for living. Nothing to show those sympathetic bones."

I looked down at my needles, spread across the table. Each one born from a hand, hands whose names I knew: Lettie, Polly, Rebecca. Mother, grandmother, great-grandmother.

And now I knew the names of other bones from other hands.

All in sympathy.

It'd been years since Ruth had ventured off her land, but that afternoon she put on a woolen skirt and coat that moths and mice had been chewing on for a decade, pinned up her long gray hair, and buttoned her blouse until those needles hanging around her neck were hid. Not that showing them would have made folks any less uncomfortable. Ruth walking amongst the good Christians of the valley might be enough to thin the blood of that hollering preacher himself.

We were real silent until the end, just before she limped out the door, and she looked back and said, "There's a man come to my attention. You go home now, come back tomorrow."

"You need help?" I asked, but she raised her brow at me, made a clucking noise, and walked on out. The poppet was in a cloth bag that swung from her shoulder.

I followed her, soon after.

Ruth had a fast limp. I had to hustle to catch up. Not that I wanted to get too close, but there was some investment on my part, and so I took a different trail that was roundabout and uneven, steep—too difficult for Ruth to walk, though I myself was too fast, sliding and flirting with loose rocks underfoot, and low-lying branches that might have taken my eye or broken my nose if I hadn't been quick to duck. All for good, though. I reached the bottom of the trail certain I was first and Ruth, somewhere above, still huffing and puffing.

I kept to the woods, lungs tight as I forced down deep breaths of cold air, and made my way to a small log cabin settled in a clearing where a man stood on the covered porch, rocking a baby. A stonecutter, still dusty from the quarry, staring at his child like she was sunshine and angels, and so much sweetness I had to look away.

I took another breath, and walked from the woods.

"Clora," he said, with a tired smile, kind as could be. "Been some time."

"I'm sorry for that, Paul." I hoped he couldn't hear the thickness of my voice. "How's Delphia?"

Paul glanced over his shoulder at the cabin's closed door. "Pain's lessened, I think. That tea you brought seemed to help her sleep. But it's this one," and he paused, holding his babe a little tighter, "that's gotten fussy."

"Etta," I murmured, peering into blue eyes that were just like her father's.

"Oh, but it's nothing," said Paul, just as gently, and kissed her brow. "I'm just glad I'm fit to care for her. What with. . . ."

He stopped. I looked away again, toward the woods. His wife was dying, eaten up by scirrhous in her breasts. No stitch could cure her of those tumors. Maybe, if caught early. But not by the time I'd heard. Not for nothing did I think it fair the needle could kill or control, but when it came to healing a mother, all that power was to no account.

"It won't be much longer," I said quietly.

Paul's jaw tightened. "Then just me and Etta. Been thinking of leaving the quarry when that happens, maybe to find work in one of the towns up north. Cutting stone is too dangerous. Can't let nothing happen to me now."

I glanced down at the baby. "You have something to live for."

Paul made a small sound. "Come inside, Clora."

"Can't." I backed away, shaking my head. "Ruth is coming."

He frowned, holding his daughter tighter. "You shouldn't spend so much time with that witchy woman. You'll get the taint on you."

"Too late," I said, making his frown deepen. "And didn't you hear me?"

"Heard." Paul gave me a disapproving look. "Got nothing to fear from an old woman. Why she visiting, anyhow?"

"Your wife sent a note. She got it in her head that Ruth could cure her."

His brow raised. "Can she?"

"No." I stepped off the porch, nearly falling, and suddenly it was hard to see past the tears blurring my eyes. "She's going to hurt you, Paul. I want you to remember that. It was *her* doing."

Her doing, not mine. Her doing, even though it was me that put the idea in Delphia's head, even though I was the one who carried the note, that note which told a story of how much a woman would give to live just a while longer so she might not leave behind a little daughter and a good man. A good man who loved her with all his soul, she said.

I knew the interest Ruth would have in a man like Paul: so good, so true. Nothing rarer. Nothing more powerful.

I walked away, and as he called my name, the baby cried.

It got done, just as I knew it would, and the stain was on my hands sure as if I'd taken a knife and cut Paul's heart.

I heard of his death from Martha, who stopped by my shack because she was terrible lonely—terrible, to come visiting a girl she'd never wanted—but even if the words hadn't come from her mouth, I'd seen the doll on Ruth's special shelf where she kept other poppets filled with death's power, and I had to turn away, not wanting to look too deep into those embroidered blue eyes. Not because I was reminded of Paul, but because all I could think of was his daughter who would soon be alone. Delphia wouldn't last the week, Martha said. Blamed the shock of losing her husband.

Sure, I'd known that, too, even if I hadn't wanted to think on it. Wasn't just power that made people greedy, but desperation. And I'd had plenty of that building inside me, years on end.

The night Paul was buried, I went and stole his hand.

Now, I was guessing that the dead might know the truth of things, that I was no innocent and that my soul was in the shadow, but I hoped these men might also recall those words I'd spoken at the end—to Edward, too—that it was Ruth, Ruth, Ruth who made the spell that killed them. They might be sympathetic, as such, to my plight. A gamble, but one worth taking.

I made the needles from their bones. One full week it took to extract and carve, and polish—and pray as I had never prayed—but when I had my little daggers I began sewing the doll.

The cloth I used was old. Old enough that I'd had to dig up my mother, grandmother, and great-grandmother for it. The oldest of them was a white wedding gown, turned brown with age; and then a black dress torn up with holes; and last, a gown made of muslin that tore so easily, I held my breath when I added it to the patchwork of poppet flesh.

Days I practiced stitches with Ruth, and nights I stitched to kill her, embroidering a fantasy of freedom upon the skin of the doll: an open road leading to its heart, and the blue sky, and birds with their wings outstretched. Black thread held the joints, but everywhere else, color sapped from forest dyes, from the walnut and woad, safflower and gold-enrod, mixed double, double, to toil and trouble.

I poured my heart into the making of that poppet. I poured what was left of my soul. And when I was done, or near so, I cut open my arm to spill my blood upon its guts: strands of hair I'd gathered, sneak-like, over years in Ruth's home; persimmon seeds she'd spit from her mouth into the yard; and chicken bones where her teeth left marks. Epsom salts for freedom, and blue salt for healing; gray talcum powder to protect from evil; and last, dirt from the graves of my mothers. Dirt from the graves of the men, along with a finger from each of their hands.

And when I was done I set a shroud upon the thing, because its eyes seemed to watch me, and I could not stand the judgment already waiting, on high and low, and inside my heart where there was no peace and never would be, even if I got what I wanted.

Even so.

"There's something different about you," Ruth said, setting down some knitting as I approached her cabin. The morning sun was on her: hair silver as frost, her skin pale, and those bone needles shining white around her throat.

"I'm tired," I said. "Been thinking."

"Dangerous." Ruth heaved herself from the rocking chair and went inside. "I'll make you tea."

She said those words with kindness. I'd heard them a million times. Comforting, warm. Ruth, who had rescued me. Ruth, who had raised me as her own. Ruth, who had been my teacher and friend.

When she turned her back on me I reached inside my satchel, grabbed the poppet, and squeezed.

Her back arched so wild she went up on her toes, a rattling cry tearing from her throat. I squeezed harder and heard a cracking sound. Bone, breaking.

Ruth crumpled, slamming down with a thud that rattled the entire porch. For a moment she was completely still, and then her fingers twitched, and her hands and arms began to move, and she clawed at the planks, panting for air. Her legs remained still.

I took a long, deep breath, and climbed the steps. My heart pounded. Dark spots floated in my vision. Ruth tried to grab my foot, hissing curses at me, but I sidestepped and went into the cabin.

I gathered the dolls on the shelf, including one with my name embroidered over the heart. My hands burned when I touched it, dizziness sweeping down, but I swallowed hard and held the doll close—burning, burning—and went back outside.

"I'll kill you," Ruth whispered, gaze burning with hate. "I should have killed you years ago."

"You held the leash and thought that was enough."

Foam touched her lips. "I *cared* for you."

I held up the doll she had made to control me. "Not in the right way."

"You would do the same!" Ruth tried to grab me again as I walked past her to the yard. I dumped the dolls on the hard frost, and then reached into the satchel for Ruth's poppet. I went back and showed it to her, crouching a safe distance away. Her eyes narrowed, and even with her back broke I saw those wheels turning, how she examined every stitch, searching for a flaw. But of course there was none. If I'd done one thing wrong, I'd be dead and she would be kicking my corpse into the refuse pile for the pigs to eat.

"Impossible." Ruth tore her gaze from the poppet. "I own you."

"I found sympathy." I pulled down my collar to reveal two necklaces of bone needles hanging from my neck. "Just enough."

Her eyes widened. "Those men."

I said nothing, and the silence was terrible and heavy, heavy on me because I saw myself in that moment: me, in Ruth's place, sprawled on the porch with a broken back and some other girl standing over me, ready to take my place with a fury. Future or not, it chilled me.

"Oh, God kill you," Ruth whispered. "God kill you, and the Devil, too."

"In time," I said, and twisted the poppet's head.

Freedom should have a tingle, some flash of light, but I felt no different afterward. Maybe I wasn't free. Maybe being free of Ruth wasn't the same thing at all.

I burned all the dolls, except mine. I was too much a coward to tempt my own death, though I deserved it in a mighty way. Shadow of death over my heart, waiting, waiting, for the needle and thread. Wicked stitchery.

I wanted to learn a different kind.

Ruth, I burned with the dolls. I broke her needles.

But I kept her house.

A week later, I heard word that Delphia had passed. No relatives nearby to care for the baby, and no one stepped in to take claim. I waited, to be sure, and then went down into the valley to take the girl. I did not ask. I held out my arms, and there was something in the way those folk looked at me, something I'd never seen before except when they looked at Ruth, but I supposed I finally had her eyes.

I took the child in, but the only doll I made for her was stitched for play, with a needle from her father's hand.

Things would be different, I promised.

All for sympathy for the bones.

"Sympathy for the Bones" is one of my favorite works of short fiction (if I'm allowed). I wrote it for the anthology An Apple for the Creature, *which was supposed to be about "your worst school nightmare," and indeed, I can't imagine a nightmare more awful than someone else owning your soul. What does one do in that situation? What is the cost of freedom? What price do you pay for a power that has been bent to one dark purpose your whole life: hurting others?*

THE BRIAR AND THE ROSE

THE DUELIST WAS AN ELEGANT WOMAN, but that was by her own design and had nothing to do with the fact that her mistress bade her act with certain manners when she was not, by law, killing her peers.

She was called Briar, but only on Sunday. Other days, she was simply the Duelist. No man had legs half as powerful or as long, and her reach with a sword was so terrifying that experienced fighters would surrender at her first lunge. A foreigner from across the sea, a brown woman in a city where she was as exotic for her skin as she was for her blade; where, after some seven years—four of which had been spent in her mistress's employ—she had settled down comfortably in her reputation and only had to draw her sword against the very young, and very stupid.

Her mistress was the most favored courtesan of the Lord Marshal, and in the evenings she was called Carmela. The Lord Marshal thought himself a special man that he knew her name, but Carmela had a talent for making every man feel the same, and each knew her by a different identity.

Even the Duelist was not privy to all her secrets, though she spent most of her waking hours attending to the woman, and even longer nights sitting by that bedchamber door, listening to her loud, dramatic lovemaking. The Duelist knew that Carmela had more respect for her sword than her intelligence, that she took delight in having a quiet beast of a woman guarding her, a woman with the same brown skin, as if they were a mismatched set.

Carmela paid the Duelist well for her sword, silence, and skin—and trusted her not to, as she put it, get any ideas.

But the Duelist, in fact, had many ideas.

Saturday had come around again, and it was almost midnight. Nearly Sunday, in fact. Which was the only day worth living, in the Duelist's estimation.

She stood at the edge of the ballroom, wearing her most imposing jacket—a stiff green silk that hugged her trim waist, held down her breasts, and enhanced the already massive width of her shoulders. No one had ever told her to dress in outfits that complemented her mistress's voluminous ensembles, but the Duelist had made it a rule. She understood Carmela's vanity, that a valued guard was also an accessory, and that it would please her mistress that nothing around her, nothing that reflected her taste, could ever be accused of anything so tacky as clashing.

Tonight Carmela was dressed in emerald silk, a gown embroidered at the bodice with gold thread and laced with rare gems as yellow as a cat's eye. Her full skirt rubbed against the stocking-clad legs of the men crowded around her. "To remind them of my hands," she'd once told the Duelist. "To make them imagine my hands stroking their legs."

Her breasts were as enormous as her waist was small: two immense, soft, ridiculous distractions that were barely covered by that petite bodice. Her brown skin looked even darker against her bright dress; dusted in gold, Carmela's flesh was nothing but supple, her face slender and delicate, crowned by thick brows. She was the only flame burning in a room full of aging pale-skinned men and women who would never be the equal of such raw beauty, not even in their wildest dreams.

She was also a proud, dangerous woman who had stayed up too late and danced far too long with the Lord Marshal. Addicted to the attention she received from him and his cronies, even as the Duelist watched her movements slow, and her words thicken.

"She'll collapse soon," said the Steward, in passing.

"Prepare the special tea," replied the Duelist, watching as Carmela missed a step in the waltz and stumbled against the Lord Marshal. He laughed, gathering her up in his arms like it was some great joke. But Carmela wasn't smiling.

"Don't tell me my job," muttered the Steward. "If you were only half as fast with that sword as I am with her tea, you'd be more than just her paid dog."

The Duelist could have drawn her sword and removed his head before he even finished that sentence, but she was beyond the age where she needed to prove a point by killing. That had been the way of her youth, but no longer.

The Duelist crossed the ballroom instead, causing a minor ripple as the much shorter guests stumbled in their dancing to get out of her way. The Duelist ignored their frowns and the deliberately loud whispers; some of it was sour grapes, anyway. She'd dueled against, and killed, hired swords who belonged to the uninvited (and now, in some cases, divorced) wives of several guests. Wives who would have been wiser punishing their wandering husbands, rather than attempting to murder the woman those men had wandered to.

Still, the Duelist felt some sympathy for those spurned wives. Carmela flaunted her conquests, vaunted her great beauty and wealth, cultivated an obsessed audience—rubbed it in, as if she wished to blind every other woman with her magnificence. In short, Carmela—unlike most others who spread their legs for coin—did not know her place.

Carmela saw the Duelist coming, frowned, and touched her brow with delicate painted nails.

"My darling," she cooed to the Lord Marshal, leaning over so that her breasts swelled even more from her dress. "I'm quite exhausted. It's time for me to retire."

"I know better than to argue," he said, with a pout that did not belong on a man in his fifth decade. "Every Saturday is the same. You throw these lavish parties in your home, then run away just as things are getting interesting."

"I'll make things very interesting for you, should you come back Monday evening."

The Lord Marshal patted her waist. "I will count the minutes."

Carmela smiled and made her way through the crowd, so graceful she might as well have been dancing. She curtsied and murmured her good-byes, encouraging guests to dance into the morning, taking a glass of wine from one of her admirers to draw her tongue over the rim (out of sight from the Lord Marshal, of course), and laughing merrily at some dirty joke that the Duelist felt certain was anatomically impossible.

Only when they were outside the ballroom, deep in the shadows, did Carmela's smile slip, and that sharp charm dissolve. She passed the Duelist, hissing something completely unintelligible beneath her breath, and made her way through the library. The Duelist always posted guards in that room to keep out roaming guests; these men straightened as they walked past, gazes firmly on the floor and not on Carmela's breasts, now spilling free of the bodice she was loosening from around her waist with frustrated, angry movements.

The Steward appeared at the foot of the stairs, accompanied by a young maid.

"Get this thing off me," Carmela snapped, but the ruddy-faced teen was already plucking at the stays. She pulled the dress down her mistress's body, which was naked underneath.

The Steward had his eyes closed, the cup of tea held out in both hands. Carmela grabbed it from him, drank the brew in one long, grimacing gulp, and tossed the cup to the floor, where it shattered against the stone.

"My lady," he murmured. Carmela ignored him and proceeded up the tower stairs with only the Duelist behind her.

The tower was high and narrow, a place for prisoners or the doomed.

One cell at the top of an endless spiral of stone steps, its dense wall broken only by slits too narrow for a woman to slip through and jump. Murder holes, the Duelist called them. No furniture, save a thick mattress upon the floor. Not even a bed frame. Too much a risk. Sheets, but nothing to tie them to. No bucket for relief, but a small closet with only a hole in the stone floor to squat over. The massive oak door took all the Duelist's strength to open, and only two people had the key: she and her mistress.

Such were the rituals for falling asleep on a Saturday night.

"Go on, go," her mistress commanded, already collapsed on the mattress and tugging on the linen nightgown that had been left folded on her pillow. The Duelist obeyed, closing the door and turning the lock. She thought she heard her mistress say something but knew better than to go back inside.

She waited until she was certain Carmela was unconscious to reopen the door and step into the darkness of the tower cell. She sat upon the floor and listened to the other woman breathe.

The Duelist always knew when her mistress was truly asleep. Not just asleep in body, but in soul—when her hold finally relaxed, and she slipped away for good. Her breathing would change in that moment, become something else. Lighter, sweeter. The breathing of another woman entirely.

Another woman, the right woman: the woman whose body her mistress had stolen.

It was in these silent moments of watching, waiting, that the Duelist had first begun falling in love.

The Duelist had bought a book the previous morning while on another errand. Something old and worn, so that the ink from newly printed pages would not rub off on the skin. Nothing that could leave a trace, not even a little, not in the slightest. She often bought books, and chose the subjects just as carefully; last week, a romantic adventure involving pirates and island temples filled with gold; today, a treatise from an ancient philosopher on the affliction of malevolence, which some believed was spread upon the breath of men. The Duelist had learned, long ago, that oppression could be defeated only through study; like a sword, the mind must always be tended to if it was to aim true.

Because it was Sunday, the town house was entirely empty when the Duelist came home from her morning walk to the port. Not one maid, not one footman, not even the Steward or the Cook. Orders from Carmela herself.

"No one else in this whole quarter has a Sunday off," the Steward boasted. "Ours is a magnanimous mistress."

Of course, the same quarter also wondered why the entire staff was turned out on Sunday—something that was just not done. The gossips couldn't decide whether Carmela used Sundays to bathe in the blood of orphans or to offer up unholy sacrifices to the Fallen Gods. After all, beauty such as hers could not come naturally.

It didn't. And yet it did.

On those secret Sundays when the entire household was dismissed, only the Duelist was allowed to attend Carmela—or even set foot under her roof. Her guard camped outside the front gate, with orders to never allow anyone else to enter the premises, not for any reason, under pain of death.

And no one ever, on any day, was allowed in the tower.

The Duelist, of course, had made herself the exception.

Light seeped through the murder holes, but the young woman was still asleep. Fallen limp among the tangled covers, a thin sheen of sweat on her brow. Long black hair clung to her skin, gleaming beneath shafts of morning light: golden and piercing. Dust motes floated.

The Duelist watched her breathe. It was one of her few joys. It was easy not to confuse the young woman for Carmela, even though they shared the same body. No acidic scowl, no cruel tension in her jaw. Even in sleep, that face was gentler, and more beautiful for it.

The Duelist sat on the floor, close to the mattress. The tower cell had not been built for a woman her size—standing felt claustrophobic, her head nearly touching the ceiling. She always feared, too, that it might be too intimidating for the young woman. The Duelist had never, until three years ago, wished she could make herself smaller.

The book was beside her, along with a basket of food: a soft, bitter cheese, a tender roast dove, loaves of crusted sourdough, and more. She unbelted her sword and laid it on the rough stone. Removed her silk jacket and unbuttoned the collar of her blouse. Unwrapped the wide black scarf that held down the graying curls of her hair, which spilled outward, against her cheek.

"Rose," she said quietly.

The young woman stirred, slow and drugged, and it was another long moment before she opened her eyes.

"Briar," whispered the girl, and even her voice was different: her accent, the way she curled the final note of that name.

Her mistress was asleep and Rose was awake.

"I'm here," the Duelist said. "It's safe. Take your time."

Rose's eyes stayed open, staring at the ceiling. "You shouldn't say that to me, Briar. There's no time at all."

"Not if you waste it," replied the Duelist, rising from the floor. "Sunday is long. And I have your favorite stinking cheese, and that nectar from the ridiculous fruit you so like. Some formerly fresh bread, too. I thought to tempt you."

A weak cough broke from between those round lips, those perfect lips. "Oh, Briar. You never change."

The Duelist frowned. "Forgive me if I offend."

Rose tilted her head to look at her, mouth tugging into a weak smile. "No. I celebrate you. I am blessed with you. As long as you're here, I am not alone."

The Duelist sat very carefully on the edge of the mattress. Rose visibly swallowed. "Anyway, I am starving. The last meal I remember was here, a week ago, with you. That's the only good in my life. You and this room, just the two of us. I'd lose my mind, otherwise. All that emptiness. All that lost time when I'm asleep and she—she has my body—"

Her voice stopped. After a moment, she held out her hand.

The Duelist almost took it, but caught herself. No contact, not even the slightest. It might wake Carmela early, which had happened once before, long ago, the same day the Duelist realized there was another woman living in that perfect skin. Just one touch, a brush of her fingers against Rose's hand, and that was enough to make those eyes change, that mouth tighten into a hard line—a shadow rising to press against the insides of that face like a demon wearing a mask made of human flesh.

"How dare you touch me," whispered Carmela.

"You were crying for help," stammered the Duelist, unable to think of a better lie in that moment. "You reached for me yourself."

"Get out," said Carmela, swaying and falling to her knees on the mattress. "I sleepwalk, you idiot. Ignore everything you hear inside this room and never disturb me again."

The Duelist had not survived so long by always taking orders—or curbing her curiosity. The next Sunday, she returned to the room. Found Rose.

They never touched again.

But the Duelist could not help making at least the gesture of a touch: she extended her hand, and their palms hovered close, heat gathering in the air between them. They stayed like that, almost touching. Until it was more than the Duelist could stand.

She placed the book onto the young woman's open palm. "She has your body, but you are still Rose. You still live."

"Stop it," replied Rose, clutching the book to her chest; and then: "I hate this sleeping draught she uses. I can barely move."

"Here." The Duelist held out the bottle of juice, but the young woman shook her head, eyes going dark in that way she knew too well, and dreaded.

"How many men this week?" asked Rose, in a quiet voice.

"This accounting does not serve you—"

"How many?"

The Duelist did not want to tell her, but long ago Rose had refused to speak to her until she revealed the truth. The silence had lasted weeks, and left the Duelist forlorn, confused. In that first year of becoming familiar with Rose, understanding what had been done to Rose, she had not often allowed herself to think of what it would mean to be possessed—did not reflect on how it would feel to have some other person inside her own body, controlling, distorting, plundering. The violation, the horror.

These days the Duelist thought of it often and the knowing, while hard, took less work than the not knowing.

That was wisdom, a storyteller had once told her.

It hurts, she had responded, almost casually.

The storyteller had nodded: Wisdom always does.

The Duelist said, "Three different men, but she was with the Lord Marshal every night, as well."

Rose managed to find her feet and was once again trying to jam her fingers through the murder holes. Just to feel the sun.

"Rose," whispered the Duelist.

"I'm fine," said the young woman in a soft voice. "I don't remember a thing."

There was a time, in the beginning, when the Duelist considered killing Rose.

It was not her idea, of course. That first year the young woman made the request often—quietly, desperately, angrily—even silently—and those appeals chased the Duelist from the tower at sunset and followed her during those long days escorting Carmela from one appointment to another, watching as lard-heavy men, pale and sweating, drooled over her mistress's figure. Sometimes they glanced at the Duelist, but only because she was a brown woman with a sword.

The Duelist was not beautiful. She had been blessed with a man's square jaw and strong nose, and though she was elegant, there was nothing fine, nothing compelling to stare at but the long scar that traveled from her temple to her throat, a duel gone wrong in her youth, a duel with a man who had fast feet. The Duelist was not sorry for that scar. Beauty had a price that she was content never to pay.

"If you wish to be more than a common street fighter, if you want to be a hero, then you must kill me," said Rose, early on, in a perfectly reasonable voice. "To stop her from doing this to another innocent girl—that would be your prize. I'm dead anyway, you know that. When she's done with my body, she won't keep me alive."

The Duelist didn't mind those conversations, much. Others were harder.

Sometimes Rose would cry, "What is wrong with you? How can you stand it? How can you watch those men, that witch—all of them using me? Raping me?"

And the Duelist would say nothing.

But sometimes when she stood guard behind her mistress, stood still and silent as Carmela sat naked in her dressing room smoothing oil over those breasts the Duelist knew so well, she thought of what it would feel like to push her sword through the delicate muscles of Carmela's back, what it would sound like to hear that gasp, smell her blood. The Duelist thought of it often, in the beginning.

She thought of killing them both, some Sunday: the young woman and herself, by sword and rope, or poison. Quick. Holding each other. Touching at last, as she desired, more than anything.

Giving in, giving up. Almost.

Then, one afternoon, Carmela remarked, "Did you see the Lord Marshal's wife in the garden when we left? The old dodder? Would you believe she was lovely once?" Quiet laughter, slow and mocking. "Beauty is always the first to die, my Duelist. It is the most fleeting of all our mortal gifts, and there is no power in this world that can save it. All we can do is steal time, when we can. Steal moments." Her mistress gave the Duelist a coquettish look that did not belong on that face, those eyes, that mouth, and gently tapped her nearly exposed bosom, which glimmered with gold dust. "This is a moment."

"You wear it well," said the Duelist in a quiet voice.

She decided, right then, that she and Rose would live.

She had not crossed thorny mountains and lifeless seas to die so stupidly. She had not humbled herself, hidden herself, forgotten herself—nor left the desert and her home—to surrender. Not once had she ever surrendered. Not in the war, not when the Torn Men had surrounded her in the Balelands and broken her sword and made her wear chains for a year until she escaped. Not then. She had not wavered. Not once.

She was the Duelist, after all.

"How do you fare?" she asked the young woman, the next Sunday they were together.

"Terribly," Rose said. "I want to die."

"You must have hope," said the Duelist.

"Hope." The girl barked a laugh. "What is that?"

"To never surrender."

There were different tellings of the tale, and all were a little true. In each there was a witch, an ancient crone. In every version a comely girl, cursed to sleep. The Duelist had heard them all as a child and scoffed at such nonsense.

Now she was older, wiser. Now she scoured books for such tales, and on those afternoons when her mistress set her free to deliver messages or buy her perfumes, or lurk menacingly upon the stoops of admirers who were a little too demanding, the Duelist always made extra time for herself: to search the city for storytellers, the ones who were blind and toothless, confined to their stools in the shade; the ones who were not fools, who knew there was truth in what they told.

In the desert, storytellers were the keepers of ancient things and could be trusted with secrets. Here, too, in this city across the sea.

There was a girl, the Duelist told them after months of tea, months of listening at their knees. The only child of a desert king. Most beloved, and graced with many blessings. Perhaps too many. Beauty has a price, after all.

Beauty draws many eyes, agreed the storytellers. Some of them unkind.

Yes, said the Duelist, and told them of a witch, a witch in the body of an aging beautiful woman, who had come to the king to seduce him—but only for the purpose of becoming close to his daughter.

A witch who craved power, yes—but who craved beauty even more. Power could be lost and regained—power was fleeting, power was part of a game she loved to play—but beauty was far more precious, far more rare. Beauty could feed a hunger inside the witch that no crown or treasure on earth could ever satiate: a hunger to be seen and adored, and desired.

Except the king was no fool, and neither was his child. Both saw the witch for what she was. Both denied her, drove her away. But not before she promised to take the girl. A curse upon her, a prophetic oath.

Time passed.

The girl became a young woman, still most beloved. But the witch had not forgotten—no predator would give up so perfect a prey. And so she hunted, and she connived, and she made her way back to the young woman, found a way into the desert fortress.

The king was away, gone into the mountains to harry his enemies. And the witch had taken a new body: a sun-wrinkled arthritic old crone who spun fine cloth, and who begged an audience with the young woman. A brief encounter, involving thorns hidden in a bolt of linen, thorns that pricked that perfect skin and drew beads of blood, blood that invoked magic, blood that sent the young woman into a slumber from which she could not wake: a slumber no one noticed because the witch had stepped so neatly into her body.

The witch fled, in that body. Fled across the desert and the sea. And in this new city, she built a home.

And in this home, she hired a guard.

The guard was another foreigner, from another desert. A woman who had lost her family in a hideous war—a war she fought for endless, dire years.

Deadened her heart, said the Duelist to the storytellers. Stripped away joy, all ability to feel the simplest of pleasures. Even love was nothing but a rumor she'd once heard, so long ago she'd forgotten what it was, and who had started it.

The guard believed the witch was nothing but a frivolous courtesan, and felt little for her, barely even loyalty. Until one day she entered the tower where the witch slept, there to perform a duty—and the princess opened her eyes instead.

Their gazes met. And in that moment—

—she remembered love, said the storytellers.

Love, echoed the Duelist. Love did not make the guard clever. She could not find a way to free the princess.

Love is powerful, replied the storytellers. Love is divine. That is the answer to every tale we tell. What sleeps can always be awakened with love.

I love her, said the Duelist, abandoning the story. But nothing has changed. I cannot see the way.

You will, they replied.

But the Duelist was not so certain.

There was a small girl among the storytellers, a bright young thing with brown hair and freckles dashed across her nose. Her grandmother, who was the eldest of the storytellers, said to her, How would you break a witch's spell, little one?

Find her true name, said the girl.

And how, asked her grandmother, do you glean a true name from one who speaks only lies?

Patience, replied the child. You listen.

The grandmother smiled. Even the greatest liar must eventually tell the truth.

One must only be wise enough to catch it.

"I had a dream," said Rose one Sunday. "Several dreams, actually. My head is full of them, Briar."

The Duelist paused in mid-stretch, palms pressed flat against the floor in front of her toes. A demonstration for Rose, who wanted to learn how she had stayed in good health after more than a decade of hard fighting. No one ever assumed that anything but her size had kept her alive all these years; for Rose to realize there was actual skill and training involved was rather unexpected. And gratifying.

"I didn't know you dream," said the Duelist.

"I don't. This is the first time." The young woman grimaced, and scooted off the mattress to her feet. She fell backward, and had to struggle again to stand.

The Duelist would have only needed to extend her elbow to help, and she almost did so without thinking.

"What did you dream?" she asked.

Rose walked with small, unsteady steps to the narrow window in the tower wall, placing her fingers in the slit. "It was all . . . unfamiliar. I was in a chamber made of smooth blocks engraved with leopards. I had many servants. My skin was golden in color, not brown, and I wore white silk."

"Was there more?"

"A different dream. Somewhere else. Carried in a litter, holding a dog in my lap, smelling the rain outside while thinking that I had better hurry or—or, nothing. I can't remember much else. The last dream is even more unclear. Standing naked before an immense bearded man wearing armor and a red sash. My body was round. My thighs rubbed."

The Duelist thought about that for a moment. "I have a surprise for you."

Rose glanced at her. "You have decided to kill me?"

The Duelist stepped over the mattress to the door. With a hard tug, she pulled it open. And stood there, waiting.

Rose stared. "What trick is this?"

The Duelist started to answer, but something hard lodged in her throat, something so magnificent and wild she felt like a child again, small and vulnerable, and consumed.

"Are you strong enough for the stairs?" she asked.

The young woman still seemed stunned, but managed a short sharp laugh. "I'll manage, even if I have to slide down each one."

But both women hesitated at the tower door. The Duelist said, "Sometimes I wonder how asleep she really is."

"That's part of her trap. Using fear to bind people in their place. I wonder if I'd been stronger . . ." Rose went silent, leaning against the doorframe. "How much of that witch's power did I hand her outright?"

"Don't blame yourself."

"Ah," she replied sadly, and sat on the stairs to scoot herself down to the step below. A long journey, just like that—scooting, lowering, bit by bit—mostly silent—until halfway down, Rose's face crumpled and the Duelist thought she'd begin to cry. Instead she let out a sharp, almost hysterical laugh that rebounded off the curved stone walls and made the Duelist blink in surprise. Rose clapped her hands over her mouth but was still shaking with laughter.

"I feel free," she managed to say. "Oh, gods, I'm a fool. But this is the first time in years I've felt free."

"Rose," said the Duelist, and then smiled—a real smile, a crooked grin that seemed to emerge straight from her heart to her face with terrifying power. She felt flush with the thrill of exhilaration and fury. She wanted to lean in and kiss Rose.

Rose said, "You're beautiful."

"Let us hurry," said the Duelist. "I want to show you something."

The house was quiet except for them. Odd, seeing Rose walking outside the tower. The Duelist felt dizzy looking at her, for a moment afraid she was wrong, that it was instead her mistress. But then she looked into those eyes and relaxed.

There was a library, but it held no books. Carmela was not much of a reader. She possessed only artifacts, sculptures, low couches covered in soft pillows; and along the walls, massive paintings of women framed by long velvet curtains that hid the empty bookshelves. Twenty portraits, twenty different faces, twenty bodies hanging. All of them, gazing out with the same sly expression, that cruel smile.

"It's her," said the Duelist. "Every one of them."

Rose shuddered. "She hasn't done mine yet."

In fact, Carmela had taken to bed the artist she'd commissioned to paint her portrait; he was scheduled to begin next month. But the Duelist kept that to herself. Instead she said, "Look around this room. This is where she keeps her treasures. See if anything is familiar."

"That," said Rose, pointing to an engraved vase perched on a small marble pedestal. "I saw the design in a dream, embroidered into a tapestry that hung beside a fireplace." Hesitation, while she looked again at the paintings. "My dreams are of these women, when the witch was in their bodies. I'm seeing her memories."

The Duelist felt pleased. "We already know there's a limit to how long she can hold you. She must rest one day a week in order to regain her strength. And now that you are glimpsing her memories—"

"—perhaps the lines between us are weakening in other ways. But that could put you in danger, Briar. What if she's dreaming of this moment, right now?"

"Rose," began the Duelist, then stopped and turned, listening.

The young woman also went very still, balanced on the balls of her feet. She'd bragged once that she was a fast runner—or had been. But there was no outrunning what was inside her. Or what had opened a door in the other room and was coming toward them with heavy footsteps.

The Duelist strode from the library. Her sword was in the tower, but her hands were strong and that unspent fury burned deep in her belly— rich and hot, and powerful.

"You," she said, entering the hall and finding the Steward just outside the parlor, holding a satchel in his chubby white hands. "You are not permitted in my lady's home on Sundays. Where are our guards?"

He gave her a startled look, but only for so long as it took him to remember who he was.

"How dare you," he replied. "You desert cunt. Our lady gave me special permission to come here today. She has errands for me to run."

"You are a liar," replied the Duelist in a cool voice. "And a thief, I think."

His mouth twisted. "It hardly matters. We'll all be turned away from her employment, soon enough. She's going to live soon with the Lord Marshal, and he has his own staff."

"What are you talking about?"

The Steward let out a laugh. "Of course you don't know. You never speak to the serving class. Our mistress is pregnant with the Lord Marshal's child."

The Duelist went still. The Steward looked past her, and his smile froze.

"Oh," he said.

Rose stood in the hall, staring at him. The Duelist watched her, every nerve on fire. Her slender body, covered in fine linen—her hands at her sides, slowly rising to touch her stomach.

"How does he know it's his?" Rose asked. And then laughed. A cruel, unhappy sound.

"M-my lady," stammered the Steward.

The Duelist slid a thin wire from the back of her belt, stepped behind him, and in one smooth motion brought it down over his head and pulled back hard on his throat. He stiffened, choking, but it was easy enough to knock the back of his knee and ride him face-first to the floor. Bones crunched. His feet kicked. The Duelist pulled back so hard she felt the wire cut through his throat.

He died quickly. The Duelist slid off his back, tugging the wire free. Blood dripped, but she cleaned the thin steel on his fine jacket. Her face was hot, heart pounding. She felt deeply troubled, and knew it was partly because Rose had finally seen her kill.

The young woman said, "Thank you."

The Duelist finally glanced at her. "He was a dead man the moment he saw you. He would have brought up this conversation." She paused. "But you knew that."

Rose gave her a cold smile.

They tossed his body into the slop pit where all the excrement flowed. It was a tight fit. The hole in the cellar was only meant for garbage, but the Duelist used a sledgehammer to break and twist his arms and shoulders until they resembled pulp, and kicked his body through. Someone else might have wavered or lost their resolve, but this was the sort of work, sadly, she excelled at. The work of eliminating foes.

She cleaned. Got down and scrubbed the stone floor where she'd cut his throat, checked the walls, the stairs to the cellar, examined every place his body had been. And then she had Rose hold out her hands, and examined her nightgown for blood.

"I can't truly be with child," Rose said.

"Your hands are trembling," the Duelist said.

"The sun has gone down. I'll have to sleep soon." She hesitated. "I was angry before, but now I'm just afraid."

The Duelist led Rose up the tower stairs. It was harder going up than down, and there were long moments when the young woman was forced to stop and rest. It was not just the drugs in the previous evening's tea—it was the arrival of night, it was the curse, it was the witch beginning to stir from her own brief sleep. The Duelist could feel Rose slipping away from her. Sunday was almost over.

In the tower, in her room, the young woman collapsed upon the bed with a groan.

"Briar," she said, as the Duelist sat on the mattress beside her. "I will try my best to dream. I will look for a way to be free."

"I will be with you," replied the Duelist. "The next time you open your eyes, mine will be the only face you see."

A month later the Lord Marshal announced he was divorcing his wife to marry the incredibly wealthy daughter of a foreign duke. The girl was rumored to be only a little better-looking than the sea sloths that spouted water in the harbor.

Within days Carmela was confined to bed complaining of a stomachache, but her bitterness prowled through the house. Maids were dismissed or beaten with hairbrushes, dishes were thrown at the cook, even the Duelist found herself nearly slapped for standing too close, but perhaps—even in anger—Carmela was not quite that stupid.

"I would have killed the child anyway, before it had a chance to grow too large inside me," she told the Duelist outright, watching her as if she half expected recrimination. "It was only a whim, nothing more. I thought it would be an interesting experience being a mother." She patted her breasts. "Thankfully, I came to my senses. I alone am allowed to cannibalize this body."

The following Sunday, when Rose found herself still spotting with blood from the miscarriage, she wept with all the force of a monsoon. Relief, yes. But grief, too, that a life had been forced inside her womb without her even realizing it.

"What am I?" she cried, scratching her own arms. "I'm not human anymore. I'm just a thing she uses."

The Duelist said nothing. Outside, the guards were shouting about an oversized cart. She left the tower early.

The angry season passed and with it the summer plague. The only person who died in the house was the new Steward, but that was the final indignity. Before the corpse cart could drag the poor man off to the pits, Carmela announced it was time to move.

"This is not a place for a woman with ambitions," she declared.

"So where do we go?" asked the Duelist.

They were standing over a map of the Known World, a gift from an admirer, his name long since forgotten.

"South," said her mistress.

The entire household fit into three barges, and they traveled down the river into the rich farmlands of the southern valleys. From the deck one could see lush, rolling hillsides over which ran countless grape arbors; local children in dusty rags played along the shore among ragged herds of goats.

It was idyllic, lovely—except for the boatloads of mercenaries heading north. The Duelist could smell them from nearly a mile off. War was coming again, perhaps. Across the sea, over the mountains, in the desert, in these perfect valleys—no place was ever quite safe enough. The Duelist had learned that the hard way. Peace rarely lasted.

Carmela turned her nose up at it all—the vineyards and mercenaries alike—and rested beneath her parasol, the latest Steward at her side. When an undine slid under the barges, she refused to come to the rail to see. The Duelist crowded with the crew, gaped at the creature's massive, graceful passage. The Duelist wished she was a painter, so that she could show Rose these sights with more than just her poor words.

Their new manse was even larger than the last, tucked within the most elite neighborhood of the capital; a steaming, sprawling riverine city where every canal and building was part of some ancient ruin. The Duelist did not care for the place; its rulers had funded the invasion of her desert kingdom, hoping to possess the endless, gnarled groves of a rare spice tree her people were famous for, which grew only in the perfect sandy soil at the base of their mountain.

She could smell that spice everywhere. It floated in the air, on the breath of everyone who spoke to her; she tasted it in every meal that curdled on her tongue, and even her clothing began to reek. To her, it smelled like ancient history. Like blood.

"I'm sorry," said Rose, when the Duelist could no longer hold her bitterness inside. "I remember hearing of that terrible invasion, their awful greed. My father was too far away to send help."

"It would not have mattered," the Duelist said, amazed at the ease with which she lied.

Carmela had no such reservations about their new city. Her target was the Regent, a man both cold and restless, and with immense power. He had the long-lobed ear of the king, some said—and most certainly held the keys to the coffer.

When the Regent came with them on the tour of their new home, he asked the Duelist, "You, with the sword. Man or woman?"

Carmela answered for her with a laugh. "Oh, how you jape. A woman, of course. I can't have a man guarding me while I sleep, can I?"

"You could leave that to me," he replied, with absolute seriousness. "Your guard won't be necessary in this city, I promise. If you must have protection, at least hire someone less . . . frightening to children. I'll pay for it."

"Oh, you," demurred Carmela; and later said to the Duelist, "The Regent is a very generous man."

"You think quite far ahead," she replied.

"A woman must," said Carmela. "Only men can surrender themselves to the Fates. If a woman is to make something of herself, she must plan. Otherwise, even the most precious gifts"—and she waved her hand over her face—"will go to waste."

This, the Duelist knew, was true.

For nine months she waited. She watched the household prosper. A stable was refurbished to house a matching pair of stallions, a gift from the Regent. The new cook tried to steal some gold, was caught, and survived the amputation of his left hand—but not the removal of his right.

And every Sunday she listened to Rose's dreams.

One day in particular when the monsoons had finally returned and the war in the south was turning from rumor to fact, they sat quietly for a long time, listening to the downpour. Rose looked up suddenly, half-shy, half-defiant. "Do you know what it's like when you have a word on the tip of your tongue and can't remember it?"

The Duelist did, having learned and forgotten three languages before the one she spoke now.

"Well, it's not a word precisely," said the young woman.

"Is it a song?"

Rose shook her head. "It's a life."

Then she stood and pulled off her shift, standing naked. And for an endless time neither of them moved, nor spoke.

The Duelist could feel the girl's breath on her, and she was sure the girl could feel her breath in return.

Storytellers knew other storytellers and were loyal only to one another—and to those who had a very particular need. The Duelist sought out the old ones who lived in her new city, but they had already heard her tale from their sisters and brothers in the north.

They had nothing new to offer, but only a word of warning: the body her mistress had stolen was still young and beautiful, but a smart woman like the witch would already be looking for a replacement. In the stories, in the lore, it was so—and once she left one body for the next, her old skin would be destroyed. The witch wouldn't even need to order it done.

The separation alone would kill the body she'd been inhabiting, drop it like a puppet, even with another soul still trapped inside.

The Duelist was deeply troubled by this. She'd told herself she could wait, wait forever, for the witch to leave Rose. And then it would be as simple as spiriting her away, protecting her from the witch and whoever she sent to kill her.

But this . . . she could not fight. Which meant there had to be another way.

And then came the Regent's ball, on a Saturday.

In the weeks preceding, the city had been abuzz with rumors of assassins, that this would be the night when western agents attempted to murder the king's right hand. Carmela laughed such things off as petty, but the Duelist clad herself in cold gray Samarin chain mail. Around her neck, a stiff collar. Even the edges of her gauntlets were ridged in iron.

"I am always gratified by your professionalism," said Carmela.

The Duelist nodded. "Professionally speaking, I find living more gratifying than dying."

The Regent had no wife, which made it less awkward when he sat Carmela at the great table, at his side. Her dress was more conservative than any she had worn at previous balls: a high collar, long sleeves, skirts that clung to her hips rather than sweeping outward like a great fondling hand. The dark red silk still served to reveal every curve of her astonishing body, but no one could complain that she showed an inch too much skin.

The Duelist stood against the wall, watching nothing but her for the entire night, studying the way she touched the Regent—or did not touch him—taking in her new restraint, how her mistress kept her seductiveness in check except for certain moments when the Regent reached for his glass and she leaned in to whisper in his ear, rubbing her breasts against his arm.

She was quite good. The Duelist watched her with the same admiration she felt for particularly cunning snakes, the ones who put their prey in a trance. It was clear, too, that this was what she'd been trying to achieve all along. There was no mistaking that cold, triumphant smile.

"Just think, our mistress could be the next queen if she marries the Regent," said the new Steward, in passing. "Should anything happen to His Majesty, that is. He's old, doesn't have any children. The Regent is his chosen successor."

"How very convenient," said the Duelist.

Unfortunately, midnight arrived. Before the musicians could really get started, Carmela's hands began to tremble, and a sheen of sweat could be seen across her entire face. The Duelist tried to hide her pleasure as she made her way through the crowd. Her mistress was surrounded by the most elite of the city: men and women whose pale skin was flushed pink from drink and dancing.

The Duelist ignored the affronted looks they gave her and locked eyes with Carmela.

"My lady," she said, bowing. "Perhaps it is time for you to retire."

Time slowed down. In that moment it was like a fairy tale come true, but only the part where the wolf eats the girl, a set of twins gets stuffed into an oven, or the ogre jams a little goat into its massive jaws. The look of malice on Carmela's face would have broken steel.

But the Duelist had faced grimmer odds.

"What is the matter?" asked the Regent, turning from another conversation. "Who are you to address my lady so?"

The sound of the Regent's voice broke the spell. Carmela's face smoothed into something sultry and affectionate. "My servant is right. I must retire."

"My love, this is nonsense—"

But the witch had already risen to her feet and, taking the Duelist's arm, allowed herself to be walked from the hall.

And that night, after the witch had fallen into darkness, Rose dreamed of a name.

They were seated across from each other at the kitchen table, holding hot mugs of tea. The chair was uncomfortable—most chairs were, for the Duelist. Far too small and unsteady. She preferred leaning against the wall, but she enjoyed sitting across from Rose, like a normal person. It was nice to pretend this was their home, and it was just the two of them.

Rose said, "I smell of roasted goat. I loathe goat."

"Hunger is much worse than goat."

"Perhaps," Rose said, and stiffened. A moment later, she rattled off a long, complicated word.

It was not a language the Duelist knew. "What does it mean?"

Rose closed her eyes. "It's a name from my dream. A name of someone powerful. An emperor, I think. But he was speaking to the witch, and she was in no other body but her own."

The Duelist straightened. "How do you know that?"

"I just do." Rose looked startled and set down her tea. She was on her feet next, pacing around the kitchen. The hearth cat, asleep by the ashes, looked up at her and meowed.

"It's a feeling," she said, rubbing her hands together. "In dreams, you just know things."

"The name you heard—it was not her name? You're sure?"

"She spoke it from her lips, addressing the emperor. It belongs to him."

"Repeat it."

Rose said it again—and a hundred times after that. The Duelist tried to say the name, but it was impossible. The language was a complex tonal tongue, more nuanced than even Stygian.

"Perhaps," the Duelist said, without too much hope, "I could bring a linguist."

"I'll do you one better," Rose said, reaching into a bag of flour, and tossed a handful onto the table. "I can see it in my head."

And in forty-seven strokes, she traced out the characters of the name.

It took the Duelist a month to find someone who could help her. A young scholar who, for three weights of silver, explained to her that this so-called emperor had ruled two hundred years before, across the sea, not far from where the Duelist's nation had fallen.

"Not a very successful emperor. Assassinated by his daughter, or perhaps his wife. His one crowning achievement? A fortress library high up on the slopes of Mount Attarra. With a peculiar covenant. No woman could set foot inside its halls, upon pain of death.

"He must not have liked women too much," joked the scholar.

"Perhaps," said the Duelist, "it was a precaution."

"Against what?"

The Duelist got to her feet. "What were the names of his wife and daughter?"

The scholar required a ten-weight of gold and sent out two dozen chiroptera. Six months passed before one finally returned. From the library, no less. "The fates have smiled on you, Duelist," the young scholar said. "They almost never honor petitions."

Such simple moments when lives change, when one world ends and another begins. She remembered another time, another place, how she stared out at a cloud and her mother, in a high voice, called her name, told her to run. The soldiers were already halfway across the field. The Duelist ran. They caught her anyway and nothing was ever the same again.

The scholar handed her the sheet of vellum, and with her hands trembling, the Duelist tucked it inside her blouse, against her heart.

That night the Regent threw a party and announced to everyone his betrothal to Carmela. At the edge of the banquet table sat his cousin's daughter, no older than fourteen, and already blindingly beautiful. She was to marry the king in less than a year.

The witch never once looked at the young princess, and that of course was how the Duelist knew. Twice the witch caught her eye, and the third time she snapped her fingers, summoned her to the dais.

"Why are you smiling so much?" demanded Carmela in a whisper. "Are you that happy for me?"

"I am a romantic at heart," said the Duelist.

Storytellers gave names to everything because they knew, better than anyone, that names were power. To name a witch was to control a witch, and, in the old stories at least, to destroy her.

The Duelist had dealt in death most of her life. If there was such a thing as a soul, hers was blacker than night. What would another stain matter? It was said that when a person died, their souls were weighed. Perhaps love would grant her some forgiveness. Such a thing happened in stories, sometimes.

She did not wonder how the scales would weigh for the witch's soul.

There was a scandal, of course. Wild, torrid speculation that occupied the elite for years and had them looking over their shoulders at night, putting new locks on their doors, shivering in their underclothes with gruesome anticipation.

Not one of them had imaginations humble enough to conceive a woman such as Carmela abandoning of her own free will the most powerful man in the south. And then, simply, disappearing. Leaving behind a household. Taking nothing with her, save jewels and gold.

Everyone blamed that female beast who was her shadow. Such an ungodly creature, more man than woman. Gone, too. Not a trace. Probably a thief who had murdered poor, beautiful Carmela and fed her dismembered body to the sewers. Or perhaps the man-woman was actually a secret agent of the north, bribed to murder the woman who had the Regent's heart, to unmake him; a most grievous attack that some called an act of war.

But war was coming anyway. It always was, always would be.

The Regent dispatched hunters. They never returned. He hired mercenaries. They never came back for their gold. He hired spies, oracles, sent letters to the Lord Marshals of cities a thousand miles away, asking them to listen for rumors of a woman who looked like a man, who bore a sword, who called herself the Duelist.

It made her chuckle, sometimes, when she'd hear tales of the Regent who had gone mad for the loss of a woman—only, the story changed, as stories sometimes do. It wasn't long before the impossible beauty he was to marry was entirely forgotten—but not the woman warrior who had defeated him, shamed him. She lived on in tales, grew in stature, prowess, mercilessness.

Even, in beauty.

"But you are beautiful," Rose would say, tucking her scarf more closely around her throat, her silver earrings chiming in the wind. Faint wrinkles had begun to touch the corners of her bright eyes and mouth, deepening when she smiled. Which was often.

"But you love me," the Duelist would reply.

Years passed. Not many, but enough.

A rumor bloomed, with an unexpected origin, carried deep from the east, in wild lands never conquered, lands ruled by nomads on fast horses. Barbarians, they were called. Fur-wearing, slant-eyed mongrels.

Who also, it was said, guarded veins of gold thick as a dragon's neck, endless gold that blinded men in the sun, filled with healing powers: gold that would make a saint go mad with avarice. Deep in the mountains. Deep in the forests. Deep where no king had ever been able to send a single spy. Not without having his head returned in a handsomely embroidered velvet bag.

Only silk and spice merchants could buy passage through those barbarian lands. Escorted, watched, gently (and sometimes forcefully) guided. The smart merchants minded their own business. Respected rules of passage. Bartered, drank, made gestures of peace with those wild men and women. Without forgetting, ever, that they would never be one of them.

And so it was quite strange—impossible, really—when a spice merchant came home to his city telling a tale of two foreign women living amongst these barbarians—dressed in furs and silk, necks wrapped in loose scarves, riding fine horses. Seen with his own eyes, he swore. One of them huge, so broad in the shoulders he would have sworn she was a man until he saw the curve of her breasts beneath her jacket. Wearing a sword against her back, and her skin dark as a desert shadow.

And then, there was her companion.

"She was not human," protested the merchant. "No human woman could be so beautiful. I thought I must be mad."

"You are mad," said his colleagues. "No foreigners would ever be allowed to live amongst those horse-riding dogs."

"No," replied the merchant, incensed. "I heard them. The mannish one told that beauty, 'I would still kill the world for you.'"

"Stop," replied the others. "You're drunk."

But the merchant leaned forward. "They held hands even when they rode. It was the strangest thing. And that fair creature, that most beautiful woman, kissed that immense mannish paw and said, 'No. We are free, forever.'"

"Fool," they said. "Idiot."

It was beyond impossible. Offensive, even. Such lunacy.

But the tale spread. It made the storytellers laugh.

Once, they said, there was a witch who cursed a beautiful girl into a deep sleep. Until a warrior found and woke her, and together they killed the witch. A witch who had spread her curse through many lands—some, where her evil was still remembered. Where her killers would be welcome.

Storytellers have a long reach.

The theme of The Starlit Wood, *the anthology where "Briar and Rose" first appeared, was simple: a fresh take on old fairytales. Sleeping Beauty was*

already on my mind. The Disney remake, which focused on Maleficent, had only come out the year before, but the troublesome nature of the source material hadn't left me.

The problem of the original Sleeping Beauty (called "Sun, Moon, and Talia" written by Italian poet Giambattista Basile in 1634) is that, ultimately, it's a story about a woman who is far more attractive "dead" than she is alive: a woman who has little agency, who is forced into an unnatural sleep, raped while she is unconscious, and then, when she finally wakes, must go and marry the man who took advantage of her. It's a bleak story, but not an unfamiliar one. It's also one of my least favorite fairy tales, which is why I wanted to reinvent it as a tale about women, and the power of women, and how women save each other and themselves through sisterhood and love.

As most women I know will tell you, they don't always sleep a lot—but they fight plenty.

THE LIGHT AND THE FURY

THERE WERE GODS IN THE SEA, but Xīng had never prayed to them, nor to any holy spirit since she had buried the tin star. Yet she found herself on the cusp of prayer as she plummeted fifty feet to the dark Pacific, a leather harness buckled around her torso and shoulders, dangling like some gristly worm at the end of a long hook. The cable was not quite long enough and when the dirigible heaved upward, caught by the first, smashing gust of the oncoming storm, Xīng was torn from the brine, swinging madly, naked toes skimming foam. She would have vomited had there been anything in her stomach, but she had emptied her gut that morning. Never an admirer of flying.

"You see it?" roared one of the lieutenants, boots securely locked within the iron braces of the hangar floor. Xīng, on the ascending portion of her dizzying, madcap swing, managed to glimpse the young man leaning down, headfirst, into the fifty feet of air separating him from the churning sea. It was night, no moon. Low clouds. He was dressed in warm silver wool and leather, and wore search-goggles over his eyes, crystal lenses lit like twin moons.

Xīng wished to remind the young man that he was in a better position to see than she; but the dirigible dipped, plunging her back into the sea. The lieutenant shouted again, though the drone of the engines drowned his words. Xīng, clinging to the cable as she kicked her legs, cast a wild glance around her.

Nothing. Impossible to see. The hull's exterior lights had been dimmed, and the waters were black. A wave slammed, rolling Xīng upward with sickening speed—and then down, sucked under. She held her breath as the ocean buried her, listening to a brief muted roar in her ears. She gripped the cable with all her strength.

When she resurfaced, the lieutenant was still calling out to her. His voice had gone hoarse. He held a knife in his hand, serrated steel reflecting the soft phosphorus glow of the night paint smeared against the wall around the exposed hangar gears. He was not looking at her, but at the sky.

Xīng twisted around the cable, searching—and discovered pinpricks of light, burning behind the clouds—growing larger, brighter. Rumbling shuddered the air, metallic groans broken with pops and low whistles that cut through her eardrums. She gritted her teeth, and threw back her head. The lieutenant was staring at her again. His knife, pressed to the cable. Xīng fumbled to free her own blade, sheathed among the sealed packages strapped to her body.

One-way trip. She had understood that, even before leaving the mountains; before saying yes; before packing her guns and memories, and her father's chemicals.

"Go!" she screamed at the lieutenant, cutting through the cable in one swipe, nearly breaking off the blade in her haste. The dirigible surged upward at the last moment, leaving her airborne. As she fell backward into the sea, swallowing a scream, she glimpsed that final surge of light through the clouds.

And then, nothing. Just down, down deep into the ocean. Her eyes squeezed shut. She lost her knife and did not care. All she could hear was her hammering heart, and another kind of pulse—longer, deeper, a single shockwave that boomed through her body like thunder. She clawed upward, lungs burning, and burst through the surface with a gasp.

The dirigible was trying to flee. It was a small air ship, built for speed and the transport of politicians, intercontinental couriers—but not war. Silver as a bullet, and slender as one, engine-fired with some of the finest core crystals the skull engineers could produce, and still, it had no chance against the vessel plunging from the clouds: an Iron Maiden, bristling with the sharp mouths of cannons, each one silhouetted like needles against the beacon lights shining from the hull. A monstrous thing, blotting out the sky as its belly rode overhead, radiating such heat from its exposed crystalline core that her face felt burned.

Xīng heard the thrumming charge before the cannons fired—felt the vibration in the water. Flinched, instinctively, at that first shot—blasted in rings of fire at the escaping dirigible, which was making a sharp ascent into the clouds. Shells tore through the silken sail, igniting hot gas. She stared, resigned and horrified, as a fireball erupted around the dirigible.

Reminded her of a man burning alive. Or a mass coffin in the oven, souls trapped inside. She imagined bodies tumbling, falling, swallowed by the sea.

Just as she was swallowed, moments later.

Hands grabbed her ankles, and yanked her under.

There had been experiments in her youth involving a pressure chamber, performed by a man on loan from the Redcoats who had something to prove. The ocean brought back those memories: all that immense, inescapable strain, as though the sea wanted to squeeze her vital organs into pudding, or implode her eyes, and brain.

Xīng had no skill for water, having never been able to stand its weight against her body. The men had to drag her along, blind, like a child. One of them, only moments after slinging lead hooks through her harness and tugging her unbearably deep, guided her hand to her nose. He forced her to pinch her nostrils shut, and then held a tube against her mouth. Bubbles tickled her lips. She opened, just enough, choking—swallowing ocean and air as her mouth clamped tight around the tube. The ache in her lungs eased, but little else.

After an interminable length of time—during which she suffered a slow-burning hysteria—the men holding her arms stopped swimming and the top of her head brushed a hard surface. The hooks were removed from her harness, and the air tube pulled from her grasping lips. The men shoved her up a long, metal column, and she kicked and clawed toward the light that burned through her closed eyelids. Strong hands grabbed the harness knotted around her body. She was hauled upward. Dragged from the ocean onto a warm steel floor.

A thick blanket was spread immediately over her body, tucked against her legs with immeasurable care. The cold had never bothered her, but nevertheless, Xīng lay for a long moment, shuddering—focused on nothing but the air in her lungs, and the pleasure of no longer enduring that unspeakable pressure. Aware, even with her eyes closed, of all the men packed into that small space around her. Every sound was amplified: the rasp of their breathing, the shuffle of boots, the hum of the crystals and the coal furnaces burning, somewhere beneath her.

"Lady Marshal," said a quiet voice. "You, MacNamara."

Xīng exhaled, going still. Suffocating again, but in a different way. Until, with all the grace and strength she could muster, she pushed herself to her knees. Her strong quick fingers tugged the blanket higher upon her shoulders so that it would not slip, and she tried to sit straight and strong. The crew would talk. Best to make a good impression, what little was left.

But it was difficult. When she looked into the faces of those silent staring boys who were crammed around the hatch—hardly a man with real years among them—she was unprepared for the awe and fear in their eyes.

She did not feel fearsome. Just wet and cold, and tired. A woman old enough to be their mother, black silvered braids dripping seawater against skin the color of sun-dried loam. She had been pretty once, or so others had said, but she had not looked at herself in a reflecting glass for more than ten years. Xīng could only guess that she had aged like her mother.

The sealskin parcels strapped to her body were heavy, as was her soaked clothing: rough cotton shirt and a man's trousers, clinging to her, perhaps indecently. Gold glinted above her left breast, hammered in the shape of a star. A new badge. The envoys from the fledgling American government had given it to her, right before she left the warm Pacifica coast of New China. She had almost tossed the badge into the sea, but at the last, decided to wear it. It meant nothing to her—but to the aircrew, it had been legend. Part of a costume. A mask.

A sinewy, brown hand appeared. Xīng stared, taking in the thick cuff of scar tissue around that muscled wrist, and then allowed herself to be pulled onto her feet. She glimpsed a dizzying blur of navy wool and gold stars, before anchoring her gaze on handsome cheekbones, a shaved head. The man had a Chinese look about him—in his eyes, mostly—but something else, too. Mixed blood, like her. Xīng searched his face with great care, finding wrinkles about his weathered eyes, and a touch of silver in the bristle around his jaw. She had been finding white in her own hair for five years, but had not thought much of it until now.

"Captain Shao." Xīng tightened her grip on his hand, as he did hers, before letting go.

He inclined his head. "I apologize for our late arrival. The British have dropped mines throughout the Pacific. We had to alter course almost a dozen times before we found a safe route."

"The air ship that brought me here," she began, and then stopped, unable to continue. Gone soft, when she could not even speak of the dead.

Captain Shao rubbed his scarred wrist. "My swimmers witnessed the attack. They're searching for jumpers who might have survived the explosion."

Xīng thought again of that aircrew, young as this one, all earnest and red-blooded, most of them too nervous to look her in the eyes. "Beijing," she said hoarsely. "The Emperor."

Captain Shao hesitated. "Best if you come with me."

Xīng gave him a sharp look. He issued a command. Boys scattered, returning to their duties—many with lingering, backward glances. She had not realized how many had come to see her until they dispersed. All of them, bursting with rumors and the damnable old stories. As she followed the captain down the corridor, every boy she passed—every single one—pressed his knuckles to his brow. None could have been older than sixteen.

"They've talked of nothing else since learning you'd be coming aboard," Captain Shao told her, gently touching one of those genu-flecting boys on the shoulder. The teen blushed, tearing his gaze from Xīng, and stooped to pick up a brush and pot of night paint. He began streaking a fresh layer into the grooves set along the iron wall, and the immediate glow was cool as winter light.

She almost reached for the captain, but pressed her fist against her thigh. "They should know better. You're all in danger now. When I dis-covered who they had sent to meet me—"

"We're always in danger," Captain Shao interrupted, glancing at her over his shoulder with eyes that were far harder than the soft, pleasant tone of his voice. "But I do believe they think you're worth it."

"They're only children."

"My men," he corrected sternly. "Don't belittle them, *Marshal Mac-Namara*. Not when you know why there's no one else left to fight. Not when they admire you so."

The admonishment cut deeper than it should have. "Call me Xīng. I stopped being a marshal after the war."

"Did you?" Captain Shao gave her a faintly mocking smile, glancing down at the gold star pinned to her shirt. "I don't think the world has quite caught up with your resignation."

He turned before she could think of an appropriate response—though there was none. Stories had been spun for years, becoming larger and more fantastic, turning her into a woman, a creature, that she could never hope to be. Legends were not flesh and blood. And she was no hero.

The corridor twisted. Steam exhaled from small valves, and when Captain Shao led Xīng past a narrow iron stairwell, she felt a wave of suffocating heat rush upward over her body. Engine room. Voices shouted below, accompanied by the mournful wail of a fiddle, and then, in counter-melody, the lilt of a penny whistle. Some Gaelic tune, the likes of which she had often heard in Albany.

Xīng raised her brow. "You play music in the core?"

"It increases engine efficiency," Captain Shao replied, peering down. She followed his gaze, and glimpsed fragments of immense crystal shards, part of a whole crown embedded in an iron cradle that left its roots exposed to the ocean itself: a natural, necessary, coolant. "The more complex the tune, the better. Musicians have become quite sought-after by the military, though each core seems to respond differently. Mine prefers strings, but I know one commander who can only make fifty knots accompanied by a harmonica."

Captain Shao opened another narrow iron door, revealing a small cabin: bed crisply made, papers stacked neatly on a narrow desk bolted to the floor. Fresh night paint had been spread over grooves in the wall, casting a cool, luminous glow throughout the crunched space. Not much decoration: just a round ink painting of a sparrow hidden among cherry blossoms, and a golden locket that hung from a hook. Xīng felt like stooping when she entered, and straightened with caution— half-expecting her head to brush against the ceiling. The air smelled humid, metallic, like blood mixed with gear grease and sweat.

Captain Shao squeezed inside, shutting the door securely behind him. He set the lock, and she was glad. For the first time in weeks she felt safe, though it was strange being together, in such a tight space. Reminded her of things she wanted to forget.

Xīng stared at the locket. "This is your cabin."

"I won't have you bunking with the crew," he replied, and then hesitated, studying her. Xīng met his gaze, remaining steady, unruffled. She might have spent the past decade lost in the mountains, but she remembered what it felt like to be judged.

"You have something unpleasant in your eyes," she said.

"This is a suicide mission," he replied bluntly. "*Your* suicide."

"Such a pessimist." Xīng turned from him, and began removing the sealskin packages strapped to her body. At least ten, of varying sizes. Beneath her bare feet the floor was warm and unsteady. When she stood in one place for too long, vibrations from the crystal core rattled her bones. She unwrapped her boots—still dry—and sat on the edge of the hard bed, turning them upside down, one after the other. She carefully shook out other small parcels, which made faint sloshing sounds when she held them up to her ear. Satisfied that the contents were still whole, she set them aside, and tugged on her boots.

"How long have you been captain?" she asked quietly, not looking at him as she smoothed her hands over the tall, worn leather shafts, poking her fingers through a bullet hole, or two.

He was silent a moment. "Several years. After the Brits were rousted from the Colonies, we were ordered into the South Pacific to work with the Chinese and their fleet. I received my command at the beginning of the opium conflict."

"You would die for your men," she said, unfolding another parcel.

Captain Shao pushed away from the door. "Who are *you* dying for?"

Xīng smiled bitterly, pulling free her gun. "I believe that would be your sister, Tom."

There was no such thing as one truth, but so far as the witnesses were concerned—and those who wrote down their stories, and couriered them across the sea to the East Americas and the Pacifica regions of New China—it seemed that some years back, British sailors had vandalized a temple in Kowloon, killing a monk, and then—after getting drunk—raged through a local village with guns blazing, taking turns with the young women, and murdering men in cold blood. It was not the first time such violence had occurred, but unlike previous encounters—

resulting, with one exception, in quick beheadings—Qing authorities were summarily denied access to the sailors. Who, with a great deal of sobriety, were set immediately to sea by their superior officers, and ferried to India on a fast ship. Given that one of the criminals happened to be the bastard son of a duke, this was not entirely surprising.

Ties, however, had long been strained between China and Britain. Not that anyone should have been surprised about *that*, either. Xīng might have been living in the mountains, but she still heard from the trappers, Cheyenne, and Chinese gold miners who occasionally visited her home. The English, she had been told, had finally found a way to take revenge on the Chinese for trading with the colonists during the war for independence, and it was a wickedness that had taken even her breath away.

Using the exclusive trade rights of the British East India Company, England had saturated Chinese markets with opium. So slowly, so insidiously, the Imperial trade authorities had not realized the danger. Not until two million were turned into addicts. And then two million had become ten million.

Efforts to halt the import of drugs would have eventually led to war—but it was said by some that the Kowloon murders were the final straw. The Emperor ordered all British sea ships seized, and their cargoes burned. Dirigibles were shot down, torpedoed with cunning gunpowder kites, and blazing missiles.

And the British, in turn, declared war.

But even the risk of China falling to England would not have been enough to bring Xīng down from the mountain. No matter how much the fledgling American government—and the Chinese officials from the Pacifica court—begged.

Until the rumors changed everything.

It took three days for the submersible to reach the southern China coast. Twice they encountered mines, and both times swimmers—Scots-Irish colony lads and former Chinese pearl divers—had to be sent out to cut the nets with their bare hands and weight the explosives with iron balls to sink them to the bottom of the sea. No other way around. The British war machine was thorough.

"The Emperor has already relocated his children and most of his wives to the Chinese colonies on the Pacifica coast," Captain Shao said on their last evening together, drinking oolong tea and snacking on dumplings that the cook had made special for Xīng. For the most part, Shao had avoided her until now; and she had obliged by keeping her own distance, mingling with him only at meals, or the few concerts she had attended in the engine room, sitting quietly in the corner while the boys played twisty jigs to the humming crystal core.

"South, in the gold country," he went on, "though I've heard rumors that his oldest sons will be journeying deeper inland to live with the Navajo. The Brits never could keep up with the natives, and the Emperor wants his heirs to learn about survival in case they must return to fight for their kingdom. He thinks his family has gone soft."

"Everyone saying yes to you all the time will do that," Xīng told him absently, studying the last of the Imperial military reports that he had saved for her, some of the complicated characters scribbled in obvious haste on rough sheets of raw silk. "The Iron Maiden that destroyed my transport could have hit, in three days, any part of New China territory. It might be there now. Our air defense is strong, but all it would take is one good strike."

He looked at her as he did only when they were alone, with thoughtfulness, a glimmer of warmth, and a sadness that Xīng could hardly tolerate. "Fears of air attacks aren't why you were called back. *Or why you agreed.*"

"The envoys told me stories," she admitted, touching the revolver holstered to her hip. No need for a weapon on the submersible, but its weight helped her think. That, and the crew enjoyed seeing it. She had used a rifle during the war, and it was her firearm of choice, but the revolver was a recent invention and Xīng found that she liked having the ability to shoot rounds in quick succession. Not that she had been aiming at much of anything but fir trees for the last decade; though occasionally, some men had thought to visit her mountain home in the hopes of murder and reputation.

"Stories," Captain Shao echoed flatly.

She gave him a hard look. "They told me things that no one could have made up."

"A trap, then."

"No." Xīng stroked the revolver, and then her thigh, feeling the puckered scars beneath the clothing she had borrowed from one of the crew. "Not this time. They know I'm alone and not a threat. Not anymore."

Captain Shao made a small sound. Xīng looked at him sharply, but he made no effort to hide the faint amusement darting against his mouth.

"Queen of the Starlight Six," he said quietly. "Most feared band of riders on the continent. I heard once from a captured British sailor that mothers still tell children stories about you, to scare them into being good."

Xīng shrugged. "They also say I'm ten feet tall, a Chinese princess who can change into a dragon. *And* that my eyes are capable of looking into a man's soul and burning it free of his bones. Which, apparently, is what I did to an entire army of Brits off the Atlantica coast, leaving corpses that were little more than ash."

"Well," Captain Shao replied, "you always terrified *me*."

"It was your sister who scared you," Xīng shot back, looking again at the golden locket hanging on his wall, and then him, searching for Maude in his face. "I was the quiet one."

He rubbed his face, and leaned back in the chair with his eyes closed. Their knees brushed, and for a moment she was a child again, sitting on the swing her father had built, and that all the children fought and made bets over, simply because it could go higher and faster than any other. A swing built for a child who possessed similar strengths of speed and power.

"Quiet, but savage," he murmured. "That's what Maude would say."

Xīng shuffled his papers into a neat pile, unwilling to remember. "We arrive tonight?"

"You know we do."

"Your orders are to wait for a day, and then go."

"With or without you."

"It will be without me." Xīng finally looked him in the eye. "You'll wait for a messenger who will tell you whether or not I succeeded."

Captain Shao stared for a moment, and then leaned forward—so quickly, with such menace, her hand flew to her gun. She moved faster than he did, and suffered a vision before he stilled: her weapon raised at his head, trigger pulled, with blood and brain and bone—and the aching silence, the terrible silence, suffocating the roar of the shot. She could taste the gunpowder on her tongue, and feel the burn of the recoil in her shoulder.

But it was not real. Not yet. Not ever. Xīng forced herself to relax, even as Captain Shao stared from her eyes to her hand, still pressed to the revolver at her hip.

"They all said you were dead," he murmured stiffly, as though he could hardly force the words past his lips. "And if not dead, then ruined. No one could imagine another reason for you abandoning your responsibilities. Not when you had so much power. Not when someone like you was needed in the rebuilding."

"Someone like me," she whispered, unable to move her hand. "I was a killer."

Captain Shao shook his head, but that was instinct, in the same way she had reached for her gun—and she listened for reassurance and heard none—watched his eyes and imagined his memories of her: covered in blood and fragments of bone, sour with the stench of decay after days of hot sun; walking away from the screams of the dying while her riders celebrated with toasts and laughter. She'd never once admonished them—always too relieved they'd survived another battle. They were only human, after all.

But there was no denying the truth. No denying how much pain she had caused in service to her country, and herself. How many families still grieved the losses, even though it had been war? Memories were long.

"It was not your fault your crew died," he said. "Maude betrayed you all."

"And you," Xīng replied tersely. "But it wasn't just that. My time was over. What people love in war, they hate in peace."

And I hated my power, she wanted to say. *I hated what people expected of my power.*

Captain Shao gave her a grim, skeptical look—so much like his sister—and the old, unbearable sadness rose again in her throat. She wished he would understand without her saying more, ashamed that she needed his compassion. She hadn't allowed herself to be honest with anyone in years. But what was the harm in a little truth between childhood friends, when there was no one else left in the world who remembered Xīng as she'd been, before the war?

There was no opportunity to say more. A bell chimed, and a sharp whine cut through the hull. The engine quieted, signaling the beginning of a steady drift. Three days, and now they were done.

"Well," Captain Shao said softly.

"I know," Xīng replied, and finally forced her hand away from the gun.

A boat was waiting for her when she broke through the surface of the ocean. A small craft, little more than a slab of wood laden down with fishing nets, and fat cormorants squatting inside bamboo cages, a boat so flimsy, a two-mast junk would have sunk it with merely a swipe. Xīng said nothing, though. It was night, and she could see the stars. She had almost forgotten what they looked like.

Captain Shao joined the swimmers who guided her from the submersible. It was against protocol for him to leave his vessel, but none of the boys who saw her off made mention of their commanding officer abandoning them, if only temporarily. They said good-bye in the same way they had said hello—with silence, and respect, and fear.

Her belongings were strapped to her body, wrapped again in seal-skin, along with a set of dry clothes. Captain Shao, who had stripped down to a special suit made of shark hide, pushed her out of the water into the boat, helped, from within, by its sole occupant: a young Chinese woman. Her hair was shorn so close to her scalp that even in the darkness Xīng could see the cuts and bruises on her skin, and a deep red welt, nearly a scar, covered her throat. Her movements were slow, and pained. Captain Shao frowned, giving the newcomer a hard, thoughtful, look.

Xīng leaned over the edge of the boat, gripping his forearm, tight as she could. He tore his gaze from the other woman, and did the same—his knuckles white, seawater streaming down his face. Beyond the harsh rasp of their breathing, and the lap of waves against the boat, she heard distant booms, one after the other, raining down into her bones.

She tried to release his arm, but he held on, pulling himself so close the boat tipped dangerously sideways.

"No mercy," he whispered. "Don't you dare."

Xīng forced herself to smile, though it was faint, grim, and felt like death. "Stay safe, Tom."

His jaw tightened with displeasure, and something else: too much like desperation for comfort. Xīng jammed her hip against the edge of the boat and reached down, ready to pry his fingers off her arm. His grip was beginning to hurt, and his men were staring.

But he let go before she touched him. Let go, as though burned, and pushed away from the boat—and her. He treaded water, holding her gaze, and she did not look away, or blink. Just held on, in the only way she knew how: with memory, and heart, and the certain knowledge that distance was always safer.

The Chinese woman began rowing. Xīng raised her hand. Captain Shao did not. He stared a moment longer, and then dove. His men followed him in silence. Swallowed, as though their flesh was made of sea and shadow. She knew better than to watch for them, but found herself doing so anyway.

"Are you ready?" asked the other woman softly. She sounded as though she was from the Mainland south, perhaps even Kowloon, which spoke a different Chinese dialect entirely, though her tone was educated, even refined. Xīng was accustomed to Mandarin, having been born to a Chinese mother in the territory of New China, but she had spent much of her adult life out east in the Colonial Americas, speaking English. Sometimes she still had trouble with the various accents of the native Chinese (and the Europeans, as well), though enough gold miners had come around the mountain over the past ten years to give her practice.

The woman's breathing turned ragged, accompanied by a faint whistling grunt every time she pulled at the oars. Her movements were awkward. Blood seeped from the deep welt in her neck. Xīng scooted forward, and without asking, placed her hands on the slender wooden grips. Cormorants clucked, shifting their wings, and in the distance, the low, crashing booms of cannons still rumbled.

"You're injured," Xīng said, as the other woman leaned slowly away from the oars. "The Emperor should not have sent you."

The woman touched her throat, and then her shaved, nicked scalp; a flick of a delicate wrist, a turn of her arm so that her frayed black sleeve fell down a fine-boned arm. Xīng would have thought her a Buddhist nun, had it not been for the fine weave of her dark clothing, as well as the look in her eyes, wild and hard. "I was uninjured in the beginning. Nor was I meant to meet you here. Everyone . . . everyone else . . . was captured. I was the only one who escaped." She swallowed heavily, looking at the birds, the ocean, anywhere but at Xīng. "You are not what I expected."

"I am Xīng MacNamara," she replied, because she had never found a better answer to that statement, not even after hearing it for most of her life. No one was ever who he or she was supposed to be; not even Xīng could say for certain that she knew herself completely. Truth rested only in action; the rest was mystery.

"I am Xiao Shen Cheng," said the woman, after a brief hesitation.

Xīng was focused on the horizon, where a faint orange glow had appeared. As such, it took longer than it should have to recognize the name. But when she did, everything stopped—everything—and the boat began to drift. She stared at the woman, letting it sink in, and suffered disbelief, and dread.

"You came too late," whispered the Empress, rubbing her pale hand against bloodshot eyes. "My husband is dead."

Xīng forced herself to breathe. "How?"

Shen Cheng gave her a disdainful look. "It was a sustained effort. We fought well. But the emperor had sent our crystal skull away with the children, and the remaining core was not powerful enough to feed the lines. When the Jugranaughts came, we could only slow them."

Xīng sat back, struck with a chill. *Jugranaughts.* She had heard that name from the envoys—heard it for the first time in a decade—and then again in the Imperial court on the Pacifica coast; from the mouths of the silver bullet aircrew, and on the submersible, whispered when the boys would see her coming. No one ever thought she could hear them, but that was the curse and the gift of being who she was. Only Captain Shao had refrained from speaking of those skull-enhanced men and women—but that was because he was also Tom, and shared the pain of his sister's betrayal.

Behind them, below, in her bones, Xīng heard a low, oppressive groan, a rumble that rose from the sea through the bottom of the boat. A despairing sound, and the answering swell that lifted them was unnatural and stomach-roiling. Something brewing in the water. More than one submersible. A battle.

Xīng tightened her grip on the oars, prepared to row again—and found herself staring down the barrel of a ruby-studded revolver. British design, new and gleaming.

Shen Cheng closed her eyes and pulled the trigger. Xīng had already begun to move, reaching out to knock aside the weapon—but the deafening blast skimmed her left arm, and sent the empress recoiling backward over the edge of the boat. She bobbed to the surface immediately, gasping for air, arms thrashing the water. Not much of a swimmer, either.

Xīng did not jump in after the drowning empress. She took a deep breath, rolling through the pain and rush of blood to her head. Ten years on the mountain. Quiet, peaceful. She could have died an old woman, with no one the wiser. A good meal for the scavengers.

She picked up the British revolver, testing its weight in her hand. "Where are the Jugranaughts?"

Xīng was not entirely certain the woman would hear—or care—but that bruised, battered face turned toward her, and a skinny hand managed to latch on to the edge of the boat. Below them, the waters swelled again, as though from the passage of a large body. Xīng thought of Shao, and Maude, and the rest of her old crew—slaughtered, ripped to pieces—and balanced the revolver across her forearm, aiming it at the woman's head.

"Tell me where they are," she said again.

Shen Cheng shook her head, though the corner of her gaze lingered on the glittering gold star pinned to Xīng's chest. Despair flickered through her face.

"I know the stories," she whispered. "You will kill me if I tell you."

"I've killed for less," Xīng agreed, and slammed the revolver butt on the woman's fingers. She howled, flailing. Xīng placed the weapon on the floor of the boat, and picked up the oars. She started rowing. The empress, sobbing, tried to follow; but it was like watching a log thrash.

"They tortured me!" she screamed at Xīng, her voice choking on seawater. "I had no choice!"

Xīng did not stop.

It was an accident, or so her father had always said.

He was a Scottish engineer, an adventurer, who had studied with the skull masters in China, before traveling across the Pacific to the Imperial colonies—a vast network of villages and cities that had been thriving for almost a century before England sent its first ships of men to hack a new civilization on the frontier of the far eastern continental tip.

By the time her father had arrived in New China, the Pacifica court and its alliance with the western native tribes was well known, but only by accident; the Chinese Empire had done its best to keep its colonies secret. Too many precious resources at stake: not just gold, but rich and verdant farmland, the likes of which did not exist in Asia.

Xīng's mother had been a skull master in her own right—the emperor's most valued musician, an operatic soprano whose voice was uniquely favored by the crystal skull that powered the Pacifica Court, and that formed the root strain of its crystalline harvests. She'd had a way with skulls—not just that one.

"I hear them . . . a hum made of light, right in the center of my head," she told Xīng, pushing her finger between her child's eyes. "And that light entered my womb and made you."

But Xīng had never heard that light, even if she was made from it. No skull had ever spoken to her.

But that was how her mother met the Scottish engineer, who quickly became a favorite of the old emperor (mostly likely because he hated the British even more than the Chinese did). A notoriously private woman, she'd never told Xīng much about that early courtship, only that her voice changed after giving birth and the Pacifica Court skull took a liking to a young Mongolian throat singer on loan from Beijing.

All for the best, as Xīng's father had decided to move his family out east to help manage the crystalline harvests of the new American colonies. A terrible decision for them all, Xīng had always thought. It might have been a different life, growing up inside the Imperial Court: a child with crystal-born powers, where she might have been protected, and seen as something more than a potential weapon.

But she knew that was wishful thinking. Power was always a weapon.

Then, and now, it was a rare honor to be allowed access to a crystal skull. Only fifteen had been found throughout the world—four of which were in Chinese possession—though rumor had it that many were yet to be discovered in the jungles of the far south. Expeditions were regularly sent—usually ending in bloody conflicts—but only one had thus far been found, and that by the new Americans themselves, raising their current possession to two—the other having been given to the colonies when they were still under British rule.

No one knew quite for certain how the skulls worked, only that some Mohammedan king of the Holy Lands had discovered three in the sands of an oasis: blocks of perfect crystal carved in the shape of human skulls, the likes of which no artisan had ever yet been able to duplicate.

Rather than declare the skulls a simple curiosity, the king had devoted himself to hours spent staring into those translucent eyes—one after the other, in patient succession. This, according to legend, went on for several years—until, quite abruptly, the king suffered a massive stroke that left him blind and speech impaired, but functional enough to declare that he had discovered the secrets to the skulls.

An overly ambitious statement. Two hundred years later, engineers were still learning what powers the skulls possessed—though it was widely known that an electrical current flowing through a skull into a special mineral bed was enough to instigate the growth of crystals that could be used to power the armadas, towns, even entire cities. Beyond that particular commonality, however, each skull was different. Some provided visions. Some made others go insane.

And some, as her father had discovered, changed the very essence of a human being.

Xīng found the shore far sooner than expected. She dragged the boat onto the beach, but did not bother hiding it. Just stood in rock and sand, staring at the ocean as she stripped off her wet clothes, and dressed in dry trousers and a shirt. The rest of her belongings were unwrapped quickly: revolver, two knives, her special bullets, and last, the vials of chemicals her father had prepared during the colonial war, and left to her upon his murder.

She loaded her gun very carefully. Then, with equal care, re-pinned the gold badge to her shirt, tracing her fingers along the points of the star. Warmth filled her, and then cold—sensations accompanied by memories of the old, tired arguments—when she'd still had a chance for a different life.

We need you. No one else but you. We will die if you cannot turn back the British. All of us, our freedom, lost. Shut your heart to the blood, shut your ears to the screams. You were born to no other purpose. You are exceptional only in death.

Xīng began walking to the rhythm of those old words, spoken in many different ways, from many different people, though the message had always been the same. Even her Chinese mother had told her future in blood, only that was to be admired, and not feared. Xīng had been touched by some great power, which her mother claimed to be from the stars, and so the stars were in her name, and as an adult, she had worn a star upon her breast in the service and protection of others: first in peace, and then in war.

The terrain was not far different from the estuaries and tangled forests that could be found on the coastlines of New China and the Colonial Americas. She smelled the sea and the spice of firs growing tangled on rocky outcrops. Listened to the booms and thunder of some not-so-distant battle. If the Chinese military realized the emperor was dead, then they might have already surrendered. She hoped not. She hoped that the fire staining the horizon was the British burning, and had a feeling she would be finding out for herself, soon enough. Shen Cheng had not been a strong rower. She had been sent from someplace near—and someone would be waiting for her to return. She could take a fine guess who.

But not long after Xīng abandoned the boat, she heard sounds that did not belong: shouts, the clunk of steel and wood. Familiar noises that sent her running. She was careful, and kept the revolver in her hand. Felt herself slipping back into the old days, except now she was alone, and the burden was only hers. Hers, knowing that it was the others in her crew who had always been the real heroes. So very human, with no power to protect themselves; driven only by courage and grit, and honor.

She missed them.

Shouts grew louder, frantic, cut with hoarse cries. Xīng burst onto a rocky beach and found herself facing boys, boys crawling from the sea, boys wearing air-filled ties made of sheep gut. She recognized all those faces, but there were so few, less than a quarter of their former numbers dragging free of the waves.

Xīng ran to them. Several cried her name, pointing. The rest let out a ragged cheer, and their smiles—those smiles of relief when they saw her—cut and burned, and twisted her heart. *As if now*, those smiles said, *everything will be all right.*

She grabbed the arm of the nearest boy, who was limping heavily across the rocks. Blood ran down his leg. He was pale, blond, just a scrap of a lad, but he was dragging a sealskin pouch behind him in a white-knuckled grip.

"Captain Shao?" she asked, running her hand over his face to push his sea-soaked hair out of his eyes.

The boy coughed raggedly into his palm. "Left 'fore him. He gave me 'is papers, he did, f' safekeepin.'"

"Bastards cracked the crystal core," added another boy, drawing near. "Had to jump before we sank too deep. Cap'n promised he'd follow."

Xīng gritted her teeth, briefly searching the faces around her. No sign of her friend. He was out of her hands. She holstered her weapon, and slung her arm around the waist of another child who was close to falling on his knees. Coughs wracked his chest.

"Come on," she said, and caught the eye of a sturdy red-haired lad, who seemed to be doing better than the others. "Go, pass on the word. Everyone needs to hurry. Something worse than Redcoats might be close."

His reaction was an infinitesimal flinch, but he gave her a sharp nod and ran down the beach, grabbing the boys who were already out of the water, and steering them back to the waves to help the ones still struggling. Xīng dragged the child in her arms as far as the brush, and then left him to go back for others. She kept count, as best she could, still searching for their captain.

She saw the red-haired boy again. "Your name."

"Samuel," he said breathlessly, still looking over his shoulder at the darkened sea. No one else was there. No one she could see.

"Samuel," she said, grabbing his chin and forcing him to look at her. "Weapons?"

"No'm," he replied, blinking hard. "Just fists."

Xīng let go of his face, and patted his shoulder. "Good. Find other sensible lads who can lead, and then break yourselves up into small groups. Scatter, but head for the hills. You'll be able to hide better there."

"But," Samuel began, stopping himself almost as quickly before continuing, "you're not coming with us?"

Xīng hesitated. "I'll be making sure no one follows."

"We can fight."

"You can live." She unsheathed one of her knives, and pressed it into his hand. "The others need you. So do I."

Samuel swallowed hard, but again, gave her that sharp nod—as though it was his way of steeling himself. Xīng watched him as he ran toward the others, and then turned away from the ocean, away and away, where her friend was not emerging from the waters. She faced the hills and the scrub, and listened to the distant sounds of air ships and gunpowder bombs, imagining the scent of smoke, finally, in the air. Her skin prickled, a focused chill that rode from her scalp down the back of her neck.

Xīng pulled out her revolver. Behind her, one of the boys shouted.

She turned, glimpsing a hulking figure looming from the shadows at the edge of the beach—moving in perfect silence. He was monstrous, a giant, more than eight feet tall and built like the side of a rock-hewn mountain. His fists were clad in iron, as was his chest, and he held a sword in his hands that could slice any of those boys in half with hardly a touch. Scalps hung from his belt, long black queues looped and tangled—still dripping with blood.

"Run!" she screamed, and dove through them as they scattered, throwing herself toward the giant. He grinned when he saw her, and took swipes at the escaping boys, his sword whistling through the air. Xīng skidded to a stop, took careful aim, and fired her revolver. The bullet hit his biceps, but he laughed at the wound and shook his head.

"Queen of the fookin' riders," he bellowed. "Bullets dinnae hurt me, lass."

Xīng holstered her gun, and withdrew her knife. Took another running leap, dodging under his sword, feeling a shift in her body as she moved—blood surging, burning, boiling in her veins. Red shadows gathered in her vision, and her heart pounded so hard she could taste her pulse at the back of her throat. Taste that, and more.

She slashed at his thighs, cutting deep, hacking and stabbing every part of him that she could. Taking her time, playing up his amusement. Distracting him.

His muscles were grotesquely shaped, distended beneath skin pocked with old burns and scars: a man who had been unnaturally grown over years of deliberate exposure to crystal light. After Xīng had entered the war, after her exploits had been proven to be more than some fantasy, the British had turned desperate for their own powered soldiers. But she'd been a lucky accident that was hard to repeat, and after losing too many quality men, the British government had turned to rapists and murderers, freed from prisons to be fed to the skull engineers and their experiments.

Few survived. But those that did were as hard to kill as Xīng. She'd found that out the hard way, the night her crew was murdered.

The Jugranaughts in front of her smelled like an outhouse, and his laugh was careless: arrogant and cruel. Oh, he thought he was going to live forever. Xīng understood. She'd felt that way herself, a time or two.

But then he made a choking sound.

Xīng darted away as his knees buckled. He fell face-first into the sand, but not before she saw his hands clutching his throat, his tongue so swollen it protruded from his mouth. His eyes bulged. Xīng could not imagine what he had looked like before the engineers had changed him, nor did she care. She watched the man choke to death—poisoned by her bullet.

Special bullets filled with special chemicals. Her father had made them while she was in her teens—when she was still the only one of her kind. Just in case the power went to her head. He had never been a sentimental man, but she appreciated that now.

Footsteps, behind her. Xīng turned, glimpsing a pale face.

And got shot in the chest.

The blast was deafening, and so was the pain. Xīng rocked backward into the sand. She tried to reach for her revolver, but a knife stabbed through her palm. Xīng glanced down, saw a hole in her chest the size of her fist, spurting like a geyser. She vomited blood.

Then stopped moving at all.

Xīng drifted. No dreams. Just darkness pricked with moments of desperate sorrow, and a terrible, aching homesickness for a life lost so long ago, it might as well have been something she never had.

Until, finally, she remembered her body—her body, which she did still have—and opened her eyes.

Overhead, stars. Xīng twitched her fingers, and then her feet. No restraints. The hole in her chest had healed, though scar tissue remained; one more to add to all the others that covered her body. She knew without looking that her revolver was gone—her hip felt too light. The bullets and the chemical vial had been removed from her pockets, as well. One knife remained sheathed against her thigh.

Her mouth tasted like raw meat. She smelled wood smoke, and listened to a fire crackling. A woman hummed, a low familiar tune that sent Xīng back to a time when she remembered how to smile.

She swallowed hard. "Hello, Maude."

The woman stopped humming. "I knew you would come."

Xīng sat up slowly, drinking in the person who had once been her greatest friend and lover. A whole childhood spent together. How many secrets had they shared? How many tears had Xīng shed that only Maude had seen, and tasted? There had never been anyone else but Maude, even when they drifted apart.

She looked at Maude's body, analyzing the muscles bulging from broad shoulders and thighs, the heavy sinews at her throat, those long-fingered hands that had once been smaller than hers, but now could easily wrap around her neck. A powerful body, not easily manufactured.

But Maude's eyes had sunken deep in her head, her cheeks hollow, skin gray and flaking like a healing scab. Her long hair had been shaved away, revealing scars where skull engineers had inserted probes. She resembled a corpse more than a Jugranaught.

Maude touched her face. "You look the same, except for the silver in your hair. I thought that would happen for me. But . . . there were other, unexpected side effects."

Xīng thought of her father, unwittingly exposing his body, and seed. Her pregnant mother, who spent too much time in the lab during his experiments. "You made that choice."

Maude smiled bitterly. "I told myself we'd be together forever. You were always worried about me when we'd ride into battle. Afraid I'd die before you. So I said this would make things easier . . . for *you*. And then I told myself it would let us grow old together, that we'd be equals . . . and I imagined how fine it would be for us as the Queens of the Starlight Six, and not just *the* Queen."

Xīng closed her eyes, unable to look at that familiar, crooked smile for one more moment. "You were jealous."

"In the end, yes. Maybe from the beginning."

Xīng's heart ached; so much raged inside her, she was afraid to speak. "Did it give you peace? Handing yourself over to the Redcoat engineers for their experiments? Were you satisfied after you came back, and killed the others?"

"I didn't—" Maude began, but Xīng surged to her feet, the knife somehow in her hand.

"You led those monsters to us while we slept," she snarled, and threw the blade at Maude's face.

The woman caught the knife out of the air and spun away through the sand. She was quick—quicker than Xīng remembered—and rammed her hard in the shoulder, sending them both into the fire. The knife slid against Xīng's side, but it was the flames that made her howl, and she rolled sideways as her hair and clothing burned. Maude did not scream, but stood for a moment in the flames, as though she did not feel them crackling at her skin. Then, she stepped out of the fire, and calmly reached down for the revolver that Xīng cursed herself for not seeing earlier among Maude's belongings.

"I heard there was a weapon that could murder a Jugranaught. But you didn't have this the last time we met," Maude said, as Xīng put out the flames on her body. "That night I watched you rip out the throats of the Jugranaughts who killed your crew. You used your bare hands, even your teeth. You were. . . ."

"Savage," Xīng hissed, trembling. "I had good reason to be."

Maude gave her a sad smile. "I dream of it every night. You chase me, and I run. Ten years running from you, when all I ever did before was run with you, toward you, after you."

She raised the revolver with its poisoned bullets, and aimed it at Xīng's stomach. She did not fire, though. Just studied Xing, with that sadness deepening in her eyes. "Why didn't you ever come looking? I expected it. I expected you at every corner, with your hands at my throat."

But Xīng said nothing. Nothing she *could* say, though the words bottled inside hurt worse that the burns along her back and scalp. Ten years thinking of that night, and nights before that, nights and battles and all of them together, like family. Xīng had hated the Redcoats, but she had been unprepared to hate Maude—and that was a cut that had never healed right.

On their left, a branch snapped. Maude glanced away, just for a moment. Xīng lunged.

No mercy. She slammed her fist into the other woman's face, and then hit her again, with all her strength. Bone smashed. Maude cried out, trying to bring the revolver back around to fire. Xīng grabbed her wrist and broke it with one swift twist. A Jugranaughts' should not have snapped that easily, but as Maude had said—there'd been side effects.

The revolver fell to the ground beside them. And just like that, Maude stopped fighting.

"I'm here," Xīng whispered, staring into her eyes, "with my hands at your throat."

"Finally," Maude breathed.

When Xīng was done—and Maude was truly, irrevocably, dead—she sat down by the fire, and found Captain Shao crouched on the other side of the flames. He was nearly naked, soaked, and a deep scratch ran down the length of his side. But he was alive—staring at the poisoned remains that had once been his sister.

"I'm sorry," she said to him, too weary and heartsick to feel anything but shame at seeing him here: shame, that he should witness her covered in the blood of the only family he had left. Anger simmered in her gut, too—and despair.

"It had to be this way," he said quietly, also without emotion. "For justice, if nothing else. But if she had seen me again . . ."

He stopped himself, and said nothing more for a very long time.

Xīng lay down in the sand, holding her revolver close. Just before dying, Maude had told her that no other Jugranaughts were close. The rest had remained in Shanghai, working with the British to overrun what remained of the emperor's southern seat. The Chinese military still fought, but not for long. They were running out of hope.

Light was creeping into the horizon when finally, softly, Captain Shao said, "I understand now why you left."

"I doubt that," she whispered, but pushed herself up and rubbed her face. "Your men are safe. As many as could be saved. We should find them."

His eyes glittered, reflecting the dying firelight. "We have no submersible. And there is a war raging."

Xīng studied the revolver in her hands. She had found the vial of poison nearby. More bullets could be made. "I suppose that's true."

A sad smile touched his mouth, again so much like his sister that Xīng's eyes burned with tears. "And I suppose it might also be true that the only way for us to survive is to fight."

Xīng sighed. Captain Shao whispered, "Can you be what they need?"

"No," she said quietly. "But I can try."

Captain Shao stood and walked to her. He did not look at his sister's body, but held out his hand to Xīng.

"Lady Marshal," he said. "You, MacNamara."

"Yes," she said, and took his hand.

"Write about superheroes," I was told, and having just seen a documentary about crystal skulls, which were originally thought to be pre-Columbian (but ended up being pre-Columbian by way of 19th century German artisans), my imagination conjured a firestorm of alternate histories: a world where China settled the Pacific Coast long before Columbus found these shores; where machines were powered by crystals, where these same crystals could alter human bodies and give them powers. In my mind there was a woman who had those powers: the Lady Marshal, a reluctant superhero committed to justice, and burdened by a past filled with war-time violence.

THE LAST DIGNITY OF MAN

"PUT ON THE CAPE," Alexander says. "Do it slow."

He sits very still, as the young man unfolds the shining red cloth. Here it is again: the old dream, a red dream—red on blue, with gold trim, and that lovely brand upon the young man's fine, fine chest. *The finest letter in the alphabet,* Alexander thinks. *A mighty letter, for a mighty myth.*

The cape will make it perfect.

But the young man grins, ruining the effect. What was to be serious, epic, suddenly feels like the farce it is, and Alexander looks away in shame. He barely notices the young man clip the cape into place, can barely stand to hear his own voice break the quiet.

Alexander does not know the young man's real name—only the one he has been given for this evening. All part of the ruined fantasy.

"Clark," Alexander says. "Clark. You may go now."

The young man frowns. "Sir?"

Alexander shakes his head. "Just . . . get your things and go."

Puzzlement, even a little resentment, insouciance, yet the young man does as he is told. This is not the situation where one acts up.

The young man gathers his belongings: a business suit, with tie; thick glasses. He is a beautiful creature: long of muscle and bone, a hint of a Chinese grandfather in that dark, wavy hair and best of all: the palest of eyes. A lucky find, and Alexander feels a moment of regret. But no, this is not right.

The young man leaves. Alexander sits in his chair by the window and stares at the city. There is enough light to cast a reflection in the glass; like a ghost mirror, he sees his face in shadow, transparent and wry.

Alexander is bald. He thinks he looks good, bald, though it's an affectation. The men and women in Alexander's family are thick-haired, but when Alexander turned eighteen he shaved all the hair from his head. Shaves it still, so that his scalp gleams polished and perfect.

It is a joke and Alexander knows it. His real name is Alexander Lutheran—Lex Luthor to the young men who visit him and try on the cape—but this is not a comic book, and there is no such thing as a Last Kryptonian.

Still, it is an old dream.

The research department at RanTech takes up an entire city block. The building squats in the center of downtown, where streets and sidewalks are a jungle during rush hour. Alexander likes the crowds; he keeps his office on the second floor so he can watch strangers pass just yards beyond his tinted windows. He has other offices, better offices, in prettier parts of town, but he has not seen them in more than five years.

Alexander's brothers do not understand this. They are not geneticists; they don't know about investment or banking instruments. It is why Alexander's father made his youngest son the principal shareholder in RanTech, why his two oldest pretend to manage sales and marketing while alternating between office and golf course, why the old man rests easy on his yacht with a third wife who is just out of college. Despite their differences in lifestyle, which have crippled communication, Alexander's father knows his son is a smart man. Eccentric, perhaps, but very, very smart.

Smart enough to appreciate the backbone of the company, to dwell close within the marrow, directing firsthand the brainiacs on his payroll. Biggest surprise of all? The employees actually like him. Some respect him, even—though he knows they make fun of his name, his appearance, the poster he keeps in his office. *Our boss, the mad scientist. Does he keep kryptonite in his shorts? Ha. Ha. Ha.*

But when he's around, the *Ha Ha Ha* stops. Rumor is that he fired a CFO who called him Lex Luthor at a meeting. It never actually happened, the firing, but the rumor is safely entrenched in the gossip biome of the company, never to be flushed out.

Alexander blames his mother. She insisted on his name, on the dignity of its sound. Alexander wonders if he would have a different kink if she had called him George or Simon or Larry. A name without power. Without expectation.

But no, he is Alexander. To his young men and himself he is Lex. And he has lived up to that name, in more ways than one.

"They're growing faster than we anticipated, Mr. Lutheran. We'll need bigger cages soon."

The lab is poorly lit. Or rather, it is well lit according to the parameters of the experiment. Batch #381 does not thrive under bright lights, so the scientists have installed lower-energy bulbs, the kind used in photography darkrooms. Everything is cast in red, blood red, and Alexander feels as though he is in the middle of a particularly nasty horror movie. The writhing masses of glistening flesh lumped in glass tanks do not help. In fact, it looks slightly pornographic.

Alexander steps close. The tanks are completely airtight, each one equipped with an isolated oxygen pump that filters and analyzes and recycles. There are also feeding slots—storage chambers built with a series of small airlocks and safety mechanisms, timed to release sludge when the sensors indicate that tank levels have dropped below acceptable feeding levels. The creatures like to swim through shit. It is the earthworm in them, this instinct to burrow deep.

But these pulsing, undulating worms are as thick as Alexander's arm, and it is not soil they are consuming.

"Have you added mercury to the mix yet?" Alexander asks.

Dr. Reynolds, a tall woman of middle years, quirks her lips. "Mercury, toluene, and just about every other heavy metal we can think of. They eat it right up, with no visible side effects. It's incredible, Mr. Lutheran. That sludge is so toxic the fumes alone could probably kill a person."

Alexander cannot tell if Dr. Reynolds is joking; the amusement in her voice does not reach her eyes. This is worrisome, because Alexander trusts her judgment.

"Kathy," he says. "What's wrong? Are the quarantine protocols—"

"No, nothing like that." Dr. Reynolds stares at the tank. One of the worms momentarily swells, ridges flaring in response to some mysterious biological cue. Its slick bulk disappears beneath a rolling heave of supple bodies that slip sideways to strain against the sludge-packed glass. "I hate looking at these things," she finally says. "Some days I'm even afraid of them."

"Good," Alexander says. "We're playing God, Kathy. We should be afraid."

"And here I thought God was fearless."

"The only fearless God is the one who doesn't have to live with His mistakes. If that were us, I wouldn't be forced to keep more than a hundred lawyers on the company payroll."

"Yes," agrees Dr. Reynolds. "That is indeed a sign of dark times."

There is little more to discuss. Alexander ends his meeting with Dr. Reynolds. The red lights and the red worms are best taken in short stints, and it will be lunch in an hour, and at the end of the day there will be interviews with the press about other, less secret, less controversial innovations. RanTech had been a slumping prospect when Alexander took over—now it is one of the technological backbones of the global economy, its products and services so much a part of everyday life that even in an apocalypse—a line that still makes Alexander's father chuckle—RanTech would be a sure bet.

That sort of meteoric success has led to the kind of attention Alexander does not crave, although in his desk he keeps a copy of a high-profile business magazine with his grimacing face on the cover.

But only for the headline: MEET THE SUPERHERO OF THE BIOTECH BOOM.

It's not what he'd call himself. It's not what he believes he can ever be. And yet. . . .

So Alexander wanders, moving through each floor of his building. He has a purpose, which is to make sure all the lead projects are progressing smoothly, these benign endeavors that he will be discussing with journalists, and that will guarantee fat Christmas bonuses—but he does not care how he gets there. It is enough that his legs are moving.

He is still thinking about worms.

It is a long-known fact that certain kinds of bacteria eat toxic waste and sewage, but such organisms are slow and require sensitive environments. More than two years ago, RanTech was given a government contract to develop creatures that are not so . . . sensitive. Not so slow. And now Alexander's team has succeeded. Or so he thinks.

Alexander will not lose sleep, either way. The government has paid for a genetically engineered solution to toxic spills, and that is what it shall receive. Only, there is a tiny fear in Alexander's heart. His alter-ego, after all, is unscrupulous. An unscrupulous man, without any counterpart in the world to balance his darkness.

There is no Superman. Alexander must be his own moral compass.

The wandering continues into lunch. Alexander had planned to eat his Niçoise in his office, but the sun is shining and his mind is still trapped in a red-lit room. He leaves the building and hits the sidewalk, carried by the crowd toward a destination unknown. A few people glance at his bald pate but he barely notices.

He knows why the worms frighten Dr. Reynolds. It has nothing to do with the way they look. It is enough that they are new and powerful and man-made. Evolution favors the strong, but these creatures are products of disparate evolutions. Distant biological paths, forced to collide into one body.

The government calls them Bio Machines: a deceptive term, meant to soothe. There are more planned, for various purposes; the contracts and proposals are locked within Alexander's safe, awaiting his signature. The government likes to dream big and it favors RanTech because the company is discreet, because it emphasizes results over everything. No fuss, ever. RanTech does not raise moral objections. Not when the price is right.

But Alexander knows there are all kinds of prices to pay—a price for every action—and he wonders about lines and points of no return, how far he can go before he becomes the man he pretends to be, how far he can push before myth becomes reality. He wonders, not for the first time, if creating that reality will not invite another collision of coincidence. Darkness, after all, often summons light.

Alexander wonders what he will attract if he becomes, in truth, *him*.

The sidewalk ends; he can turn left or right, but ahead of him is a vast expanse of green, and he decides that grass might be a nice change from concrete and glass. He crosses the street, passes through the open iron gate, and enters the park. The sounds of traffic fade instantly. Alexander feels cocooned by sunlight and the scent of fresh-turned soil.

Alexander finds a concession stand and buys a wilted sandwich, chips, a large soda water. The surrounding benches are taken, so he wanders off the path onto thick grass, plopping down in the shade cast by a gnarled oak. He does not sit there long before he feels a presence at his back, the subtle hint of shuffling feet.

The man is middle-aged, with a dusting of silver in his hair. He has a feral sort of look, which has nothing to do with his somewhat scruffy clothes, his tangled beard, or the limp backpack in his hand. His eyes are hollow, hungry, but there's a hint of grief beneath that gaze, and Alexander feels an impulse to run from that sorrow. But then he remembers the worms and the papers in his safe, the other projects percolating in his labs, and he thinks, *I am much more frightening than this man's sadness. And he, at least, is human.*

Alexander nods at the man, who hesitates for just one moment before setting down his backpack and slumping to his knees in the grass. Alexander does not make him ask; he gives the man half his sandwich, and pushes over the drink and chips.

"Thanks," he says. Alexander can hear the desert in that voice, which carries the dry timbre of sand. Elegant and coarse, like its owner. "My name is Richard."

"Alexander."

Richard nods. The two men say nothing more. They eat and watch joggers and mothers with strollers; children on leashes and dogs running without; teenagers slinging Frisbees, shouting obscenities at each other with adolescent affection. It is a very nice afternoon.

"Tell me about yourself," Richard finally says, finishing the last of the chips. "What kind of man are you?"

Alexander studies Richard, but the man's eyes are stronger now, more full. He even looks belligerent. Defiant. Alexander smiles.

"I'm not a very nice man," he says.

Richard grunts. "So, you're an honest man."

"When it suits me."

"My statement still stands."

Alexander chuckles. "What about you?"

"Ah, see, I'm a very good man."

"Liar."

"Oh, the insult." Richard slurps down the soda and wipes his mouth with the back of his hand. "What are you? Thirty, thirty-five?"

"Around there."

"You're wearing a nice suit. Bespoke, by the thread count. And yet you're sitting in the grass, getting it dirty. If I had on that suit I wouldn't even drink water, I'd be afraid to mess it up. You must be doing all right."

"You could say that."

"I thought you were an honest man."

"I own half this city."

"That's more like it." Richard grins. "Did you earn it?"

"I plan to."

"Well, we all have to dream." Richard climbs to his feet, brushing crumbs off his clothes. Alexander stands with him; he senses their conversation is over, and it leaves him awkward. He has not asked his own questions.

Alexander feels like they were just getting started, but that is not right, either.

Richard holds out his hand and Alexander takes it.

"You have a good life, kid. Stay honest." Richard releases him, stoops to pick up his backpack, and begins shuffling away with a good deal more dignity than at his arrival. Alexander stares after him. Something moves through him, so faint it could be easily brushed off, ignored. He imagines that's how the entire world gets by—by ignoring intimations of their hidden selves. But he's not a normal man, he reminds himself.

"Wait," he calls out. "Do you . . . do you need money?"

Richard fixes Alexander with a pointed stare. "I'd rather have a job."

Alexander thinks for a moment, and says, "I can do that."

Richard will not talk about himself, who he was before losing home and livelihood. Alexander finds him work at the physical plant. He is probably overqualified to empty bins and mop floors, but that does not matter. According to Richard, the past—that life—is done. Besides, being a janitor at RanTech pays well. Alexander takes care of his employees. Even the private school down-with-the-man types don't bring up unionizing after they see the healthcare benefits.

And Richard, in turn, attempts to show his gratitude. Small things, only. Words more than actions. Alexander does not have many friends—actually, he has no friends. Sometimes he has drinks with the woman who perfected the process of regenerating human skin—a former herpetologist turned doctor—and she's kind and reads comics, and tells funny stories about the pythons she still keeps—but she's the one who does all the talking. He almost never tells her anything about himself that matters.

His own family rarely speaks to him unless they want a salary hike, or access to some Hollywood event—or maybe a week at the estate he bought in Hawaii, which is the only property he's told them about. They never ask how he's doing. They're afraid of him and now that he's taken the company into the stratosphere they can hide it under envy.

Which is one of the reasons Alexander enjoys talking with Richard. He might not count as much more than an acquaintance, but Richard always, with zero malice, ridicules him to his face.

"You have problems," Richard says, the first time he sees Alexander's office, the poster of the Great Hero on the wall.

"I like comics," Alexander says, stung. "How is that a problem?"

Richard gives him a look. Alexander suddenly feels as though he has been caught in church with both hands on his dick.

"Kid." Richard stares at Alexander's naked scalp, still moist from a recent shave. "It's not the comics. It's everything else. You can't help your name, but the rest . . . it's a little on the nose, don't you think?"

"It's how I keep things fun."

Richard studies him a moment. "I think you're the last person in this building enjoying yourself."

He might as well have kicked him in the teeth. Alexander says nothing.

Richard points at the poster. "Why, *really?*"

Alexander hears himself say, "Because I believe men can fly."

The worms are ready.

They have passed all initial tests, and except for their size—which is startling, unusual, and somewhat disturbing—they are ready for a real-world scenario. The government has selected a field inspection, and if the worms succeed within the parameters set for them, the government will take possession of the creatures, and what happens next even Alexander can't imagine.

Which is why Alexander is encased in a rubber suit, standing thigh deep in open sewage, trying not to gag behind the oxygen mask strapped over his face.

He is not the only one struggling for balance in the sludge. Dr. Reynolds and her team are present, along with "experts" from the federal government. This section of the city sewer system is completely blocked off, sealed tight to prevent any of the worms from escaping into the main line. Alexander objects to the use of a public facility for this test, but the government wants to make sure the worms will thrive outside a controlled environment.

Alexander does not worry about them thriving. Quite the opposite.

These particular worms, which are waiting to be released from the plastic containers carried by Dr. Reynolds and her assistants, are young and small, fresh from the incubator. The others, the mammoths of Batch #381, have been destroyed, their bodies conserved for study. Alexander's skin prickles, remembering those massive bodies, heavy with sludge, resting torpid at the bottom of their enlarged tanks. Still alive, still healthy, and still growing.

Alexander catches Dr. Reynolds' worried glance. They share a moment of perfect doubt. This is a lot of sludge and they are releasing a lot of worms. When the experiment is over, the government's plan is to carefully drain the remaining sludge from the system, thereby revealing—and trapping—the worms for easy collection. Alexander does not think it will be so easy, but the government scientists have insisted.

For the first time, Alexander wonders if evil villains are only beards to hide what's truly septic about the world.

Dr. Reynolds inches close. "You really don't have to be here for this, Mr. Lutheran. Once they have the containment calibrated, all we're going to do is insert the worms into the sediment." Alexander hears an odd thumping sound. Dr. Reynolds tightens her grip on the container.

"Me, leave?" Alexander drawls, eyeing the cloudy plastic. "And miss all the fun? You shock me, Kathy."

Dr. Reynolds snorts, but her face is pale, her eyes just a little too large beneath her mask. She has seen what the creatures become; her fears have outgrown them.

"Kathy," he says, touching her arm.

"I'm all right," she says. "I just don't know what we're doing."

"Science, Kathy. We're doing science."

"Science." She draws the word out, low and hard. "And here I thought we were playing at theology."

Dr. Reynolds turns away toward the other scientists. Alexander watches her go, unable to call her back. She is right, of course, and he wishes he had chosen this moment to be honest, to speak again the truth voiced in the red-lit room when he told her it was all right to be afraid because yes, what they were doing was too big for mere mortals, too much responsibility to put on human shoulders.

We're doing more than science, Alexander thinks. He watches Dr. Reynolds flip the locks on her rattling container. *We've crossed the line into something bigger.*

But we can't go back. Not now.

Dr. Reynolds opens the lid and Alexander hears a hiss that is not human, a sound that exists only because he pressed a button and moved resources from one line item to another.

The worms fall free in a tangle, smacking the sludge, writhing against the surface before sinking, sinking, out of sight. The other containers open: worms are unceremoniously dumped. Alexander imagines them working their way through the darkness, feeding, growing. He feels something brush his ankle and it takes all his strength not to shudder.

Everyone begins to clamber out of the sludge. Alexander realizes he is being left behind. It is a short climb up the ladder to the wide shelf jutting from the sewer wall. Dripping shit, Alexander is greeted by a man wearing a yellow rain slicker over a dark suit. A nameless government liaison paying his dues in a crappy assignment. His eyes are bloodshot and he keeps swallowing hard. Even better, then. A puker.

Alexander rips off his mask; he almost doubles over from the smell, but manages to maintain his composure better than the other men and women removing their facial protective gear. Amidst a symphony of gagging, Alexander forces a smile. The puker grunts, his gaze sliding sideways to the sludge below them.

"So those things really eat heavy metal and human shit?"

"Like the finest chocolate," Alexander says, still smiling. He wants to run, to scratch this man from his path and fight for sunlight. He hates this place.

The puker grimaces. "No kidding? So what comes out the other end?"

A stupid question. Alexander imagines the worms in their liquid heat, sucking in filth and growing large and strong. It is the bacterial strain in them, this unexpected and fortuitous ability to process sludge without creating any. Alexander would say that it defies the laws of nature, except Dr. Reynolds has assured him there is waste—only, it is processed at an extremely slow rate, released in non-toxic dribbles. Very alluring. Very practical.

Very dangerous.

The government has been given reams of intel on this subject: data, photographs, samples, and even more data. Nothing has been held back, nothing, but this fool—this dangerous fool who is their liaison—remains ignorant. Alexander cannot stand it.

He steps close and it works; the man retreats, unwilling to entertain shit on his rain slicker and shoes. Alexander keeps moving, faster and faster, dangerous on this narrow path, these close quarters, his smile wider and brighter and the puker's eyes narrow, hands fumbling for air, for a gun, for something to stop this strange, strange, man from coming too near.

The puker stumbles. He cries out. Alexander grabs his rain slicker, keeps him from falling off the ledge into the sewage with its hidden worms. He holds the puker close, smearing him with filth, and whispers, "Nothing, you idiot. Nothing comes out the other end. The worms just suck it in and keep it there, growing pregnant on the stuff. They could probably eat you, when they get big enough. Imagine that."

He releases the puker, who gasps and clings to the wall. He vomits.

Alexander does not feel compelled to apologize. No one seems to have noticed what happened. He does not worry about the puker complaining. The puker is a little man and Alexander is powerful, untouchable.

Sunlight beckons, and this time his smile is genuine.

Alexander pulls his old comics out of storage and spends the evening thumbing through the varied adventures of the caped wonder, lingering over those stories that pit him against his human nemesis. A childhood habit: Alexander has sought comfort in these pages since he was four years old, the age he discovered the meaning of his name, the purpose to his life.

"At last!" the archvillain says to the hero. "I have you now!"

If only, Alexander thinks. But that is the thing about the Last Kryptonian. In the comics, no one ever really has him. Not even the intrepid gal reporter, who must share her man with every bleeding body and broken soul to cross his path. The Last Kryptonian is a paragon, the best kind of man, and that means he never truly owns himself. Pure compassion cannot live in isolation. It demands the world.

And the world demands it back. The world needs more compassion. The world needs the kind of man Alexander knows he will never be.

The government proposals are still in Alexander's office safe, waiting to be signed. All of them require the creation of new life, creatures as of yet beyond the ken of man. Their desired purposes are varied, innocuous on the page. Alexander is not fooled. These organisms, should RanTech succeed in making them, will alter the world—just as the worms—when their existence is finally, inevitably, revealed—will alter the way people view bioengineering. It is not enough to say one supports science. The real test is to see the finished product, fat and glistening, and not flinch.

Even Alexander is incapable of that, which should be all the answer he needs, but still he keeps the papers, and still he promises the government that yes, any day now, he will sign and return them and once again begin the process of evolutionary quilting, piecing together scraps of biology into a useful fabric.

Because if he does not do this, someone else will, and while Alexander does not entirely trust himself, he has even less faith in those who would take his place. It is a strange sensation, wanting to save the world—while at the same time creating the very things that will irrevocably change it, for better or worse. Sometimes he wishes he could talk to his father about these things.

Of course, it helps that the money is good.

The next morning, he signs the papers.

A week passes, and then two. Dr. Reynolds provides daily reports, which are along the lines of, "The worms are still down there." A complete and accurate statement, which tells Alexander everything he needs to know.

The worms are down there. They are eating. They are growing.

Alexander hopes the government understands what it is doing, though he himself does not fear reprisals, bad press, or protesters on his doorstep. The government provides anonymity to keep RanTech free and clear to run its experiments, a cordon so all-encompassing, violent, and complete that even Alexander, who can imagine a lot, is not worried about being betrayed. It is very liberating, this lack of oversight, though Alexander still feels his moral compass with its needle a-quiver. The ethical and the not-so-ethical, holding hands.

He wishes he really could hold someone's hand, just once.

He almost messages the woman who handles his nighttime affairs. *I found several great candidates*, she had written that morning, with photos attached. Beautiful men, with chiseled jaws and perfect, wavy hair. The ache in his chest is unbearable when he looks at them, and he imagines, as he always does, that one of these men might make him feel less lonely—if only for a moment.

He stares at the photographs. Picks up his cell phone. But for once, he doesn't give in. Instead, he thinks of sitting in the park with Richard, sharing that tasteless sandwich.

Richard has been spending more time in the general vicinity of Alexander's office. Alexander knows this because he pays attention to the man. Even if Richard does not care about Alexander in any special way, Alexander cares about Richard and what he has to say. Richard is not afraid of Alexander.

If only Alexander's other employees were straightforward.

Alexander hears them talking on a day when he wanders through the labs, peering into instruments and poking around spreadsheets, enjoying—for once, without guilt—the simple pleasure of great imaginations applied to science.

His employees return late from lunch and do not know their boss is communing with sea slugs behind a pile of newly arrived supply crates.

"He's a freak," says a man.

"If you got a red cape I bet you he'd let you fuck his fortress of solitude."

They laugh, and walk away.

Alexander does not follow them. He stares at the sea slugs in their tank, his chest growing tighter. Time passes and he knows he must leave; someone will find him, and he cannot bear to face the owners of those voices.

Holding his breath, Alexander listens hard and carefully slips out from behind the crates. He takes one step, two, and just when he thinks he is free to run, movement catches his eye. Too late; he has been seen.

It is Richard, holding a wet vacuum.

The two men stare at each other. Alexander cannot fathom Richard's expression, but his silence is confirmation enough. He has heard every word of that awful conversation.

Heat suffuses Alexander's face; he cannot meet Richard's eyes. Staring at the wall, he turns and walks quickly to the door.

Dignity bleeding, Alexander returns to his office.

Alexander does not dwell long on the incident. He has overheard many variations of that particular conversation, and while each one cuts raw, he recovers quickly. Life is too short to waste on insults.

Still, he wonders what Richard makes of it, what else the man has heard during his time at RanTech.

Alexander does not have to wonder long.

He is in the private gym down the hall from his office, swinging a one-hundred-pound kettle bell, when Richard knocks on the door and walks in. The secretary knows not to stop him. Richard is free to come and go as he pleases, though he has never been told this explicitly.

"That would break my spine," Richard says, and bounces on a fitness ball.

Alexander grunts, finishing his last rep. "Being fit projects a strong corporate image. Also, I am not naturally charismatic. Looking good makes it easier to convince people to do what I want."

Richard snorts and something about it makes Alexander laugh. A chuckle, really, but it's rare enough that it startles him. He points to his briefcase.

"Front pocket. There's an envelope."

Alexander stretches out on his toes and elbows to do a plank. Richard peers inside the envelope. "Baseball tickets?"

"I'm told the Dodgers are playing."

Richard gives him a crooked grin. "You noticed my hat."

Alexander gives up exercising. It's hard to focus, when he's suddenly so embarrassed. Richard leans back, folding his arms over his stomach.

"My old man liked the Dodgers, so I wear the hat to remember him. He's worth remembering. I lost a bunch of his stuff some years back, so I make do with what I can." He hesitates. "But I'm a basketball fan, myself. Never even been to a baseball game."

"Oh," Alexander says, and then: "Neither have I. My dad didn't . . . well, I guess I wasn't into sports."

He reaches for the envelope, but Richard waves it in the air. "You can't take back gifts. Two tickets in here, right? So, we'll go together. Maybe we'll both learn something."

Alexander blinks. "I'd . . . like that."

"Good. Because you need some mentorship, kid. You need some time with regular people."

"The people who work here are pretty regular. I guess."

"They ain't regular. They're your employees. Shit, I'm your employee. But you're the least regular of all. In fact, you're a mess."

"A . . . mess?"

"You heard me."

"I can tell you've been giving this some thought."

"Enough to make me crazy."

Alexander does not know whether to be pleased or worried. "So. I'm making you crazy. Why is that?"

Richard shakes his head. There are shadows under his eyes, new lines around his mouth. Alexander wonders if perhaps Richard *has* been going a little crazy thinking of him.

"I don't get you. Haven't from the beginning, but I could tell you had a good heart. And after I was here for a while and saw how you run this place, I knew you had more than that. Real brains. Talent. One of those bright futures you hear people bragging about, but don't really deserve." He narrows his eyes. "I still don't know if you deserve it, but I know you ain't wasting it. And that's rare. Most of us blow every chance we get. I did that. I was an attorney for twenty years, a good one. Then I slipped.

Kept slipping. Didn't care. Deliberately fucked up because I was angry and grieving about stupid shit that couldn't be fixed. Kid, I had a long tantrum that ruined my life."

This is not what Alexander expected. Richard leans forward and drums his fingers on his knee, a harsh, rough sound.

"But here's what I don't understand. You let your employees talk shit about you—real abuse—and hard as I try, I can't feel sorry for you. You know why? Because you ask for it."

"I ask for it," Alexander echoes, tasting those words.

Richard's gaze is pained. "Little things add up. Like your head, the way you shave it. What, three times a day?"

"I like my scalp," Alexander says, soft.

"Yeah, we know." He points at all the posters of the Last Krypto-nian hanging on the gym walls, along with other memorabilia from his private collection. Alexander's private gym has always seemed like an acceptable place for that sort of thing. "The other idiots think you're just a rich nerd who wants to look like a supervillain. Nothing wrong with that. I'd tell them to go fuck themselves, if that was the case. But I think it goes deeper. This isn't a fashion choice. You *want* to be Lex Luthor. You think this world is a comic book and you want to be him."

"Want to be?" Alexander laughs weakly, something raw and bitter rising in his throat. "I think I already am. And . . . so what? It doesn't hurt anyone, does it? It's my life, my choice, if . . . if I feel more alive when . . . when . . ."

He stops, stunned that he's close to tears. He turns his head, takes a deep breath.

Richard says nothing for a long time. He merely stares at Alexander, and then—to the young man's relief—turns his gaze on the window, look-ing down at the hordes of nameless, nearly faceless, people tramping down the sidewalk. Alexander grows light-headed from holding his breath.

Richard says, "I had a son. He died. He'd be about your age now. You don't drink and drive, do you?"

"I don't drink alcohol."

"I didn't think so." Richard glances at him. "You told me once you believe a man can fly."

Some men can, Alexander thinks. *Somewhere, there has to be that man. For me.*

And maybe it shows on his face because Richard straightens and looks hard in Alexander's eyes. Alexander senses a fissure between them: closing or opening, he cannot tell. Only, that he wants to cross the distance and does not dare.

Richard stirs. "You ain't no super-villain, kid. But you believe. You really believe it all, like it's not made up. Like you could touch it with your hands."

"Yes," Alexander breathes, because to say it louder would feel coarse, like a desecration of the truth, the myth. "Yes. I've always believed."

Believed in the perfect essence of the myth, the stark lines between good and evil. How one must have the other to survive.

He can't help himself. He looks at a poster of the Last Kryptonian, just for a moment.

Perhaps Richard is psychic. Perhaps Alexander has revealed more than he thought possible: in his face, his words. Richard looks at the poster, too. His eyes grow dark with understanding, and he says in a deep, strange voice, "My son once told me he was in love, and I mean, in *love* with Prince. That's you, ain't it? You're in love, not with Prince, but with *him* . . . the man who flies."

Surprising, to hear those words out loud. Surprising and thrilling.

Alexander sits up, steady and full and ready to speak. But someone knocks on the door.

It is Dr. Reynolds. Her face is flushed.

"There's a problem," she says.

Richard follows them to the Mayback. When Dr. Reynolds slips into the back seat, he places a strong hand on Alexander's shoulder, holding him still. His eyes are clear and hard.

The two men do not speak, but it is enough. Their conversation remains unfinished and neither man dares let the other out of his sight until some final word has rung. What has already been said is too strange. Like a dream, it might fade if not held tight.

Alexander steps aside and motions for Richard to precede him into the Mayback. Dr. Reynolds looks on with some surprise, but Alexander does not explain. He is the boss and today he will take advantage of it.

They drive from downtown into an un-financed part of the city. Not so worn as to be inhospitable, but not so up-and-coming as to be frequented by anyone whose questions about the odd comings and goings of windowless utility vans, the frequent descent of uniformed men and women into the shadows below the street, might be listened to.

It is just the city government doing work, the locals think. Special maintenance. Very special. The ones who know better—well, no one listens to the people in that neighborhood, anyway.

Dr. Reynolds says, "Everything was fine on Friday. The sludge levels were getting low, but the federal scientists promised—those idiots—they promised me they would put more in over the weekend."

"Kathy—"

"They did it on purpose, Mr. Lutheran." Her voice breaks. Alexander wonders if he will lose this woman after today's work. "They wanted to see what would happen."

Alexander closes his eyes. Richard remains silent, watching them both.

A member of Dr. Reynolds' team meets them at the site, bearing enough protective gear for two people. Alexander sends the young man back for another suit; Richard is coming with them. A bad decision, perhaps, but it is part of Alexander's reckless drive toward honesty. He cannot stop, no matter the price.

Richard asks no questions when Alexander gives the order—he says nothing at all—but his eyes are sharp, sharp, sharp.

Alexander helps Richard dress. The protective gear—suit, mask, oxygen—are tricky for the uninitiated. Alexander does not look at Richard's face as his capable hands zip and tug and button. The moment is inappropriate for words.

And what can Alexander say? *Don't be afraid of my touch. Don't be afraid of me. Please, don't be afraid.*

Dr. Reynolds bounces on her toes, agitated. "We don't have time for this. Please, Mr. Lutheran."

"I'm done." Alexander steps back from Richard. Their eyes meet and Alexander turns away, toward the sewer entrance. "Let's go."

They descend. Down, down deep into shadow, Alexander leading the way. His mask is off, his ears keen for screams, shouts—cries of horror. Nothing. He hears nothing human.

Nothing human. Nothing coherent. Just flesh, whispering, dry and cool; the sucking of large mouths.

He smells shit. Shit, and something stronger, bitter.

Bitter, like blood.

"Fuck," Richard whispers, as they make their final descent into the sewer, stepping onto the concrete platform.

An appropriate response. Alexander would say something similar if he could, but his mouth will not work. Nothing seems to work but his eyes and mind, and how lovely—how miraculous it would be, if Alexander could somehow turn those organs off. At the moment, they are vital to nothing but nightmare.

And the nightmare is this, what the government could have prevented, what they should have known would happen: the worms have grown. Grown large and long and strong. Their sludge is gone.

And they are still hungry.

The experiments at RanTech, repeated time and time again, have shown that the worms have only one instinct, and that is to feed. Reproduction is asexual and infrequent, stimulated by solitude: a single worm, immersed in large amounts of sludge, will grow buds of baby worms across its body. When the worms emerge, they spill into the sludge and begin to feed.

And so the cycle goes. Feed, feed, feed—it is always feeding with them. Even when the food runs out.

Alexander watches a mouth bang against dry concrete; diverted, the orifice sucks air, seeking purchase, anything soft and wet. Flesh will do. Flesh will do just fine. It is warm, it yields to sharp lips, and just below the surface is blood, and deeper, the remnants of sludge. It is as good a meal as any, and better than death.

Alexander notices the government scientists huddled in a group, taking notes and casting surreptitious glances in his direction. Some of them look sick, but even nausea seems to take on a dispassionate quality in their faces. The worms are eating each other alive, spraying blood with each bite, tearing flesh in mighty chunks, and the scientists are doing nothing to stop it. They do not want to stop it. They will let these creatures torture each other, and simply watch.

Alexander's hands curl into fists. "Who's in charge here?"

They stare. A dark-suited figure in a rain slicker pushes clear. The puker, his black eyes small and smug. He looks as though he has been ill, but power, it seems, is a fine medicine.

"You have to stop this," Alexander says.

"I don't have to do anything," says the puker. "These creatures are government property and this is our experiment. You're a guest here, Mr. Lutheran. I suggest you act like one and stay out of the way."

"A guest?" Alexander feels Richard and Dr. Reynolds close against his back. "RanTech designed these worms. Until the hand-over is official, their well-being is our business, and they are clearly unwell—due to your mismanagement, I assume."

"I won't warn you again." The puker is angry. "The government paid a high price—"

"And having paid that price, what will your superiors say when they discover there is nothing left of their experiment but a few dozen corpses? Will you impress them with a barrel full of remains? Lovely. Be my guest. Go right ahead."

"Look," says a government scientist. "There was no other way to move their bodies. They're too large and the kill-gas is too slow. This way, we manage everything at once. It's not like you can't make more. That's your job, isn't it?"

"My God," Alexander hears Richard whisper. Alexander wonders if God plays the same game: a disinterested observer watching His creations in their sewer-world, watching death and malice and love and conception, waiting to see which side will win, waiting to see if there will be any side, or just clumps of blood and flesh, waiting at the very end of a failed experiment on a tiny little septic tank of a world.

No, Alexander thinks. *No, we are more than that.*

Behind the government scientists is a valve; if turned, it will release sludge into the trench below. Experiments have shown that the worms prefer sludge to flesh—bathe them in it, let them wallow in shit, and they will stop consuming each other.

Alexander strides forward. The puker does not back away. He meets Alexander with arms outstretched, blocking the path.

"Not this time," he says, as though that is enough, as though his word is law.

The government scientists are smarter; they know what is behind them and can guess what Alexander plans to do. One of them says, "He's going to stop the experiment! Don't let him near that valve."

Dr. Reynolds shouts at them. Alexander cannot understand what she says because his ears are roaring, his head buzzing with rage. The worms are writhing in blood and it is another red-lit room—red with fluid, dark and dirty—and he must stop this, he must stop this torture because the worms cannot stop it for themselves.

Alexander is lean and strong. He pushes the puker aside, but the man is ready for him and has his own rage, his own bruised pride. The puker strikes Alexander hard in the gut, a sharp thrust. Alexander staggers backward.

Back into Richard, who has followed close to help.

Alexander hears a gasp, a startled cry. He turns in time to see Richard teeter on the narrow ledge, flail and swing and fall. He does not hit concrete. He hits worm.

Alexander cannot see Richard's face; he lands facedown, limbs entangled in shifting flesh. Richard tries to stand but the worms are too large. All he can do is straddle, stay on top, struggle to keep from slipping into crushing darkness.

It is the worst kind of Hell Alexander can imagine, but he does not hesitate. He jumps into the trench. Alexander lands hard but the worms cushion his fall—a grotesque trampoline made of firm flesh. He lunges forward, slithering and bouncing over thrashing bodies, thick as oaks. The worms are slippery, greased with blood and shit. Alexander swallows filth. His eyes burn.

Richard sees him. There is a moment when Alexander imagines something more than fear on the man's face—a shadow beneath the terror and disgust that looks like concern. And then a tail rises up and slams into Richard's head.

Richard disappears.

Alexander fights. His life narrows down to one thin line and he pulls his soul over this line, hand over hand, slamming fists into hard bodies, into searching mouths, razing his skin on sharp lips while his lungs fill with the hot stench of shit and blood, shit and blood in his mouth, on his tongue, gritty and slimy and metallic. He fights and fights, the worms tearing open his suit, crushing him between their surging bodies, squeezing him like a lemon. Ribs crack, but he pushes forward, slithering. He glimpses a white suit.

Alexander screams as he wrenches his torso against undulating muscle. His broken ribs shift against skin. The worms move, pull apart, and Alexander dives to the ground, scrabbling on all fours until he reaches Richard.

Richard is curled tight, his chin tucked against his chest, hands over his head. The suit around his upper thigh is ripped. Alexander sees bone.

Alexander covers Richard with his body, placing his hands against Richard's filthy hair, the bare skin of his neck. Richard turns his head just a fraction; his eyes are bloodshot, terrible.

"Get out of here," he says, and Alexander can hear the desperation in his voice, the despair.

"No," Alexander mouths, because he cannot make his lungs work past the pain in his ribs. A worm rolls over his legs and Alexander swallows a cry.

"Please," Richard begs.

Alexander says nothing. He does not have the strength to stand, to fight. Everything he had, he has given in his battle to reach Richard. All he can do now is curl around the body beneath him and hold on tight. He presses his cheek against Richard's hair. He closes his eyes.

The worms come up hard against his back, their mouths seeking flesh.

After the accident, the government takes possession of the worms and all associated technology. It does this in a matter of days. Alexander does not fight when Dr. Reynolds gives him the news. He hopes the government has learned a lesson, that it will be more careful in the future. But hope is just that. It does not mean very much.

"When you stop being optimistic," Richard says, "the veil that hides the cruelty of things is removed."

"Then I've never been optimistic," Alexander says, and pushes down a button. The bed whirs and his upper body propels slowly forward until he can look Richard in the eyes. Richard is in a wheelchair. He wears a hospital gown that does not quite cover the thick bandages wrapped around his upper left leg. Alexander remembers bone every time he looks at that leg, but he is paying for the best regeneration-grafts money can buy, the ones made by his acquaintance, the former herpetologist. Richard will be able to walk again in a year. It will take Alexander much longer. The doctors must repair his organs so he can live beyond the machines knitted into his body.

Richard rubs his sallow face. Flowers surround him: roses, lilies.

They are pleasant substitutes for Alexander's parents, who have visited their son only twice since he entered the hospital. Alexander does not remember either visit. He was asleep.

"You're the most optimistic person I know," Richard tells him.

Alexander does not feel like arguing. Instead he says, "Did you see Dr. Reynolds on her way out?"

"Yes. I thanked her." Richard looks at his palms, rubs his knuckles with one finger. "I suppose she's the reason we're still alive."

"Yes," says Alexander. "I didn't know she had safety protocols in place. I thought the lockers were full of scientific equipment. Not stun rods." Stun rods powerful enough to take down an elephant. Powerful enough for the worms. Dr. Reynolds and her team, who jumped into the trench, stunning the worms long enough to drag Richard and Alexander to safety. A miracle. Her resignation email is still in his inbox. He hasn't had the heart to open it.

Richard stops looking at his hands. His gaze is bleary, haunted. "You didn't have a stun rod."

But Alexander barely hears him. "I've been thinking about what you said."

"I say a lot of things." But then Richard goes still. "Ah."

Alexander finally looks at him. "I always wanted to be Lex Luthor . . . really be him, for real . . . because wherever he is, there's Superman. And the world needs something of Superman to exist, even if it takes his worst enemy to draw him out. The world needs someone good."

I need someone good, Alexander thinks.

"He's a fantasy."

"He doesn't have to be."

"Well, he does, actually." Richard frowns. "But let's call it a dream of better things. Is that what keeps you going?"

"People need to be reminded of what they can become, not what they are."

Richard sits back. "You've chosen a pretty passive way of doing that, haven't you? Pretending to be a comic book character? Telling yourself that if you play at being that character, the comics will come to life and everyone will have a happy ending?"

Alexanders flushes with shame. "Richard—"

"You're not happy, kid. If you weren't so high-functioning in every other part of your life, I think you'd have killed yourself by now—just like my son killed himself. He couldn't face his own life, either." Richard takes Alexander's hand, and squeezes it gently. "People don't care if you're actually Lex Luthor or if Superman exists. *I* don't care. The only person who cares is you. And I guess that's okay, kid. But," and Richard leans forward, so close Alexander can feel the heat of his breath on his face, "being in love with something that isn't real won't keep your heart from breaking."

Alexander swallows hard. He remembers the worms tearing off chunks of his body and wishes that he was back in the sewer, because being eaten alive is easier than telling the truth to this man. Alexander forces himself to look into Richard's eyes.

"Yes," he whispers. "But it's not just him I'm in love with."

Richard goes very still. Alexander listens to the slow thrum of his aching heart.

"I can't be something I'm not," Richard finally says, carefully, gently. "I love you, kid. Just not like that."

"I know," Alexander says, and his eyes feel hot, as hot as his body, burning with shame.

Richard rests his hand on top of Alexander's head. He has not shaved since the accident. He has hair again. It has been such a long time, he had forgotten the color.

"I'm tired of being alone," Alexander says, throwing away the last of his dignity.

Richard's eyes are kind, so kind. He leans in, hugs Alexander, and does not pull away.

"Don't worry," he says. "You're not alone."

I wrote "The Last Dignity of Man" in 2004 at the Clarion Writers Workshop in Ann Arbor, Michigan. I had just turned twenty-five, and I don't know what came over me, except I was a nerd, imagining another nerd, but one with vast wealth and intelligence: someone consumed by desperate loneliness.

In some ways, this story is far timelier now than it was then, given the rise of corporate billionaires whose companies have inserted their products and services into every part of our lives. More than ever, they've become essential—and now, more than ever, the lack of boundaries has become clear, as has the soft power these corporations wield over us. When I hit the "buy" button on my browser, I often joke, "Here I pay fealty to my corporate overlords," but that's actually kind of true.

And so here we have a corporate overlord who wears the costume of a villain, living out a fantasy driven by one desperate hope: that somewhere in the universe . . . there's a hero who will love him.

WHERE THE HEART LIVES

When Miss Lindsay finally departed for the world beyond the wood, it meant that Lucy and Barnabus were the only people left to care for her house and land, as well as the fine cemetery she had kept for nearly twenty years outside the little town of Cuzco, Indiana. It was an important job, not just for Lucy and Barnabus, but for others, as well, who for years after would come and go, for rest or sanctuary. Bodies needed homes, after all—whether dead or living.

Lucy was only seventeen, and had come to the cemetery in the spring, not one month before Miss Lindsay went away. The girl's father was a cutter at the limestone quarry. Her brothers drove the team that hauled the stones to the masons. The men had no use for a sister, or any reminder of the fairer sex; their mother had run away that previous summer with a fortune-teller, though Lucy's father insisted his absent wife was off visiting relatives and would return. Eventually.

When word reached the old cutter that a woman named Miss Lindsay needed a girl to tend house, he made his daughter pack a bag with lunch, her comb, and one good dress from her mother's closet—then set her on the first wagon heading toward Cuzco. No good-byes, no messages sent ahead. Just chancing on fate that the woman would want his daughter.

Lucy remembered that wagon ride. Mr. Wiseman, the driver, had been hauling turnips that day, the bulbous roots covered beneath a burlap sheet to keep off the light drizzle: a cool morning, with a sweet breeze. No one on the road except them, and later, one other: an old man who stood at the side of the dirt track outside Cuzco, dressed in threadbare brown clothes, with a thin coat and his white hair slicked down from the rain. Pale eyes. Lost eyes, staring at the green, budding hills as though the woods were where his heart lived.

In his right hand, he held a round, silver mirror. A discordant sight, flashing and bright; Lucy thought she heard voices in her head when she saw the reflecting glass: whispers like birdsong, teasing and sweet.

Mr. Wiseman did not wave at the man, but Lucy did, out of politeness and concern. She received no response; as though she were some invisible spirit, or the breeze.

"Is he sick?" Lucy whispered to Mr. Wiseman.

"Sick and married," said the spindly man, in a voice so loud, she winced. He tugged his hat down over his eyes. "Married, with no idea how to let go of the dead."

"His wife is gone?" Lucy thought of her mother.

"Gone, dead. That was Henry Lindsay you saw. Man's been like that for almost twenty years. Might as well be dead himself."

Which answered almost nothing, in Lucy's mind. "What happened to her?"

A sly smile touched Mr. Wiseman's mouth, and he glanced sideways. "Don't know, quite. But she up and died on their wedding night. I heard he hardly had a chance to touch her."

"That's *awful*," Lucy said, not much caring for the look in Mr. Wiseman's eye, as though there was something funny about the idea. She did not like, either, the other way he suddenly seemed to look at her: as though she could be another fine story, for him.

She edged sideways on the wagon seat. Mr. Wiseman looked away.

"People die, Miss Lucy. But it's a shame it happened so fast. I even heard said they were going to run away, all fancy. A honeymoon, like they do in the cities."

Lucy said nothing. She did not know much about such things. In her experience, there was little to celebrate about being husband and wife. Just hard times, and loss, and anger. A little bit of laughter, if you were lucky. But not often.

She twisted around, looking back. Henry still stood at the bend in the road, his feet lost in deep grass, soaked and pale and staring at the woods, those smoky green hills rising and falling like the back of some long, fat snake. Her heart ached for him, just a little, though she did not know why. His loss was a contagious thing.

Honeymoon, she thought, tasting the word and finding it pretty, even though she did not fully appreciate its meaning. And then another word entered her mind, familiar, and she murmured, "Lindsay."

Lindsay. The same name as the woman she was going to see. Lucy looked inquiringly at Mr. Wiseman.

"His sister," he replied shortly, and smiled. "His very pretty sister, even if she's getting on in years." He stopped the wagon and pointed at a narrow dirt path that curled into the woods. "There. Follow that to her house."

Lucy hesitated. "Are you certain?"

"There isn't a man, woman, or child in this area who doesn't know where Miss Lindsay lives." He reached behind him, and pulled out a bulging cloth sack. "Here, give this to her. Say it was from Wilbur."

Lucy clutched the sack to her stomach. It felt like turnips. She slid off the wagon, feeling lost, but before she could say anything, Mr. Wiseman gave her that same sly smile and said, "Stay on the path, Miss Lucy. Watch for ghosts."

"Ghosts," she echoed, alarmed, but he shook the reins, tipped his hat, and his wagon rattled into motion. No good-byes. Lucy watched him go, almost ready to shout his name, to ask that he wait for her. She stayed silent, though, and looked back the way they had come. Home, to her father and brothers.

Then she turned and stared down the narrow track leading into the woods. It was afternoon, but with the clouds and misting drizzle it could have been twilight before her, a forest of night. Birdsong rattled; again, Lucy thought she heard whispers, voices airy as the wind.

Ghosts. Or nothing. Just her imagination. Lucy swallowed hard, and walked into shadow, the wet gloom: dense and thick and wild.

She thought of her mother as she walked. Wondered if she had been this frightened of leaving home, or if it had been too much a relief to unburden herself of husband and children. Then Lucy thought of the old man, Henry Lindsay, and his lost eyes and lost wife and lost wedding night, and wondered if it was the same, except worse—worse, because her mother had chosen to go, worse because her father did not have eyes like that man, or that sorrow. Just anger. So much bitter anger.

The path curled. Lucy walked fast, stepping light over rocks and vines. In the undergrowth, she heard movement: a blue bird broke loose from the canopy, streaking toward the narrow trail of gray sky; to see it felt like she was watching some desperate escape, as though the leaves on either side of the track were walls, strong as stone and insurmountable. She half expected a hand to reach from the trees and snatch the bird back.

A chill settled between her shoulders. Lucy heard a whisper, wordless but human. A hush, heart-stopping. She paused in mid-step and turned. There was no one behind her.

Lucy heard it again, and terror squeezed her heart. Ghostly, yes; a voice like the wind, high and cool. She caught movement out the corner of her eye—cried out, turning—and saw a face peering from the shadows of the underbrush.

A woman. A woman in the wood, pale and fair, with eyes as blue as cornflowers. Lucy stared, trying to make sense of it—unable to speak or move as she met that terrible gaze, which was lost and so utterly lonely, Lucy felt her heart squeeze again, but softer, with a pang.

"Help me," whispered the woman. "Please, help me."

Lucy tried to speak, and choked. Around her, other voices seemed to seep free of the wood; whispers and hoarse cries and birds screaming into the cool wet air, a rising wind that blasted Lucy with a bone-chill to her heart, swelling like her insides were growing on the hum of the wood, engorged on sound.

She heard a shout—a man—but she could not turn to see. His voice felt far away, and the woman cried, "*She's coming.*"

Something broke inside Lucy: she could move again. She tried to run—heard another shout, desperate, and turned in time to see a brown, flailing blur, a streak of silver, a shock of white hair.

Arms caught Lucy from behind. She cried out as she was lifted into the air, screaming as the sky and trees spun into a blur, so sickening she closed her eyes. She heard the woman sobbing, a man crying a name—*Mary, Mary*—and then nothing except a heartbeat beneath her ear, sure and steady as a hammer falling.

Her heart hurt. Lucy opened her eyes and found the world changed.

She was no longer caught on the path in the woods. A meadow surrounded her, small and green and lush with grass and wild daisies, scattered with heavy oaks; somewhere nearby, a creek burbled and goats bleated. Lucy saw a small, white house behind a grove of lilac trees, and beyond, again, the rising forest, only gentler, without the dense shadows that seemed to live and breathe. No women lost in the leaves.

There were arms around her body, and movement on her left. Lucy struggled, managing to pull away until she could dance backward, staring.

Two men stood before her, one young, the other older. The elder man was Henry Lindsay. Lucy remembered his face. Up close, however, he did not look quite so aged. His body was straight and hard and lean; he had few wrinkles and his eyes were bright, startling, the color of gold. His white hair was the only symptom of age, but that seemed a trivial thing compared with the fire in his gaze, which was so alive, she thought she must have imagined the man who had stood at the side of the road with a face as slack and dead as a corpse.

The young man with him had quieter eyes, but just as bold. He wore a faded blue cotton, a complement to his blue eyes, his shirt patched with bits and pieces of rags, the stitches neat, made with thick red thread, his skin brown from the sun, hair dark and wild like a scarecrow. He glanced at Henry, just before the older man lurched toward Lucy: a half step, the edge of a full run, stopping before he reached her as though pulled back by strings. His hands clenched into fists. The silver mirror jutted from his coat pocket.

"She spoke to you," said Henry, his voice deceptively quiet, easy—frightening, because Lucy could tell it was a lie. She said nothing, uncertain how to answer him. In her head she could see the woman in the wood, her pale face and lost eyes: a mirror to how this man had looked while standing on the road.

Henry said it again, louder: "She spoke. Tell me what she said."

Lucy stared, bewildered, and he rocked toward her with a low cry, hand outstretched. She staggered back, holding up her arms, but the young man stepped between them and caught Henry before he could touch her, holding him back with his size and easy strength. Lucy readied herself to run.

"Stop this," said a new voice. "*Henry.*"

Lucy turned. She had to steady herself—all of this was too much—but she dug her nails into her palms and gazed at the newcomer: a woman who stood a stone's throw distant, her mature face a reflection of Henry Lindsay, who quieted and stilled until the young man let him go.

Black hair, threaded with white; golden eyes and an unlined face; a small, narrow body dressed in a simple dark red dress, finely mended. The woman stood barefoot in the grass, hair loose and wild; proud, confident, utterly at ease. Lucy felt drab as a titmouse compared to her. In the trees, crows shrieked, raucous and loud.

"Miss Lindsay," she whispered, following her intuition. "Ma'am."

The woman tilted her head. "I don't know you."

"My father heard you were looking for a girl," she replied, hoarse.

Henry swayed. Lucy forced herself to stay strong, to look him in the eye as her father had always said to do, that eyes were important when dealing with strangers, especially men.

He said, "She spoke to Mary. She spoke to Mary in the woods."

"Did she now?" asked Miss Lindsay slowly, her gaze sharpening. She moved close, hips swaying gracefully. "Did you speak to someone in the woods, child?"

"No," Lucy said softly. "But the woman . . . the woman in the trees spoke to me. And I heard . . ."

She stopped. Miss Lindsay stood near, her golden gaze like fire: hot, burning. She reached out and touched Lucy's forehead with one finger, just between the eyes, and whispered, "What did you hear?"

"Voices," Lucy replied, compelled by those eyes, that searing touch. "Many voices."

"Mary," said Henry, in a broken voice. "Tell me what she said."

Lucy looked at him, and finally could see again the man from the road, lost and dull. She was sorry about that, and said, gently, "The woman asked me to help her. And then . . . then she said . . . someone was coming."

She's coming, echoed that urgent voice, inside her head. Lucy felt a chill race through her body. Miss Lindsay flinched, and moved away. She turned her head until her hair shifted and Lucy could not see her eyes.

"You'll do," said the woman softly. "Yes, if you like, I'll hire you."

"If she wants to stay," said Henry, also turning away, his voice rough, shoulders bowed. His hand was in his coat pocket, clutching the mirror. A wedding ring glinted on his finger.

Lucy stared at them, helpless, unsure what to do. Her gaze finally fell on the one person who had said nothing at all—the young man, who was calm and steady, who watched her with that same straightforward regard. Lucy imagined a clear, pure tone when she looked at him, and it was an unexpected comfort.

"I'll stay," she found herself saying—two words that could have been a leap off a cliff for the falling sensation she felt on uttering them. It was dangerous—something was not right; there were ghosts in the woods and spirits unseen, and here, here, these people knew of such things. And she was joining them, would cook and clean for them.

But it was better than going home.

Lucy imagined a whisper on the wind. Miss Lindsay briefly closed her eyes, then held out her hand and gave the girl a long, piercing look.

"Come," she said, in a voice gentler than her eyes. "I'll show you the house."

And that was that.

Nothing happened that first week, except that afterward, Lucy's life felt irrevocably changed. The sensation crept on her slowly, nudged along by little things that she had never had a chance to experience: reading as a leisure activity, for starters (Miss Lindsay insisted on it, in the evenings), or being treated as a thinking person, something more than a girl or daughter or sister or future wife. Something beyond drudge. An equal, perhaps.

It was a fine house, much larger than anything Lucy was accustomed to, with a second floor and an actual parlor and fireplace just for sitting and warming the feet. There were books shelved against the walls, more than she had ever seen—a library of them, all around—as well as journals and odd paintings, and stacks of newspapers bound with string. Most of those were crumbling and yellow; Lucy was careful as she cleaned around them, gazing as she did upon faded images of President Lincoln, as well as cramped headlines about the War, some fifty years past.

Lucy had her own room with a lock on the door, just off the kitchen. Miss Lindsay slept upstairs, as did her brother, Henry. The young man, Barnabus, kept his bed and belongings in the work shed off the garden. He was like her—there for odd jobs—although unlike her, he was treated more like family, though Miss Lindsay explained that he was not. Or rather, not by blood.

"A child of the forest," the woman called him, that first night. "Found in the woods as a boy, living wild as the coyotes and foxes.

Folks brought him here. It was that or the circus, with those men. So I raised him. Taught him. Oh, he's a good one, that Barnabus. Talk to him as you like—he's as smart as you and I—but don't expect a word from his mouth. He can't speak. Not like us. The forest stole his voice."

Given what Lucy had experienced, she thought that might be the literal—if not fantastical—truth. And it disturbed her greatly. She did not know what to make of it. The forest was dangerous—she knew that in her heart—and while it went unspoken that she should not walk near the tree line, ever, the others did so all the time.

No one ever explained the threat she felt so keenly. She tried asking, but Miss Lindsay always managed to change the subject—so smoothly, Lucy hardly realized what she was doing until it was too late and she was off scrubbing a floor or cooking or weeding, and thinking hard about why she was there, and how Miss Lindsay had managed, yet again, to deflect a question about a situation that Lucy found threatening and frightening and undeniably odd.

She dreamed of the woman at night, the woman in the wood, and listened to her pleas for help beneath a wail of wind and whispers, endless and cold and pained. Sometimes she sensed another voice beneath the other—*Mary, Mary*, she would hear Henry cry—and something else, bells and the pound of hooves, and music playing high and wild like a storm of thunder and fiddle strikes.

And sometimes in her dream she would open her eyes and Miss Lindsay would be sitting by her bed, with that cool hand pressed against her forehead and her golden eyes shining with unearthly light. And in those moments of fantasy Lucy would think of her mother, and stop feeling afraid, and slip into softer, gentler, dreams: buttercups and horses, and afternoons by the river with her feet in the sun-riddled water. Sometimes Barnabus was there, holding her hand. She liked that, though it scared her too. In a different way.

There were several surprises that first week, the biggest one being that Miss Lindsay had a cemetery on her land, only a short walk away along a narrow wagon track. Her family was buried there, but mostly other folk—from town, the surrounding areas—anyone who did not have the money to be planted in one of the church plots near the bigger towns. Miss Lindsay called it a service to the public, and several times Lucy saw strangers exit the trail through the forest bearing gifts of cloth and food. Payment served.

Folks never lingered, though. They visited the graveyard, then left quick, hardly looking around, as though afraid of what they would see. Lucy wondered how they managed to make it through the forest unmolested, and said as much to Henry, whom she found one afternoon in a rare moment of responsiveness—sitting in the sun, reading a book by someone with a long, rather familiar, name. Shakes Spear, or something of the kind. She settled down beside him with a pile of mending in her lap. Barnabus was nearby, chopping wood. His shirt was off, draped over a low tree branch.

"The forest has a mind of its own," Henry replied, after some deep thought. He gazed at the tree line, and his eyes began to glaze over, lost. Lucy pricked him—accidentally, of course—with her needle. He flinched, frowning, but his expression cleared.

"You were saying?" Lucy prodded.

"A mind, a spirit. This is the forest primeval," murmured Henry, "darkened by shadows of earth." He looked at her. "Longfellow. Do you know him?"

"We never met," she said, and then blushed when she realized that was not at all what he meant.

Henry smiled kindly, though, idly tapping the book in his hands. Lucy, in part to hide her embarrassment—but mostly because she was suddenly quite motivated to educate herself—pointed and asked, "What are you reading?"

"The Bard." Henry handed her the book. "Specifically, *Romeo and Juliet*. A great and tragic love story."

Lucy made a small sound, savoring the smooth feel of the slender red volume in her hands. "Seems like tragic is the only kind of love there is."

Henry tilted his head. "Broken heart?"

She frowned. "Oh, no. Not me, sir. Never been in love. Just . . . I've seen things, that's all."

"And I suppose you've heard of *me*," he said with a hint of darkness in his voice. Lucy felt a moment's panic, but then she looked at him and found his eyes thoughtful, distant—but not lost. Not angry.

"I heard something from someone," Lucy said slowly. "First time I saw you on the road, coming here."

"You saw me?" Henry looked surprised. "Ah. Well."

"You were . . . distracted," Lucy told him, not wanting him to feel bad. "Staring at the forest."

A rueful smile touched his mouth. "That happens."

Lucy hesitated. "Because of the woman? Mary?"

She knew it was a mistake the moment that name left her mouth. Too much said, too fast. Henry's expression crumpled, then hardened; shadows gathered beneath his eyes, which seemed to change color, glittering like amber caught in sunlight. Lucy had to look away, and found Barnabus watching them with a frown. He put down his ax and began walking toward them.

"I'm sorry," Lucy said to Henry. "Please, I'm—"

He cut her off, leaning close. "You saw her. In the forest. What did she look like?"

Barnabus reached them. He sat beside Lucy, the corner of his knee brushing her thigh. He was big and warm and safe, and she was glad for his presence.

"She was beautiful," Lucy said simply, and then, softer: "She was your wife."

"My wife," echoed Henry, staring at his hands. "She is still my wife."

Lucy stared. "I thought . . . I thought your wife was dead. What I saw . . . just a ghost." The ghost of a woman lost in the forest; the walking, speaking dead; an illusion of life. Nothing else made sense. Not even the forest, a forest that had almost captured her—a terrible dream full of ghosts, spirits.

Barnabus went still. Henry exhaled very slowly. Lucy felt a whisper of air against her neck, a chill that went down her spine. Miss Lindsay was behind her. She could feel the woman, even though she could not see or hear her. Lucy always knew when she was close.

Miss Lindsay said, "Perhaps you'd like to walk with me," and Lucy rose on unsteady legs, and joined the woman as she turned and strode away toward the cemetery.

"I'm sorry," Lucy said.

Miss Lindsay raised a fine, dark brow. "Curiosity is no crime. And you have a right to know."

"No." Lucy shook her head. "I'm just the house girl. You didn't hire me for —"

"Stop." Miss Lindsay quit walking and gave her a hard look. "Close your eyes."

The demand was unexpected, odd. Lucy almost refused, but after a moment, Miss Lindsay's gaze softened and she said, "I will not hurt you. Just do as I say. Close your eyes."

So Lucy closed them, and waited. Miss Lindsay gave her no more instructions, which was curious enough in itself, though the girl did not break the silence between them. The darkness inside her mind was suddenly fraught with color, images dancing: not memories, but something new, unexpected. Like a daydream, only as real as the grass beneath her feet.

She saw a thunderstorm, night; felt herself standing in a doorway, staring at the rain. A warm hand touched her waist.

And then that touch disappeared and she stood in the forest, within the twilight of the trees, and the woman was once again in front of her—*Mary*—hands outstretched, weeping.

Gone, again, gone. Other visions flashed—feathers and crows, golden glowing eyes—but they were too quick and odd to make sense. Except for one: Henry, younger, standing beneath a bough of flowers, holding hands with the woman from the wood. Mary. Smiling. Staring into his eyes like he was where her heart lived.

Then, later: Henry and Mary, riding away in a buggy. Henry and

Mary, kissing. Henry and Mary, in the dark, his hands shaking against the clasps of her wedding gown, the white of the cloth glowing beneath the dappled moon. On a blanket, in the forest.

Lucy saw a shadow behind them, something separate and unnatural, creeping across the forest floor. She tried to shout a warning, but her throat swelled, breath rattling, and all she could do was watch in horror as that slither of night spread like a poison through the moonlight, closer and closer—until it nudged Mary's foot.

And swallowed the rest of her. One moment in Henry's arms—in the next, gone. Gone, screaming. Henry, screaming.

Lucy, screaming. Snapping back into the world. Curled on her side in the thick grass. Arms around her. A large, tanned hand clutching her own and Miss Lindsay crouched close, fingers pressed against Lucy's forehead.

"You're safe," said the woman, but that was not it at all. Henry and Mary were not safe. Henry and Mary had been torn apart, and Lucy could not bear to think about it. Not for them, not for herself—not when she suddenly could remember so clearly the night her own mother had disappeared, swallowed up by the world. Her choice to go—but with the same pain left behind.

"Ah," breathed Miss Lindsay, and her fingers slid sideways to caress Lucy's cheek. "Poor child."

Lucy took a deep breath and struggled to sit up. The world spun. The arms around her tightened—*Barnabus*—and she closed her eyes, slipping back into darkness.

She woke in her bed. A candle burned. Outside, strong winds rattled the house; rain pattered against the roof and window. Miss Lindsay sat in a chair. Her hands were folded in her lap, and she wore a man's robe that smelled of cigar smoke.

Lucy tried to speak, found her voice hoarse, hardly her own. "What happened?"

A sad smile edged Miss Lindsay's mouth. "Impatience. I pushed you too fast."

The girl hesitated. "Was it real, then? What I saw?"

Only after she spoke did she realize the foolishness of that statement; Miss Lindsay could not possibly know what she had seen. But the older woman denied nothing, nor did she look at Lucy as though her mind was lost.

"Real enough," she replied softly, and then, even quieter: "Did you understand what you saw?"

"Some of it. Except at the end . . . what took Mary . . ." Lucy's voice dropped to a whisper as a chill swept deep. "That was not human."

"So little is," murmured Miss Lindsay, but before Lucy could ask what that meant, she said, "The woman you saw in the forest the day you came here is my brother's wife, Mary. She did not die, as others have said, but was stolen away. Captured, with the woods as her cage. She cannot leave, and my brother . . . my brother cannot enter. He cannot see her. He cannot speak to her. But he knows she is there, and so he stays and watches, for just one glimpse." Miss Lindsay looked at her hands. "He loves her so."

Lucy curled deeper under the covers, staring. "I don't understand how any of this could happen. It's not . . . normal."

"Normal." Bitterness touched Miss Lindsay's smile. "Some would say the same of the moon and stars, or the wind, or a flight of birds, but all those things are natural and real. We accept them as such, without question." She leaned close, candlelight warming her golden gaze. "You should know, Lucy, that I hired you on false pretenses. Not merely to cook and clean and stay silent in your room. You live here, my dear, because you are the first person in twenty years to see my brother's wife. And *that*, if one wished to speak of such things, is *not* normal."

Lucy shook her head against the pillow. "The driver, Mr. Wiseman, told me about ghosts. That's all I thought she was."

"Ghosts." Miss Lindsay's fingers flexed. "To tease a child about ghosts is simple because of the cemetery I control. Because of the dead that people bring. Not because of Mary. Those in town think she's buried here. And she is, in a way. But the woman you saw is flesh and blood."

"How?" Lucy breathed, thinking of Mary—Mary in the forest, so lost—Mary in the forest twenty years past, so in love. "Why?"

Miss Lindsay closed her eyes. "Tomorrow. Tomorrow, I will tell you that story."

"No," Lucy protested, but the older woman stood.

"Tomorrow," she said again, and blew out the candle. Lucy reached out and caught her hand. Miss Lindsay gently disengaged herself, swept her fingers over the girl's brow, and walked from the room. She closed the door behind her.

Lucy lay in the darkness for a long time, listening to the old house, the rumbling storm. It occurred to her, briefly, that she could leave this place and go back to her father and brothers, but the idea made her heart hurt, and she realized with some surprise that this place, despite its mystery, felt like home. A better home than what she had left behind, what she had been forced from by her father.

Mother was forced to leave, in a different way, whispered a tiny voice inside her mind, but that was too much, and Lucy pushed back her blankets to rise from bed. She still wore her clothes from that afternoon, but did not bother with her shoes.

The house was quiet. Lucy walked silently through the kitchen. She wanted water, but as she reached for the pump above the sink, she noticed a warm glow against the wall in the parlor, and heard the sound of pages turning. She peered into the room.

Henry and Barnabus sat before the small fire, reading. Her heart jumped a little at finding them; she was not quite certain she was ready to face the older man, not after what she had seen inside her head. And Barnabus . . .

The young man looked up from his book. He had not been long from the rain; his hair was damp, as was his shirt, which strained against his shoulders. She tried to imagine him as a child, wild in the forest— still wild, maybe—and it was easy, as simple as looking into his eyes.

She felt shy, looking at him. He was handsome, breathtakingly so.

Barnabus stood and gestured for her to take his seat. When she did not move, he held out his hand to her, and she let him take it and guide her. His skin was warm. His touch, gentle. Her heart beat a little faster.

Henry closed his book. "Are you better?"

"Yes," she said, hardly able to look at him. But she did, and though she found terrible sadness in his eyes, there was also compassion. Barnabus very quietly settled himself on the floor beside her chair, the edge of his hand brushing her foot.

Lucy fidgeted, staring at the fire. Henry said, "You want to ask me something."

She hesitated. Henry frowned, laying his book on the floor. "I'm sorry for earlier. I scared you this afternoon. I didn't mean to."

Barnabus sighed. Lucy glanced down at him. "I'm sorry, too."

"So? Ask me what you want." Henry smiled gently. "I am here, Lucy."

You are with your wife, she thought, and summoned up her courage. "Please . . . why was Mary taken?"

Henry paled. Barnabus' hand shifted against her foot. A warning, perhaps. Lucy ignored him, refusing to take her gaze from the older man's face. She watched his struggle—battled one of her own, resisting the urge to take back her question—and thought instead of Mary. Mary in her wedding gown. Mary in the forest, begging for help.

Lucy thought of Miss Lindsay, too. She was defying the woman; she doubted that would end well. But she needed to know.

Henry looked at the fire; for a moment his eyes seemed to glow. "Mary did nothing. It was me. I was . . . foolish. I had a temper, and there was a woman who had too much interest in me. I rejected her, badly. And because she could not hurt me . . ."

He stopped. Lucy forced herself to breathe. "Does this woman live in the forest?"

Henry closed his eyes; a bitter smile touched his mouth. "She *is* the forest. She is a witch and its queen."

"A witch," Lucy murmured, thinking of fairy tales and crones, women in black hats with cats in their laps, cooking children for supper. "How do you stop a witch?"

"You don't," Henry said heavily, and picked up his book, tapping his fingers along its spine. "None of us are powerful enough."

"She couldn't hurt *you*," Lucy pointed out, and Barnabus once again touched her foot—yet another warning.

Henry's jaw tightened; his eyes were quite bright. "Do you have any more questions?"

"Just one," Lucy said softly, thinking of her mother. "What is it like to be married?"

Barnabus went very still. Henry glanced at him and said, "It is a sacred art. A union of souls. To be together is the grandest adventure."

Lucy shook her head, trying to picture Henry and Mary as her father and mother, to imagine what that would be like, to have parents who loved. It was difficult to do, and disheartening. "It seems like a lot of work."

Henry studied her. "And?"

"And, nothing," she said, but hesitated, still chewing on her memories. "I heard a word once, talking about such things. *Honeymoon*, someone called it. I liked the word, but I still don't know what it means."

"It doesn't mean much by itself," Henry replied slowly, with a distant look in his eyes. "It's a symbol, I suppose. You're married, so the both of you run away where no one knows you, no one can find you, and you make a world that is just your own. For a short time, your own." He smiled gently. "A month, the span of the moon. Sweet as honey. And if you're lucky, perhaps you turn that honeyed moon into something longer, a lifetime."

"But I still don't see how it makes a difference," Lucy said, feeling stubborn. "If you're married, you're together anyhow. Happy or not. You don't need to be all . . . sticky about it."

Barnabus shifted slightly, but not before she saw his small smile. Heat flooded her face; she felt deeply embarrassed to have said so much in front of him. She had forgotten herself—was far too comfortable in his presence—far too at ease with all these people who were supposed to be her employers. Not her family.

As if you were ever made so welcome by your own flesh and blood.

Lucy stood. Barnabus caught her ankle in a loose grip. The contact seared her skin.

"The heart loves," Henry said softly, so gentle, it made her chest ache. "Listen to your heart, Lucy. Don't be afraid of it."

"I'm not," she whispered, feeling captured, trapped; Barnabus' hand felt too good. She nudged her foot, and he released her.

"Good night," she said, not looking at either man, and fled the parlor for the kitchen. She almost went straight to her room, but she needed air and flung open the kitchen door that led into the garden. Wind blasted her, as did rain. She worried about others feeling the draft and began to close the door behind her. It caught on something. Barnabus.

Thunder blasted. Barnabus touched her waist, drawing her back until heat raced down her spine, and her shoulders rubbed against his hard chest. His hand closed over hers, and they held the door together, blasted by white lightning and tremors of sound.

Barnabus shut the door when the rain began coming in. Cut off from the storm, the air inside the house felt closed, uncomfortably warm. No lightning, no candle, no way to see except by touch and memory.

Barnabus still held her hand. He guided her across the kitchen until she touched the door of her room, and there he eased away. Lucy listened to his soft retreat, the creak of the floorboards, the rustle and whisper of his clothing, the faint hiss of the wind as he left the house for his bed in the work shed. Her hand tingled with the memory of his fingers. Her waist still felt the pressure of his palm.

Lucy lay down on her bed and closed her eyes. She dreamed of a world that was her own, and a sweet moon made of honey in the sky.

Lucy rose early the next morning. Barnabus was already awake; she could see him in the distance, in the cemetery, digging a grave. Lucy vaguely recalled Miss Lindsay mentioning a death in town. She watched him work, and then went about her business, feeding the chickens and milking the goats. Crows gathered along the eaves of the house, watching her.

They made a ruckus only once, and Lucy looked up at the sky just long enough to see a streak of golden light in the shape of a bird fall behind the work shed. She did not know what to make of it—again her imagination, perhaps—until she heard a rustle of clothing and Miss Lindsay walked out from behind the small structure, buttoning the top of her dress.

She did not appear surprised to see Lucy, but merely said, "Good morning," and walked into the house. The girl stared after her, perplexed. So much was odd about this place. Or perhaps Lucy was just odd herself. That did not bother her as much as it should. As much as it would have, not so long ago.

The funeral took place that afternoon. Few people came, but one of them was Mr. Wiseman, hauling a coffin in the back of his wagon. Lucy did not feel any great pleasure in seeing him. He was a very real reminder of the world beyond the wood—a world that felt like a distant place—and the sight of his face made her stomach twist with dread.

"I see the ghosts didn't get you," he said loudly, with that same sly smile.

"Ghosts are for children," said Miss Lindsay, coming up behind his wagon. She stood beside Lucy, and rested her hand on the girl's shoulder. "Don't you have something better to do with your time, Wilbur, than tease young girls?"

Mr. Wiseman tipped his hat. "Helena, you're still as handsome a woman as I've ever met. I don't suppose your brother would consent to me courting you?"

"I believe my brother would have very little say in the matter," replied Miss Lindsay dryly, "nor would your wife be all that pleased with the arrangement."

His smile was all teeth. He tore his gaze from Miss Lindsay and looked at Lucy. "Got a message for you, girl. Your father's come down with some kind of sickness. He wants you to come home straightaway to care for him."

Lucy stared. "He was fine when I left."

"But he's not now. You're to ride with me after I'm done here."

"No," she said without thinking.

Mr. Wiseman's smile slipped. "Maybe you didn't hear me."

"I heard you." Lucy drew in a shaky breath, swept away by such hard emotions that she almost quivered with tension. "No, I won't go."

"He's your father."

Desperation rode over guilt. "I'm doing a job. He wouldn't give up his place at the quarry for me. I know that. He told me often enough."

Mr. Wiseman's jaw flexed. "You'll do as you're told, girl."

Miss Lindsay's hand tightened on Lucy's shoulder. "Wilbur. You and I will discuss this later."

"No time for that," he snapped, eyes narrowed. "You been twisting this girl's mind, making her turn from her family?"

"I like working here," Lucy told him, voice rising. "And my brothers are still at home. They don't need me. They don't even *want* me."

"Go on, now," Miss Lindsay said to Mr. Wiseman, drawing Lucy away. "There are people waiting on that body."

He looked ready to argue, but it was true—there were mourners dressed all in black standing at the little cast-iron gate in front of the cemetery, and they were watching Mr. Wiseman with a question in their eyes. The old man grunted, giving Lucy a baleful glare.

"You be packed by the time I get back," he told her. "Or else I'll take you as you are."

Lucy flinched. She saw Barnabus running toward them, and caught Mr. Wiseman also staring at the young man. Something passed through his gaze, and he slammed the reins against his horses, jolting them into motion.

"Coward," Miss Lindsay murmured, but Lucy hardly heard her. All she could do was stare at Barnabus. He looked dangerous, furious—like he was ready to fight, something she had never imagined of him. He touched the small of her back, his mouth set in a grim line that only grew deeper, darker, as he gazed past her at the old man's retreating wagon.

And then he looked at her, and in his eyes, a question. Uncertainty.

"If I go, I won't be back," Lucy said, speaking to them both, but looking at Barnabus. "I know it."

Knew it like the truth. Just as with those visions of the day before, she could feel inside her head the future tumbling away into a dark, cold place, and if she went with Mr. Wiseman, that would be her fate. Something lonely and awful. Like having her wings cut after a taste of flying.

Miss Lindsay's eyes flashed golden, and this time Lucy was certain it was not her imagination. "You want to stay here? You're sure of it?"

Lucy nodded, struggling with her fear. She knew it was terrible—*she* was terrible—and her father, her father would think *she was just like her mother*—but she did not care. She had to stay. Something would break inside her if she left this tiny world within the forest—this dangerous forest—this little place with these strange and wonderful people who made her feel safe and welcome. If her mother had felt this way, all those years ago, then Lucy could forgive her. She understood now, what could drive a woman to abandon all. She understood, and if it was selfish, then so be it. She would be selfish, and happy.

"Barnabus," said Miss Lindsay crisply, "take Lucy to the pond at the bottom of the hill. I'll handle Wilbur. When he's gone, I'll come fetch you both."

"I'm sorry," Lucy said, suddenly regretting the trouble she was causing the woman. "If *you* don't want me—"

"No." Miss Lindsay brushed her fingers across the girl's forehead. "You are no trouble to me or this family. This is your home."

And with that, she turned and strode away toward the cemetery, where Mr. Wiseman was helping the mourners unload the coffin. Barnabus tugged on Lucy's hand. It took her a moment to follow; she kept hearing those words, seeing those golden eyes, and felt inside her a flush that could have been what Henry spoke of, that sense of running away.

The grand adventure. Making a new world from the old. She was not married, but it felt the same: a union, in its own way.

She and Barnabus crossed the meadow, chased by crows. They climbed a gentle slope through scattered oaks, and at the crest of the hill gazed down upon a body of still water, blue from the sky and filled with lily pads and brown ducks. The forest nudged the northern edge of the pond, but the sun chased back the shadows, and the grass was tall and green.

A rough dock jutted from the shore. Barnabus and Lucy sat at the end of it, careful of splinters, and dangled their feet in the water. After a short time, he reached over and held her hand.

She liked that, and felt a stab of fear that she might have to give it up. But then she remembered Miss Lindsay's calm strength and said, "They're good people, aren't they? Henry and Miss Lindsay. But they're not . . . like other folk. Regular, I mean." She had been about to say *normal*, but recalled Miss Lindsay's feelings about that word.

Barnabus nodded, squeezing her hand. He did not appear at all perturbed by her question or the implication, but rather, seemed comfortable with the truth: that Henry and Miss Lindsay *were* different, inexplicably so, and that it was natural. Like the wind or the moon. She liked that too.

"How long have you lived here?" Lucy asked him, jumping slightly as fish nibbled on her toes.

He spread out his fingers. Five, then two. Seven years.

"And before that? Did you really live in the forest?"

Barnabus shrugged, gazing past her at the dense tree line. His mouth moved, but not a sound emerged except the whistle of his breath. He looked, for a moment, frustrated—and Lucy wondered what it would be like to have no voice, to have a lifetime bottled up inside her without words or sound. She reached out, unthinking, and touched his lips with her fingers. She only meant to tell him it was all right, that he did not need to explain, but his face was so close and his eyes were so deep and blue, that she found herself leaning, leaning, until she felt the heat of his breath and her fingers slipped away, only to be replaced by her mouth.

Lucy had never kissed a boy before. His taste was sweet and hot—toe-curling, a delight. It frightened her, but not enough to give it up.

It did not last. Lucy heard a weeping cry, and broke away, staring at the woods. She heard it again, a voice calling out, and it took her only a moment to find that pale feminine face, luminous in the rich green shadows of the forest. Lucy leapt to her feet and ran. She felt Barnabus behind her, but did not look back, afraid if she did, the woman would disappear.

Mary. She heard a crow shrieking above her head—an animal caw that sounded very human—but she ignored that, as well.

She reached the edge of the forest just as Barnabus caught up with her. She thought she heard Henry shouting, but Mary was there—right in front of her—and the woman whispered, "Please, help me."

Lucy sucked in her breath—fighting for courage—and jammed her hands through the underbrush toward Mary. Barnabus grabbed her waist—another set of hands joined his, as well—but it was too late. Something took hold of her wrists, yanking hard—and the face in front of her changed. It stopped being Mary, and became instead a shadow, a gasp of night, like that slithering tendril of nothingness she had witnessed in her vision.

Raw terror bucked through her body. She tried to pull back, fighting with all her strength. Whispers rose from the trees—all those voices she had almost forgotten, soaring into her head like a scream.

Lucy was pulled into the forest.

The first thing she noticed, when she could see again, was that the world around her seemed quite ordinary. She was in the forest, yes, but she had been inside forests before, and this was no different. The shadows were long and the canopy thick, and the twilight that filled the air was neither gloomy nor particularly menacing. It was simply dense—with vines of wild rose and new spurting growths of seedlings: poison ivy, ferns, tiny bowing cedars, and those massive trunks of oak that spread fat like squatting giants all around her. She smelled the earth, something else—like rain—and the air was still and warm and humid.

Lucy turned in one slow circle, trying to find the edge of the forest. She was close; she knew she should see Barnabus or Henry—at least hear voices—but even the birds did not sing, and all she could see was leaf and branch and shadow.

"Hello?" she called out, thinking of the creature that had pulled her inside the wood. Fear clutched her throat, pounding against her heart, but she steadied herself, fought herself, and regained control. She thought of Mary, too. Trapped here for twenty years. She wondered if the same would happen to her.

She heard something, and turned in time to see an immense pale figure part the gloom. A white stag. Tall and broad, with a deep chest and a long neck that glittered as though sprinkled with dew. Its hooves had been polished to the sheen of pearls, and its eyes glowed with a wild, raging light. Tiny bells hung from its silver antlers, and the sounds they made were those same whispered voices Lucy had heard in her head—now louder, cries and sorrow ringing with a delicate knell.

A woman sat upon the stag. She was divine: pale and slender, sparkling as though spun with stars and diamonds, her hair so long it almost swept the ground. A Snow Queen, with a manner that begged a bow. White furs and silks crisscrossed her high breasts, which were quite nearly exposed, though covered with faint lines of pale rose, curling like poems and wings upon the skin below her throat.

She held herself with such lightness, Lucy imagined she might float to fall, and as the stag stepped near, Lucy saw that the woman was perched on a fine dainty saddle shaped like a frog.

"Witch" was not the right word for this woman, Lucy thought. A witch was human. And this . . . creature . . . most definitely was not.

"You are trespassing on the land of the *Sidhe*," said the woman, her voice strong, ringing. "What say you?"

"I say no," replied Lucy awkwardly, fighting for courage. "You brought me here. So I was invited."

A faint smile touched the woman's mouth. "You thought you were saving a heart that belongs to me. So you are a thief. Much worse, I think."

Lucy steeled herself. "You're talking about Mary. Mary doesn't belong to you."

The stag shook its head, and the bells wept. Lucy thought she heard Mary's voice within those tones. She closed her eyes for just a moment, searching. Listening hard, but when she looked again at the woman, she was gone from the stag.

A cold hand caressed the back of Lucy's neck, and she flinched, whirling. The woman stood before her, impossibly tall, peering down like a snowy owl about to bite a mouse. The hunger in her gaze was implacable and terrifying.

"All that enter the forest belong to me," said the woman softly. "And now you, as well."

"No," Lucy said. "I want to go home."

"Home." The woman smiled. "This is home."

"There are people waiting for me. For Mary, too."

"Mary," she said quietly. "Mary betrayed my trust. She tried to fetch help. You. Quite shocking that you were able to see and hear her. I find that fascinating."

Lucy did not. "Let us go. Please."

"For what reason?" The woman smiled, tilting her head. "Shall I tell you a riddle and have you guess the answer? Or perhaps have you perform three impossible tasks, each more harrowing than the other. Oh, better still, tell me stories to keep me amused. Be my fool, my jester of the wood, and *perhaps* in a year or twenty I will release you."

Lucy doubted that. So she said nothing, instead waiting, watching, refusing to let herself feel a moment lost. The woman's smile faltered, just slightly, and that momentary weakness humanized her presence in a way that made her seem less regal than ridiculous—as though her shocking appearance was nothing but an attempt to awe, and intimidate.

Lucy suddenly felt stronger. "I won't beg you. I won't be a fool."

"You already are," said the woman darkly. "You are nothing."

"No more than you," Lucy replied recklessly, following her intuition. Perhaps too well: a cold hand grabbed her chin with crushing strength, yanking up until she stood on her toes, forced to look the woman in the eyes.

"You love," she whispered harshly. "I can smell it on you. Should we test that love? Do you truly think the one your heart cares for would wait? That handsome young man who used to be mine?"

"Barnabus," Lucy said, hoarse.

"*Barnabus*," she hissed. "I raised him long before that old crow sank her claws into his heart. He was *mine*. My *son*, in every way but one. But *that* one . . . he remembered."

"He did not love you." Lucy could feel it, see it, a little boy with blue eyes running naked and wild, engaging with the woman, but never with emotion. Never with affection, or a smile.

The woman glanced away, and then, softly, almost to herself: "He would never call me mother. He refused. And so I punished him."

"You took his voice."

"I could not have him calling another by the name he refused me."

"So if someone refuses you, you hurt them? What good does that do?"

The woman gave her a sharp look. "Respect must be shown. I am a queen."

"You are a queen who is alone," Lucy said, and the woman released her so quickly, she staggered, rubbing her aching chin. The woman—the queen, the *Sidhe*, whatever that might be—watched her with cool, steady eyes, a gaze she now knew Barnabus copied well. Lucy met those age-less eyes, letting her thoughts roam, picking up as she did tendrils of some alternate vision: the woman in her finery, wandering the endless expanse of forest, alone. So very alone.

"You wanted Henry to love you as a man loves a woman," Lucy whispered. "You wanted Barnabus to love you as a mother. And there have been others, haven't there? People who caught your eye. You brought them here, and then you hurt them because you couldn't understand why they didn't return what you feel."

"Love," whispered the woman. "It is a myth that belongs only to humans, and those who pretend to be like them. It cannot last."

"I used to think that," Lucy told her. "Until I met Henry, and I saw how he loves."

"Henry will give up his wife."

"Henry will love her forever."

The woman smiled coldly. "Forever does not exist for mortal love."

"It doesn't exist for immortals, either," Lucy said, still listening to that little voice inside her head. "Or maybe that's just you."

The woman sucked in her breath; the stag backed away, eyes keen on its mistress. Lucy did not retreat. She took a step, overcome, as though she could hear her soul humming, as though the world was in her veins, alive and strong. Her heart, full to burst—and she thought of Barnabus, Henry, Miss Lindsay. People who cared for her. People *she* cared for, in ways she had not known possible.

She loved them. She *loved*. And she knew what love was now, even if it was never returned. Even if one day, it all fell away.

The woman flinched, staring at her. She began to speak, then stopped. Light burned in her eyes, but Lucy did not falter, nor did her heart dim. The woman turned, stopped, and in a muffled voice said, "Go. Leave. You have your freedom. I give you my word."

Lucy blinked, startled. "And Mary."

The woman stiffened, her back still turned. "I have blessed Henry with a gift. I would have returned Mary sooner, but she stopped loving him as she should. She is not worth his heart. He will be hurt, he will be broken. He has loved an idea for all these years."

"Because of you," Lucy said, and then, softer: "Henry loved the woman before the idea. Let him find his own way."

The woman's light seemed to dim, her radiance faltering beneath the gloom. Lucy, in a moment of pity, said, "You could leave this place if you're so lonely."

That flawless head turned just a fraction, enough to show the corner of an eye, the curve of a high cheek.

"We all have our homes," she said quietly. "The ability to choose yours is not a gift to take for granted."

The woman plucked a silver bell from the stag's antlers and tossed it at Lucy's feet. A heartbeat later she was perched high on the fine saddle, her composure fixed and utterly regal.

"Give my regards to Barnabus," she said coldly. "The crows, as well."

And then she was gone. Vanished into the forest twilight.

Lucy picked up the bell and shook it. Mary's voice echoed, like an eerie chime. She held it tight after that, steady in her hand—scared somehow of hurting the woman, no matter how odd it was to think of a woman as a bell—and chose a direction to walk in. Voices whispered all around her, and what filled her ears and head tasted like music, a delightful mix of laughter and argument, lilting into a bustle that burst and billowed like bubbles, or birdsong. The queen—the woman—alone. Or not. There were things living in this place, in this entire world, that Lucy imagined she would never understand.

Twisting trees grew before her, and after a moment, it seemed a path appeared, grass rimming its edges. Ahead, light. Lucy ran.

She pushed out of the forest into a sunlight that felt like holy fire, bright and hot and clean. She was not beside the pond any longer, but on the meadow across from the old house. She could see Barnabus in the distance, with an ax in his hands. Miss Lindsay and Henry were with him. Above her head, in the branches of the trees, crows began to shout. And after a moment, so did Henry.

The bell in her hand rattled. Lucy released the silver charm, unable to hold it. She instantly felt light-headed—had to close her eyes to keep her balance—and when she opened them, there was a woman on the ground.

Mary. Still in her wedding dress. Looking not one day older.

Again, Henry shouted. Lucy was not able to see the reunion. She staggered, eyes closing. Inside her head, voices, bells, a woman whispering. The dizziness was too much; her muscles melted.

She fell down and did not get up.

Lucy dreamed. Of women and men who turned into crows, and other creatures with burning gold in their eyes; of beings who grew tails like fish, and dragons that breathed fire; dark figures with green shining eyes, and the woman, the queen herself, with a similar gaze, effortlessly regal and unrelenting in her stare.

"Truce," said the woman, in Lucy's dream. "Never ask me why, but between us, a truce. For one who loves."

And Lucy woke up. She was in her bed. Miss Lindsay was seated beside her, as was Barnabus. There were shadows under his eyes, as though he had not slept in days. She wondered, fleetingly, if he might speak to her—if perhaps there were other gifts in her release—but when he picked up her hand and brought it to his mouth with that silent, gentle strength, she knew instantly that was not the case.

"Henry?" Lucy breathed. "Mary?"

Miss Lindsay briefly shut her eyes. "Gone. Already gone. Henry wanted to stay to see you wake, but Mary . . ." She stopped, hesitating. "Mary wanted away from this place, immediately. She said to give you her thanks."

Miss Lindsay made the words sound flat, cheap. Barnabus looked unhappy. Lucy did not know what to think. She felt an aching loss for Henry. She wanted to see him, but thought of Mary, twenty years trapped, and knew why the woman had run—and that where she went, so would he. No choice. She was his home.

Miss Lindsay seemed to read her mind—she was good at that, Lucy mused wearily—and said, "For both of us, thank you. From the bottom of our hearts, thank you, always."

"It was her, not me," Lucy pointed out. "She gave us up."

Miss Lindsay looked sideways at Barnabus. "She does that, sometimes."

Lucy shifted, uncomfortable. "What is she?"

"I don't know," said Miss Lindsay. "She is old, though. Her kind always are. So old, they don't have children anymore. Not with each other, anyway."

"She's lonely."

"Tell Henry that."

Lucy held up her hand. "He and Mary have their time now. Time to make their own way." Time to finish what they had started, if such a thing was possible. To have their honeymoon, their marriage, their life.

Miss Lindsay murmured, "Patience. I told Henry—both of them—to have patience. They've been through so much. Neither is the person the other married. Not anymore." She glanced away, bitterness touching her mouth. "Is it wrong to wonder whether I should be happy for them?"

Lucy closed her eyes, savoring the warmth of Barnabus' hand. "Did you ever marry?"

Silence, long and deep. Finally, Miss Lindsay said, "A woman like me rarely does."

Lucy opened her eyes and gave her a questioning look. The woman sighed. "I'll tell you some other time, perhaps."

Some other time, Lucy thought. *Like how you read minds? Or how sometimes you are a woman, and sometimes a crow?*

Miss Lindsay stared at her, startled, and then laughed out loud.

"Yes," she said, still smiling. "Just like that."

But she never did. At least, not for a long while. One morning soon after, she approached Lucy and Barnabus as they were weeding the garden, and said, crisply, "I think I will go away for a time. There's a world beyond the wood, you know. I've been here my entire life, already."

"Yes," Lucy said, though she herself had no desire to go elsewhere. Barnabus put down his rake and regarded the older woman thoughtfully, with no small amount of compassion in his steady gaze. He nodded once, finally, and held out his arms. Miss Lindsay fell into them, hugging the young man so tightly, Lucy thought his bones might break. And then Miss Lindsay did the same for her, and she was quite certain that was indeed the case.

"Tend this place for me," whispered Miss Lindsay, her eyes glowing golden as the sun. "For all of us. We'll be back. And we might bring others. There is so much in this world I have yet to explain to you."

And then, with no shyness or hesitation, she did a shocking thing—stripping off all her clothes, right in front of them, with hardly more than a smile. Golden light covered her body. Feathers black as night, thick and rich and hot, poured up from her skin and rippled like water. Lucy could not help but gasp; her knees buckled. Barnabus caught her, and she glanced at his face. He did not appear at all surprised by what he was seeing.

He nudged Lucy, gestured for her to look again—and she found Miss Lindsay shrinking, narrowing—until she was no longer a woman, but a crow.

A crow who stared at them with golden eyes—cawed once—and leapt into the air, followed by a flock of companions that shrieked and beat their wings in raucous sympathy.

Quite a sight. But it was not the last time Lucy ever witnessed it.

Time passed. Lucy and Barnabus did as Miss Lindsay asked—maintaining the house and land, as well as the cemetery—though they married soon after to keep local tongues from wagging. She kept the name of her birth, since Barnabus had none to give. Lucy Steele. They called their son William, who also, on occasion, exhibited peculiar talents.

And sometimes Lucy would take a book and sit on the edge of the woods, and read out loud. She never knew if the woman, the *Sidhe* queen, was listening, but she liked to think that the trees were, and that through them the immortal could hear another voice, speaking just for her.

It was a good life for Lucy and Barnabus, a happy life. A life together, a grand adventure, and one that lasted many moons, over many secret stories—each as sweet and golden as honey.

I had to write about a honeymoon from hell (yes, that was the assigned theme), but when this story was first released, astute readers probably noticed the honeymoon part was sort of . . . jammed . . . in there. I wasn't interested in honeymoons. I was interested in heartbreak, and what happens when someone who has never experienced love and family begins to let those two things into their life—how it makes a person vulnerable, but also stronger than they've ever been.

That openness to love was a running theme in my Dirk & Steele paranormal romance series, about a "detective agency" that acts as a cover for supernatural creatures who use their powers to help others—as well as build a community built on trust and friendship. I so enjoyed writing those novels, which was how I got started as an author: the first book I sold when I was just twenty-four years old was Tiger Eye, the beginning of the series.

In the Dirk & Steele universe, it didn't matter if you were human, merman, or witch; a shape-shifter, or a gargoyle: learning how to trust in love, be open to love from others . . . and to love in return . . . was the scariest thing of all.

"Where the Heart Lives" takes place many, many decades before the beginning of the series—here is the origin of the Dirk & Steele detective agency, and its founding principles of friendship and family.

AFTER THE BLOOD

Lost in the forest, I broke off a dark twig
And lifted its whisper to my thirsty lips . . .
                                    —PABLO NERUDA

I DIDN'T HAVE TIME to grab my coat. Only shoes and the shotgun. I had gone to sleep with the fanny pack belted to my waist, so the shells were on hand, and jangled as I ran. I had forgotten they would make noise. Not that it mattered.

No moon. Slick gravel and cold rain on my face. Neighbor's dogs were barking, and I wished they would shut up, but they didn't, and I kept expecting one of them to make the strangled yip sound like Pete-Pete had, out in the woods where I couldn't ever find his body. I missed him bad, nights like these. So did the cats.

The cowbell was ringing when I reached the gate, and I heard a loud thud: a hoof striking wood. Chains rattled. I raised the shotgun, ready.

"They're coming," whispered a strained voice, murmuring something else in his old Pennsylvania Dutch that I couldn't understand. "Amanda?"

"Here," I muttered. "Hurry."

Hinges creaked, followed by the soft tread of hooves and wheels rolling over gravel. Slow, too slow. I dug in my heels, hearing something else in the darkness: a hacking cough, wet and raw.

"Steven," I warned.

"We're through," he said.

I pulled the trigger, gritting my teeth against the recoil. The muzzle flash generated a brief light—enough to glimpse a hateful set of eyes. And then, almost in the same instant, I heard a muffled scream. I fired again, just for good measure.

Steven slammed into the gate. I ran to help him set the lock—one-handed, shotgun braced against my hip. I heard more coughs—deeper, masculine—and got bathed in the scent of rotten meat and shit. All those unclean mouths, breathing on me from the other side of the fence. A rock whistled past my ear. I threw one back with all my strength. Steven dragged me away.

"Son of a bitch," I muttered, breathless—and gave the boy a hard look, his body faintly visible, even in the darkness. "What the hell are you doing here?"

Steven let go. I couldn't see his face, but I heard him stumble back to the horses. I almost stopped him, needing an answer almost as much as I feared one—but I smelled something else in that moment.

Charred meat.

I stood on my toes and reached inside the wagon. Felt a blanket, and beneath, a leg.

When? I wanted to ask, but my voice wouldn't work. I clung to the edge of the wagon, needing something to lean on, but that lasted only until Steven began leading the horses up the driveway. I followed, uneasy—trying to ignore the sounds of rocks hitting the fence and those raw, hacking coughs that quieted into whines. Sounded like dogs crawling on their stomachs, begging not to be beaten. Made me think of Pete-Pete again. My palms were sweaty around the shotgun.

Steven remained silent until we reached the house. Lamplight flickered through the windows, which were crowded with feline faces pressed against the glass. It felt good to see again. Steven dropped the reins and walked to the back of the wagon. He was a couple inches taller than me, and slender in the shoulders. Just a teen, clean-shaven, wearing a dark, wide-brimmed hat. His suspenders were loose, and his pants ended well above his ankles. A pair of old tennis shoes clung precariously to his feet.

"They hurt him bad," said the boy, unlatching the backboard. "Even though he saved their lives."

"He didn't fight back?" I asked, though I knew the answer.

Steven gave me a bitter look. "They called him a devil."

Called him other things, too, I guessed. But that couldn't be helped. We had all expected this, one way or another. Only so long a man could keep secrets while living under his family's roof.

I tried to hand my gun to the boy. He stared at the weapon as though it were a live snake, and put his hands behind his back.

"Steven," I said sharply, but he ducked his head and edged around me toward the back of the wagon. No words, no argument. He did the job I was going to do, taking hold of those blanketed ankles and pulling hard. The body slid out slowly, but the cooked smell of human flesh curdled through my nostrils, and I had to turn away with my hand over my mouth.

I went into the house. Cats scattered under the sagging couch and quilt, while kittens mewed from the box placed in front of the iron-bellied stove. I left the shotgun on the kitchen table, beside the covered bucket of clean water I had pulled from the hand pump earlier that evening, and grabbed a sheet from the line strung across the living room. I started pulling down panties, too, and anything else embarrassing.

Just in time. Steven trudged inside, breathing hard—dragging that blanket-wrapped body across my floor. He didn't stop for directions. Just moved toward the couch, one slow inch at a time. A cat peered from beneath a quilt and hissed.

I helped sling the body on the couch. A foot slipped free of the blanket, still wearing a shoe. The leather had melted into the blackened skin. Steven and I stared at that foot. I wanted to cry—it was the proper thing to do—but except for a hard, sick lump in my throat, my eyes burned dry.

"What about you?" I asked Steven quietly. "They know you brought him here?"

"I put the fire out," he replied, and pulled off his hat with a shaking hand. "Don't know if I can go home after that."

I rubbed his shoulder. "Put the horses in the barn, then take my bed. This'll be awhile."

"Our dad," he began, and stopped, swallowing hard. Crumpling the hat in his hands. He could not look at me. Just that blackened foot. I stepped between him and the couch, but he did not move until I placed my palm on his chest, pushing him away. He gave me a wild look, haunted. I noticed, for the first time, that he smelled like smoke.

But I didn't have to say a word. He turned and walked out the front door, head down, shoulders pinched and hunched. Some of the cats followed him.

I stayed with the body. Sat down at the bottom of the couch, beside that exposed foot. It took me a long time to peel off the shoe. Longer than it had to. I wanted to vomit every time I touched that warm, burned skin. I peeled and pulled, and finally just cut everything away with a pair of old scissors. Steven passed through only once, from the front door to my bedroom. If he looked, I didn't know. I ignored him.

I unrolled the body from the blanket. Worked on all those clothes—and the other shoe. Stripped off what had been hand-sewn pants made of coarse denim, and a shirt of a softer weave. The beard I knew so well was gone. So was that face, except for blackened skin and exposed bone. His mouth was open, twisted into a scream so visceral his lower jaw had unhinged.

"Stupid," I whispered to him, rubbing my eyes and running nose. "You had nothing to prove."

Same as me. Nothing to prove. Nothing at all.

I had brought in a knife with the scissors—sterilized in boiling water and wrapped in a clean rag covered in some faded drawing of a black mouse in red pants. I did not want to touch the blade, but I did. I did not want to hold my arm over that open mouth, but I did that, too.

Sucked down a deep breath. Steeled myself. Cut open my wrist.

Nothing big. I wasn't crazy. But the blood welled up faster than I expected. My vision seemed to fade behind a white cloud, and I almost lay down on that burned body. But I took a couple quick breaths, grit my teeth, and stopped looking at the blood.

Just that mouth. Just that mouth I held my wrist over. Swallowing all those little drops of my life.

It took a while. I didn't want to make a mistake. This was the worst I had ever seen. So bad I began to wonder if this was the end, the last and final straw. Got harder to breathe after that. My throat burned. Cats pawed my legs and took turns in my lap, butting my chin and kneading my thighs with their prickly little claws. One of them licked a charred finger, but didn't try to chew, so I let that go.

My wrist throbbed. So did my head, after a time. I kept at it. Until, finally, I noticed a little color around his lips. A hint of pink beneath the blackened skin. I closed my eyes, counting to one hundred. When I looked again, it wasn't my imagination. Pink skin. Signs of life.

I pressed my wrist against his burned mouth and felt his lips tighten just a hairsbreadth. Good enough for me. I was exhausted. I didn't move my wrist, but stretched out on the couch beside him, ignoring the smell and crunch of cooked skin. A cat walked up the length of my hip, while another perched on the cushion above me, licking my hair. Purrs thundered, everywhere.

And that mouth closed tighter.

I closed my eyes and went to sleep.

I woke choking, water trickling down my throat.

But there was also a hand behind my head and something hard on my lips, and both flashed me back to the bad days. I sat up fighting, heart all thunder. My fist slammed into a hard chest.

A naked man squatted in front of me, gripping a cup of water in his hand. Scared me for a moment, terrified me, part of me still asleep—but then I took a breath and my vision cleared, and I saw the man. I saw him.

He was bald, scorched, raw. Not much better than a half-cooked chicken, and certainly uglier. But his eyes were blue and glittering as ice, and I smiled crooked for that cold gaze.

"Henry." I wiped water from my mouth, trying not to tremble. "Aren't you a sight?"

"Amanda," he replied. But that was it. Only my name. That other hand of his still held the back of my head. I looked down. My wrist had been bandaged. I saw other things, too, and dragged the quilt from the couch to toss over his hips. His mouth twitched—from bitterness or humor, I couldn't tell—but he leaned in to kiss me.

Just my cheek. Slow and deliberate, lingering with our faces pressed close. I slid my arms around his neck and held tight.

"Don't make me cry again," I whispered.

Henry dragged in a deep breath. "How did I get here?"

"Steven."

He leaned harder against me. "Did anyone see him?"

"We haven't talked about what happened. But I'd say yes." I pulled away, speaking into his shoulder, a patchwork of pink and blackened flesh. "He said you saved lives."

"I gave in." Henry's fingers tightened in my hair. "I killed."

"Monsters."

"I killed," he said again, shivering. "I violated God's rule."

You did what you had to, I wanted to tell him, but those were cheap words compared to what he needed, and that was more than I could give him.

Bedsprings creaked from the other room. I glanced toward the window. Still dark out, but it had to be close to dawn. I heard birds, and the goats, and farther away, that dog barking. I tried to stand. Henry grabbed my wrist. "You need to rest. What you did last night—"

"I'm fine," I lied, blinking heavily to keep my vision straight. "Stay here."

But he didn't. He wrapped the quilt around his hips and limped outside with me, followed by several cats, bounding, twining, pouncing in the grass. Little guards. Cool air felt good on my face, and though Henry did not take my hand, our arms brushed as we walked.

I had built the rabbit hutch inside the barn. Horses stirred restlessly when we entered, and so did the goats in their dark pen, but the chickens were quiet. I felt all the animals watching as I undid the latch and reached inside for a sleek brown body. The rabbit trembled. So did Henry, when I handed it to him.

"I wish you wouldn't watch," he murmured, but almost in the same breath he bit the rabbit's throat. It screamed. So did he, but it was a muffled, relieved sound. I looked away. All the other rabbits were huddled together, shaking. I could hear Henry feeding, and it was a wet, sucking sound that made my skin crawl and my wrist throb.

I counted the seconds. Counted until they added up to minutes. Then I took another rabbit from the hutch and held it out, head turned. Henry took it from me and walked away. No longer limping. I heard the rabbit scream before he reached the door.

I did chores. Freshened the water for the goats, brushed the horses down with handfuls of hay and the palms of my hands. Thought, again, about building a pen for some pigs and how much I'd have to trade upriver for several in an upcoming litter I'd heard about in town. I wanted to get set before winter. Trees needed cutting, too, for firewood. I had been putting that off.

When I left the barn, I found Henry near the garden, digging a hole just large enough for two dead rabbits. Soil was wet and smelled good, like the tomatoes ripening on the vines. I saw light on the horizon.

"I'll finish that," I said. "You need to get inside."

"I need a walk," he mumbled. I realized he had been weeping. "I don't want to see Steven."

"Too bad." I crouched, taking his hand. His skin appeared healthier, burn marks, fading. "You may be all he has now. Besides, it's too close to dawn for a walk. Don't be stupid."

"Stupid," he echoed, and pulled his hand away. "You should have seen how my dad—how they—looked at me. How they'll look at Steven now. My fault, Amanda. I was too weak to leave."

The rabbits were still warm, but hollow, flattened. Drops of blood coated their throats. I tossed them into the hole Henry had dug and pushed dirt over their bodies.

"Staying was harder than leaving," I said, but that was all. The house door creaked open, somewhere out of sight, then banged shut. Henry tensed. I backed away. I doubt he noticed. Too busy watching his brother, who strode down the path toward us—just a shadow in the predawn light, shoulders hunched, hands shoved deep in his pockets, hat tilted low over his eyes.

I left them alone. Went back to the house for my shotgun and a coat, and then headed down to the fence. Looking for monsters.

Cats followed me.

The land had been in the family a long time. Long enough for stories to be passed down, stories that never changed except for the weather, or the animal, or the person: stories involving my kin, who were neighbors and friends to the Plain People. Or the Amish, as my mother had called them, respectfully.

She was dead now, gone a couple years. She and my father had both survived the Big Death, though cancer and infection finally killed them. Mundane, compared to what had destroyed most everyone else: a plague that struck cities, a virus that killed in hours or days. My brother was lost that way—gone to college in Chicago, which didn't exist anymore. It was for him that I didn't like hearing stories about the Big Death, though some refugee survivors seemed to get kicks from the attention they received when telling the tale. Blood in the streets, and riots, and the government quarantining the cities and suburbs with tanks and barricades, and guns. No burials for the millions dead, no burials for the cities.

Just the forests that had grown up around them. An unnatural growth, some said. Cities of the dead, swallowed by trees. And, in the intervening years, other strange things. Unnatural visitations.

But folks didn't like to tell those stories. Plague was easier to swallow than magic.

The fence around my land was made of wood and planks instead of strung barbed wire. Maybe my great-grandfather had built the thing, or his father—I didn't know for sure—just that it was older than living memory, and had been tended and mended over the last hundred years by people who knew what they were doing, so many times over, there probably wasn't much original wood left in the damn thing.

It was a good fence. And I'd made my own additions.

Still dark out. Skies clearing, revealing stars. I checked the gate at the end of the driveway. Couldn't see much on the other side, except for a splash of something dark on the gravel. Blood, maybe. No body. Dragged away into the woods with Pete-Pete's bones. I undid the lock, crossed over. Shotgun held carefully. Cats walked with me, but didn't hiss or flatten their ears. Just watched the shadows beyond the road, in the trees. I didn't hear anything except for birds.

"Hiding from the light," said a quiet voice behind me. I didn't flinch. One of the cats had glanced over its shoulder, which was warning enough.

Henry stepped close, still naked except for the quilt. I said, "You should be in the house."

"I have time. Not safe here, all by yourself."

"Got an army." I held up my gun and glanced at the cats. "Steven?"

He said nothing. Just took a few jolting steps toward the woods. I grabbed him, afraid of what he would do. He didn't fight me, but the tension was thick in his arm. I pretended not to see the sharp tips of his teeth as he pulled back his lips to scent the air.

"They're in there," he said, his voice husky. "I tasted their blood last night."

I tightened my grip, both on his arm and the shotgun. Cats twined around our legs. "Did you like it?"

Henry looked at me. "Yes."

"It's not a sin," I said, "to be yourself. You told me that."

"Before I was turned into this." He touched his mouth, pressing his thumb against a sharp tooth. "I was called a demon last night. Dad put the torch to me himself, and I didn't stop him. I kept hoping he would stop first."

I squeezed his arm. "Come on. Before the sun rises."

"I have time," he said again, but gently, holding my gaze. "Please, let's walk."

So we did. On the dangerous side of the fence, outside the border of the land: my cornfields, and the potatoes, and the long rows of spinach, green beans, tomatoes, and cucumbers. I didn't have a rabbit problem. Cats strolled along the rails and through the tall grass, which soaked the bottoms of my jeans. Henry did not notice the wet, or chill. He watched the forest, and the sky, and my face.

"Stop," I said, and knelt to examine a weather-beaten post. It was hard to see. I had no batteries for the flashlights stored in the cellar, but I had traded for some butane lighters some years back, and those still worked. I slipped one from my pocket, flipped the switch. A little flame appeared. I needed it for only a moment.

"It looks fine," Henry murmured.

"You always say that," I replied, and held out my finger to him. He hesitated—and then nipped it, ever so carefully, on the sharp point of his tooth. I felt nothing except a nick of pain, and maybe sadness, or comfort, or affection—*love*—but nothing as storybooks said I should feel: no shiver, no lust, no mind-meld. I had done my research in the library, which still stood in town, governed by three crones who lived there and guarded the books. I had read fiction, and myths, and looked at pictures on the backs of movies that couldn't be played anymore. But in the end, none of it meant much. Problems just had to be lived through.

I smeared a spot of my blood on the fencepost and said a prayer. Nothing big. It was the feeling behind the words that mattered, and I prayed for safety and light, and protection. I prayed to keep the monsters out.

We moved on. A hundred feet later, stopped again. I repeated the ritual. Weak spots. No way to tell just from looking, but I knew, in my blood, in my heart.

"They got through last night," Henry said, watching me carefully. "Past the fence to the front door. That's what started it. I was in the barn, cleaning the stalls. I heard Mom scream."

"I'm sorry." I glanced at the sky—lighter now, dawn chasing stars. Sun would soon be rising. "I'll swing around the farm today and see if I can't shore up the line without your folks seeing me."

"Take Steven with you."

I shook my head, patting the tabby rubbing against my shins. "Won't do that. If they try and hurt him—"

"Then we'll know. It's important, Amanda."

I started walking. "Have him talk to me about it. His choice. No pressure from you."

Henry stayed where he was, clutching the quilt in one hand. His broad shoulders were almost free of burned skin, and so were his arms, thick with muscle. He had been teethed on hard labor, and it showed.

But Henry was a good-looking man when he wasn't burned alive, and it hurt to feel him staring at me. Staring at me like I wanted to be stared at—with hunger, and trust, and that old sadness that sometimes I couldn't bear.

I looked away, just for a moment. One of the cats meowed.

When I turned back, he was gone.

No one knew, of course. About the blood on the fence. Prior to last night, no one had known about Henry's affliction, either. Just Steven and me.

Small town. Caught on the border of a government-registered Enclave, one of hundreds scattered across the former United States. Not many official types ever came around, except a couple times a year with fresh medicines and other odds and ends—military caravans, powered by gas. No one else had fuel. Might be some in the quarantined cities, but I couldn't think of anyone who would go there. The virus might still be active. Waiting on the bones.

Twenty years, waiting. Little or no manufacturing in all that time; no currency, no airplanes, no television or postal service, or ice cream from the freezer; or all the little things I had taken for granted as a kid and could hardly remember. Just stories now. Lives that were and would never be again. The past, gone unmissed.

Maybe it was for the best. Survivors of the Big Death had to make do with leftovers. Farming experience was more valuable than guns. So was living without electricity and plumbing. Which meant—to the dismay of some—that Amish, and folks like them, now held the real power. Government was encouraging them to spread out, establish new agricultural communities—from Atlantic to Pacific. Nothing asked for in return, though it had created an odd dynamic. I'd heard accusations of favoritism in business dealings, complaints about cold shoulders and standoffishness. Other things, too—bitter and sour.

But not all communities were the same, and if you were a good neighbor, the Plain people were good to you. Even if, when you knew them too well, they had their own problems. Religion was no cure for dysfunction.

I rode in the wagon beside Steven. Brought my shotgun—unloaded in case anyone checked. Shells were in my pockets. Knives, hidden inside my boots. We weren't the only ones on the road, which had been one of those two-lane highways back in the old days. Still a highway, just not for cars—which rusted at the side of the road. Relics of another age. None had been dumped in the fields. Plenty of land, but it needed to be used to grow food. Vast vegetable gardens and grazing cattle surrounded several battered trailer homes. Little kids playing outside waved to us, and went back to chain the dog.

Steven and I didn't talk much until we reached the border of his family's farm. I made him stop twice and each time, pricked my finger for blood. Blessed the fence.

"God has a plan," Steven murmured, watching me.

I glanced at him. "I hate when you and Henry say that."

"Better God than the alternative." He leaned forward, studying his hands—his trembling hands. "I want God to be responsible for what changed us. I want God to have a reason for us being different. We're not demons, Amanda."

"I agree," I replied sharply. "Now let me concentrate."

"You don't even know how to do it," he murmured, still not looking at me. "Or why your blood works against . . . them."

Because I will it to, whispered a small voice inside my mind. But that was nonsense—and even if it wasn't, years of considering the matter had given me nothing worth discussing. The same instincts that had led me to dot fence posts with my blood seemed just as powerful as the driving urge of birds to fly south for the winter, or cats to hunt—or Henry to drink blood.

I worked quickly, and climbed back into the wagon. Steven clucked at the horses. I kept my gaze on the fence, watching for weak spots—listening for them inside my head. But it was near the gate where I saw the breaking point.

"Those boards are new," I said, jumping down and crouching. "Or were, before last night."

"Dad replaced them. No one told Henry or me." Steven's voice was hoarse, his face so pale. He looked ready to vomit. "Found out too late."

"You don't have to do this. We can go back."

He closed his eyes and shook his head. "I need them to understand. None of us could stop what happened."

Not before, I imagined him adding. *But we could stop it this time.*

I stared past Steven at the woods. "It's been hard for you, these past few years. Helping your brother pretend he's human. Keeping up the illusion, every day, in your own home."

A strained smile touched the corner of his mouth. "Lying all the time. Praying for forgiveness. Wears on the soul."

"Cry me a river," I said. "You know you're a good person."

"By your standards, maybe."

"Ah, my weak morals. My violent temper. The jeans I wear." I gave him a sidelong glance. "I thought pride was a sin."

He never replied. I finished blessing the fence and pulled myself back in the wagon. Less than a minute later, we turned up the drive, almost a quarter-mile long, from the fence to the house. It was a sunny day, so the bright white clapboard house glowed with light. Purple petunias grew in tangled masses near the clothes line; chickens scattered beneath the billowing sheets, pecking feed thrown down by a little girl dressed in a simple blue dress. A black cap had been tied over her head, and her curly brown hair tied in braids. She looked up, staring at the wagon. Steven waved.

"Anna is getting big," I said, just as the little girl dropped the bowl of chicken feed and ran toward the house—screaming. I flinched. So did Steven.

He stopped the horses before we were halfway up the drive. I slid out of the wagon, watching as a man strode from the barn. He held an ax. My unloaded shotgun was on the bench. I touched the stock and said, "Samuel, if you're not planning on using that cutter, maybe you should put it down."

Samuel Bontrager did not put down the ax. He was a stocky, bow-legged man: broad shoulders, sinewy forearms, lean legs, and a gut that hung precariously over the waist of his pants. He had a long beard, more silver than blond. Henry might look like him one day. If he aged.

Last time I had seen the man, he had been admiring the new horse, a delicate high-stepping creature traded as a gift for his eldest daughter. Smiles, then. But now he was pale, tense, staring at me with a gaze so hollow he hardly seemed alive.

"Go," he whispered, as the house door banged open and his wife, Rachel, emerged. "Go on, get out."

"Dad," Steven choked out, but Samuel let out a despairing cry, and staggered forward with the ax shaking in his hands. He did not swing the weapon, but brandished it like a shield. Might as well have been a cross.

I took my hand from the shotgun. "We need to talk."

Rachel walked down the porch stairs, each step stiff, sharp. Her gaze never left Steven's face, but her husband was shaking his head, shaking like that was all he knew how to do, his eyes downcast, when open at all.

"Out," he said hoarsely. "I saw a crime committed last night that was against God, and I will not tolerate any who condone it."

"You saw a young man save his parents from death." I stepped toward him, hands outstretched. "You saw both your sons take that burden on their souls." *To keep you safe*, I didn't add. *Making amends for what they couldn't do years ago.*

I might as well have spoken out loud. Rachel made a muffled, gasping sound, a sob, touching her mouth with her scarred, tanned hands. I saw those memories in her eyes. Samuel finally looked at his son, his gaze blazing with sorrow.

"You held them down," he whispered. "You held those men down . . . for him."

I gave Steven a sharp look, but he was staring at his father. Pale, shaking, with some strange light in his too-bright eyes.

"They were going to kill you," he breathed. "I did nothing wrong. Neither did Henry. We did not forsake the Lord."

"You held them down," Samuel hissed again, trembling. "And he ripped out their throats. He used nothing but his mouth to do this. We all saw it. He was not human in that moment. He was not a child of God. He was . . . something else . . . and I will not have such a monstrosity in my home. Nor will I bear the sight of any who would take that monster's side."

"Samuel," I said, looking past him at his weeping wife, who swayed closer, clutching her hands over her mouth. "Those were not human men he killed."

"Then what was my son, if those were not men?" Samuel tossed his ax in the dirt and rubbed a hand over his ashen face. "I would rather have died than see my own child murder."

He was telling the truth. I expected nothing less from a man of his faith. Nor could I condemn it. He believed what he believed, and it was the reason so many towns and Enclaves had become safe places to live. It was also why so many local men of the Amish were gone now, in the grave.

And why Anna Bontrager did not look like either of her fair-haired parents.

"Steven," I said quietly. "Get out of the wagon. We're going."

"No," he whispered, flashing me a desperate look. "Tell them, Amanda." *Tell them what happened years ago in the woods.*

But I looked at Steven, and then his parents, and could not bring myself to say the words. Not yet. Maybe not ever.

"Steven and Henry's belongings," I said instead. "We'll take them."

"Gone," said Rachel, so softly I could barely hear her. She drew close to her husband's side, and her bloodshot gaze never left Steven's face. "Burned."

Steven sank down on the wagon bench. Breaking, breaking—I could hear his heart breaking. I suddenly hated Henry for not being here. For asking me to do this.

I grabbed my shotgun off the wagon and touched Steven's leg. "Come on. Let's go."

He gave me a dazed look. Samuel, behind me, cleared his throat and whispered, "Take the wagon and horse. I don't want anything he touched."

I ignored him, still holding Steven's gaze. I extended my hand. After a long moment, he took it, and I pulled him off the wagon. He kept his head down and did not look back at his parents. I pushed him ahead of me, very gently, and we walked down the long driveway toward the road.

Samuel called out, "Amanda."

I stopped. Steven did not. I glanced over my shoulder. Samuel and his wife were leaning on each other. I wanted to pick up handfuls of gravel and throw it at their faces. I wanted to ask them to remember the bad days, and that violent afternoon. Maybe the choice not to act had always been clear to them, but not to Henry. Not to his brother.

"If you keep the boy with you," Samuel began, but I held up my hand, stopping him.

"Don't," I said. "Don't threaten me."

"No threats," Rachel replied, pulling away from her husband, pushing him, even. "We care about you. Our families have always been . . . close."

More close than she realized. Close enough that she would not want me here, should the truth be known. All those little truths, wrapped up in lies.

All I could do was stare, helpless. "Then don't do this to Steven. No matter what happened last night, you have to forgive him. Isn't it your way?"

Rachel's face crumbled. Samuel clamped his hand down hard on her shoulder.

"Forgiveness isn't the same as acceptance. Steven will be held accountable," he said, with ominous finality.

Rachel shuddered. For a moment I thought she would defy her husband, but she visibly steeled herself and gave me an impossibly sad look that reminded me of my mother when she would dig out old pictures of my brother.

"I know about the violence that was committed against you," she whispered, so softly I could barely hear her voice. "But don't let that be an excuse to harbor violence in your heart."

"Or my home?" I gave her a bitter smile. "There are just as many kinds of violence as there are forgiveness." I looked at Samuel. "You set Henry on fire. You killed your own son. No one's free of sin in this place."

I turned and walked away. Steven waited for me at the end of the driveway. I grabbed his arm and marched up the road, holding him close. Even when the Bontrager farm was out of sight, I didn't let go.

I said, "You told them what happened to me?"

"She just knew," Steven whispered. "It was the same man and she knew."

I didn't want to think about that. But I did. I had time. It took us more than an hour to walk home. Longer, because I detoured to check other parts of his family's fence; and then mine. No need to bless any other borders in these parts. Folks had their own problems, but not like ours—though the road, between his place and mine, had a reputation among locals: few travelled it at night. Years ago, men and women had gone missing, parts of them found at the side of the road, chewed up.

We walked slowly. Met only two other people, the Robersons: a silver-haired woman on a battered bicycle, transporting green onions inside the basket bolted to the handlebars, and her husband, ten years younger, riding another bike and hauling a homemade cart full of caged chicks. On their way to town central. Mr. Roberson wore a gun, but his was just for show. I was the only person in fifty miles who still had bullets, but no one knew that either, except for Henry and Steven.

Steven kept his head down. I forced myself to wave. Mrs. Roberson, still a short distance away, smiled and raised her hand. And then glanced to the left, to the young man at my side.

Her front tire swerved. She touched her feet to the road to stay upright, but it was rough, and she almost spilled her onions. Her husband caught up, deliberately inserting himself between his wife and us. He touched his gun.

And then they were gone, passing, pedaling down the road. I stopped, turning around to stare. Mr. Roberson looked back. I felt a chill when I met his gaze.

"Amanda," Steven said.

"What," I replied, distracted, thinking about the farm and the land, and those crops I would need help harvesting. I thought about the pigs I wanted to buy, and all the little things I needed that only town businesses—businesses run by Amish—could provide.

"I'm sorry," he said, and then, even more quietly: "Everyone is going to know. My parents have already told the Church about Henry and me. We won't be able to stay here."

"They think Henry is dead."

"Doesn't matter. You won't have it easy, either."

"I don't care," I lied.

We got home. A small part of me was glad to see it still standing. Cats waited at the gate. Several perched on the posts, watching the woods.

And one of them—a scarred bull-necked tom—laid a dead mouse on my boot when I stopped to undo the lock and chain. I thanked him with a scratch behind the ears, and nudged the small corpse into the grass.

Steven did not talk to me. He headed for the barn. I didn't ask why. I went into the house, trying not to trip on the cats, and set my shotgun down on the kitchen table. Blinds had been pulled. Henry sat on the couch in the dark room. He still wore the quilt. Kittens squirmed in his lap, chewing the fingers of his right hand. In his left he held a small heart carved from wood.

"I wondered all these years where this had gone," he said softly.

"You could have asked."

"Maybe I was afraid of the answer." He tore his gaze from the heart, and looked at me. "You had it hidden under your mattress."

I tilted my head. "Been going through my things?"

"It was an accident," he said, unconvincingly. "Why was it there?"

So I could touch it at night without having to see it, I almost told him. *So I could remember watching your hands as you made it.*

Instead I said, "Today went badly. But we both knew it would."

Henry stared down at the kittens. "I hoped otherwise."

I hesitated, watching him, wondering how so much had changed. Seemed too far in the past—too painful—but I remembered, in clear moments: fishing on Lost River; eating corn fresh from the stalk under the blazing sun; holding hands in secret, while hiding under the branches of an oak during some spring storm. We had loved being caught in storms.

I walked to the cellar door, grabbed a candle off the shelf, and lit the wick with the butane lighter. Down the stairs, into the cold, dark air. Shadows flickered, some cat-shaped: fleeting, agile, skipping across the cellar floor, in and out of the light as they twined around my legs. I passed crates of cabbage and potatoes, and dried beef. Walked to a massive chest set against the wall and knelt in front of the combination lock. A new, shiny lock, straight from the plastic, part of a good trade from an elderly junk woman named Trace who rode through a couple times a year.

Cats butted their heads against my hips, rubbing hard, surrounding me with tails and purrs. I opened the chest. Held up a candle so that I could see the boxes of bullets, and guns wrapped in cloth. Two pistols. One rifle. One hundred boxes of ammunition. Twenty alone were for the shotgun, making a total of two hundred shells. My father's stash. He had been a careful man, even before the Big Death.

And now I was a rich woman. But not in any way I wanted to make public.

"Going to battle?" Henry asked, behind me.

"Make love, not war," I quoted my father, and shut the chest, nudging aside paws that got in the way. I locked it one-handed, and turned to face Henry. He still wore nothing but the quilt. Candlelight shimmered across his smooth chest and face. His gaze was cold. Had been for years, since the change.

"Been a while since I saw you without a beard," I said.

"I never could bring myself to shave it," he replied softly. "I didn't want to look unmarried."

I tried to smile. "Too bad. I've heard you're a catch. Aside from an aversion to the sun, and all the blood."

"Aside from that." Henry's own faint smile faded. "About today. Whatever happened, I'm sorry."

"Talk to Steven." I walked to another metal chest, the one unlocked. Inside, clothes. I set down a candle and pulled out my father's jeans and a red flannel shirt. Musty, old, but no mice had been in them. I fought back a sneeze, and held out the clothing to Henry. He did not take them. Just stared.

"You're a dead man," I said bluntly. "To them, you're dead. Would've been that way even if your father hadn't set you on fire. You couldn't pretend forever."

His gaze was so cold. "That doesn't change who I am."

I tossed the clothing at his feet. "You changed years ago, even before what happened in the woods. You've just been slow to admit it."

I picked up the candle, stood—and his fingers slid around my arm. Warm, strong grip. I closed my eyes.

"Wife," he whispered.

I flinched. "Don't call me that."

Henry tried to pull me closer. I wrenched my arm free, spilling hot wax on the stone floor and myself. Cats scattered. Upstairs, a door banged. Footsteps passed overhead. I stopped moving. So did Henry. My eyes burned with tears.

"Amanda?" Steven called out from the cellar door. "Henry?"

"Coming," I croaked, stumbling toward the stairs. Henry grabbed my arm again, and pressed his lips against my temple. He whispered something, but I couldn't hear him over the roar in my ears and my thudding heart.

"Not again," I finally heard, clearly.

"What?" I mumbled.

But Henry did not answer. He let go, and passed me. I heard him say something to Steven, but that was nothing but buzz, and I pushed him aside, running up the stairs, from the darkness, from him.

Steven stood in the kitchen. He had been crying. His eyes were red, same as his nose and cheeks. He glanced from my face to Henry—who appeared behind me at the top of the stairs—and his expression twisted with grief or anger. I could not tell.

"I made a bed in the barn," he said.

"I'll cook something," I replied, because it was the right thing to say, and I couldn't think. "Then we'll talk about where to put you. The attic will be too cold in the winter, but so will the barn."

"Won't be here that long," Steven said. "Not me, not any of us."

I stared at him. Henry said, "Steven."

But the young man gave us a look so hollow it chilled my bones. He backed away, across the living room to the front door, whipping off his hat and crushing it with his hands.

"I see what I see," he said, and then turned, stumbling from the house. Henry started after him. I grabbed his arm, yanking hard.

"Sun," I said.

"I don't care," Henry replied harshly, but stayed where he was, staring at the door. I did not let go. My hand slid down his arm until our fingers entwined. He squeezed hard.

"What happened?" he whispered. "Out there? What changed us? We were human, Amanda. And then we weren't."

"We're human," I said. "Just different."

"Don't be naïve." He tried to pull away from me, but this time I was the one holding on, stubborn.

"It wasn't our fault," I told him. "Everything was out of our control."

"Not everything," he replied, and grabbed the back of my neck. "I made a bad choice. Crawled on my stomach back to what was familiar and normal. I should have stayed instead. Stayed for good, instead of returning to you only when something was wrong."

"Something was wrong almost once a week," I reminded him. "I pushed you away. We both needed time."

"And now this." Henry's fingers slid into my hair. "What do you want, Amanda?"

"Nothing," I told him. "You're here only because you have to be. You're like a fox smoked out of its den. Secret marriage, secret life. You're good at pretending to be something you're not. Ask yourself what *you* want, Henry. But don't ask me."

I pulled his hand off my neck, and walked toward the front door. He didn't stop me. I escaped into the sunlight.

I walked through the fields and ate a tomato fresh from the vine, biting into the red flesh like it was an apple. I ate a carrot, too, and some raw, ripe corn, then threw down the cob after only a few bites. Restless, aching, heartsick: a man in my house, a boy in my barn, and a world beyond the fence, threatening me now, in more ways than the woods could harm me.

I stood on the border of my land, staring over the fence at the dense shadows beyond the trees. Cats twined around my legs and climbed the boards and posts. Watching the woods.

You're not free, I told myself, holding still, holding my breath. It had always been Henry who was caught—in his own lies, his confusion, his conflict. Before, after. And me, trapped in limbo. Waiting. Not for him, but for myself. Years, waiting, to wake up from the haze and bad dreams. Waiting for a little peace.

I had built my fortress. Guarded it with guns and blood. Told myself it would help. Bit by bit, help. Only nothing had changed. Until now.

What do you want, Amanda?

A cat hissed. I glimpsed movement deep in the woods. A flash of white twisted around two dark spots and a moving hole. I saw it again, never still, but always facing me. Restless and hungry.

I stood for a long time, staring, prickly with heat. Burning up, burning, hardly breathing. *Caught, trapped. Caught, trapped.* Two words that filled my head, droning on and on, until I forced myself to grab the fence, fingers digging into the wood.

What do you want, Amanda?

I climbed the fence. Stopped halfway up, swaying on the rails, and then kept going. Relentless. I jumped down on the other side, the wrong side, tasting blood as I bit my tongue. Cats followed, yowling, ears pressed flat against their skulls. I ignored them and walked across the grass toward the woods. This was my neighbor's land, but his house was far away on the hill. I heard his dog barking. I didn't know if the old man ever entered the woods, but his nights were safe. He had not been marked like me—and Henry, and Steven.

It was late afternoon, sun leaning west, lines of light falling away from the trees. Only a matter of time before the shadows grew thick and long. My feet bumped cats—spitting, hissing, growling cats—but I kept walking. Sweating, heart thudding, stomach hurting so badly I wanted to sit down and vomit.

Instead I stood on the other side of the sunlight, a golden barrier bathing the grass between the woods and me. Less than a stone's throw from the dense tangle of branches, vines, knotting together like awful fingers, an undergrowth that seemed made to scratch and bind and close around bodies like barbed, clawed nets. Forests had become strange places after the plague—not just here, I had heard, and not just around the dead cities, but everywhere. Made me wonder, sometimes, if there were others out in the world like me and Henry, and Steven. Others, like *them*.

I forced myself to look at the pale monster that waited in the shadows, holding my breath as it licked the edges of its lipless mouth with a long, pink tongue. No eyelids. Hardly a nose, just a stub that looked partially melted, as though it had frozen in mid-drip off that ashen face.

We stared at each other. Years rolled. Memories. I remembered the woods, and the coarse laughter, and the fear. I still felt those hands on my body. I felt naked again, without my shotgun.

"I know you," I breathed, trembling—and then, again, louder. "I know you. It doesn't matter how much you've changed, I still know who you were, before."

I picked up a cat, hugging its quivering body against mine. No purrs. Just a deep-throated growl. I watched that monster in the woods tilt back its head, cutting its cheeks with long nails that sank into its thin skin. That pit of a mouth made a rasping sound, like a sob.

"Yeah. You cry," I whispered, scrubbing my wet cheeks with the back of my hand. "Living for night so you can finish what you started. But I'm not going to let you."

Cats pushed hard against my legs, reaching up to claw my thighs. I backed away from the woods, gaze locked on the monster. Branches broke somewhere deeper behind it, and wet coughs hacked at the air, followed by a faint whine. Sun was sliding lower. The cat in my arms struggled free, hitting the ground with a hiss. I continued to retreat. Never breaking that gaze, though the terror crept on me, harder and heavier with each slow step, something building in my throat—a scream.

Until finally, my back hit the fence. I climbed it, flew over it, tumbling over the rails and landing on my ass. I sat there, light-headed, heart pounding. Sweat-soaked. My finger throbbed, and so did my wrist. I looked down. Blood seeped through the white bandage and dotted the end of my index finger, which I had been nicking all day. All my fingers were lightly scarred.

I looked through the rails. The monster was gone, but I heard wet coughs and the struggling movements of slow-waking bodies. Men, rotting, rising from their day graves: pushing aside leaves and brush; ripping the sod pulled over their bodies. Cats gathered close. I petted heads and tried to stand. Took several attempts. My knees were weak, and my skull throbbed.

But I made it. Sun was sitting pretty on the horizon. I walked, slowly, staring at the land and the fence, and those long rows of crops I had planted with my own hands. For a moment it didn't seem real. I should have been somewhere else. I didn't know where—all I'd had were books and pictures from old magazines, conversations with my parents—but I knew there had been universities and jobs, once—all kinds of work that needed doing, and that had to be easier than growing food to stay alive.

The world had been smaller, before—and brighter. Faraway cities that took only hours to reach. Endless streams of music and art—so much brilliant color—and those never-ending aisles in the pharmacies and grocery stores where nothing ever ran out and no one ever went hungry. A world with laws and justice, and safety. Where being . . . a little different . . . was not a mark on the soul.

The Big Death had stolen away that simpler life.

I saw the house long before I reached it. Small, white, just a box beneath the golden haze of the sky. Red roses grew in massive bushes that surrounded the neat rows of my herb garden.

Henry stood on the porch, dressed in my father's clothes. They looked strange on him—almost as odd as seeing him bald, without a beard. I stopped walking, caught differently than I had been earlier when facing the monster—another kind of heartache.

He saw me standing on the hill, and strode to the edge of the porch. He held a knife and a small block of wood, which he pushed into his pocket. Sun was almost down, but not quite, and I was too far away to stop him as he walked down the steps. Smoke rose from his skin. I started running. Henry did not return to the porch shadows. He teetered, but kept moving toward me. Walking, then stumbling. He fell before I reached him, fire racing across his smoking scalp.

I barreled into his body, rolling us both into the grass. Fire went out before we hit the ground—a little patch hidden from sunlight by a low-rising knoll. I lay on Henry anyway, covering him, pressing my hands against his partially charred face. Blisters formed on his scalp, and his lips were pressed together in a tight white line of pain—but he stared at me, stared as if none of it mattered—just me and him, me and him, like the old days.

"Stupid," I whispered. "Sometimes you make me hate you."

"I hate myself," he said, grimacing as I pulled my hands from his head—taking some of the burned skin with me. It was disgusting. I tried to sit up, but he touched my face, sliding his other arm around me. He was stronger than I remembered, and I closed my eyes, holding my breath as he brushed his lips over mine. Brief, warm. I relaxed, just a little; and the next time he kissed me, I kissed back.

Henry pulled me down beside him. I lay against his chest, listening to his heartbeat. The sky had darkened. I saw the first hint of stars in the purple east. Purrs rumbled as cats pressed near, settling warm against our bodies.

"You were in braids," he murmured. "My first memory of you. Sitting on a white sheet in braids and a dress, playing with a doll. My mother told me to look after you. I remember that."

"I remember other things." I fingered a button on his flannel shirt. "Maybe we didn't have vows ordained by any minister, but we made promises to each other."

"Which I broke," Henry said quietly. "I failed you. Not just that night, or after—but all those years before, when I loved you and never said a word to anyone. You deserved better than that. And now I'm supposed to be dead."

I unsnapped a button and slid my hand inside his shirt to press my palm against his bare skin, above his heart. Henry stopped breathing; he fumbled for my hand. He held it tightly against his chest.

"You're not dead to me," I said. "But I don't know what to do, Henry."

"If I was a better man, I would take Steven and leave."

Bitter laughter choked me, and my eyes started burning again. "Don't start doing the right thing now. I don't think I could take it."

"Neither could I," he whispered, and reached into his pocket. He pulled out the small block of wood. I thought it must be a scrap from the stove bin. He had started carving into it. I could already see the promise of what it would become.

"It's not much yet," he said, turning it around in his large hands.

"It's going to be a heart." I reached out and touched the edge, lightly.

Henry cleared his throat. "I wanted to make you a new one."

A warm ache filled my chest. I tried to speak, lost my voice, then whispered, "Don't take your time."

Henry exhaled slowly, closing his eyes. I kissed the edge of his jaw—once, twice. When I kissed him again, he turned his head and caught my mouth with his. Gentle at first, then harder. His sharp teeth cut my lip. I tasted blood. He broke away.

I grabbed his jaw. "Don't."

Henry shuddered, twisting out of my grip. "Amanda—"

He stopped, looking sharply to the east. A moment later, I heard the neighbor's dog begin to bark. Distant, urgent. Cats scattered. I sat up, Henry following me—both of us holding still, listening.

"They've left the woods," I said. "Hunting."

Henry made a small, dissatisfied sound. "Hunting just us. I've always wondered why they never actively sought out other families. If all they wanted was to kill—"

I cut him off. "That's all they want."

He frowned but made no reply. Simply tilted his head, as though listening to something beyond us.

"Where's Steven?" he asked, suddenly.

We stared at each other—and I stumbled to my feet, running toward the house. I called Steven's name. He did not respond.

My shotgun was on the table where I had left it. I grabbed the weapon and the fanny pack full of shells. Henry appeared in the doorway. I took one look at his face and knew.

"He's not here," I said breathlessly, belting the ammunition around my waist.

Henry's expression darkened. He turned and disappeared. By the time I reached the porch, he was already at the gate. I followed, running hard down the driveway. Cats bounded alongside me.

Henry glanced over his shoulder, eyes glinting red in the shadows. I almost slipped, went down—and he was there in a heartbeat, holding me up.

"Steven must have gone home," he hissed.

"Why?" I asked, even as Henry dragged me to the gate. "Why would he do that?"

"To warn our parents, to make certain the fence is locked. Just in case those creatures don't follow us here. On his own, Dad always left the gate open at night. Steven and I were the ones who made certain it was shut."

"You should have told them the truth," I muttered. "*I* should have."

"They wouldn't have listened." Instead of fumbling with the lock and chain, Henry climbed the fence, straddled the top—and reached down to pull me bodily over. I held the shotgun tight across my chest. Cats followed, over and under.

I was ready when I hit the ground, my finger on the trigger. Listening for monsters in the dark. I heard nothing. Not a breath, or a cough, or the dragging slough of bellies on the road.

We ran. Henry was faster than me, but I did not tire. Cats raced at my side. I lost count of them. They had never left the land before this night, and I did not know why, now, they came with me. The wind was soft. So was the night, and the light of stars behind the thin veil of gathering clouds. Henry was pale and his legs so quick—just a blur.

I heard the screams a long time before we reached the farm. Henry made a strangled sound and burst ahead of me. I lost sight of him in moments. Somewhere distant, that dog was barking. I ran harder. I could hear the roar of my blood, and feel it pulsing like fire beneath my skin. My wrist throbbed. So did my fingers.

I felt more heat when I finally saw the Bontrager farm. Real fire, licking the shadows, climbing wild up the side of the barn. Horses were screaming, and so were children. I could hear those young, shrill voices, and part of me kept waiting for them to cut out the same way Pete-Pete had, the same way I kept expecting my neighbor's dog to stop barking, strangled and choking. Caught. Dead.

The gate stood open. Blood pooled beside the road, trailing into a smear that covered the broken concrete toward the woods. I glanced at it but did not slow. Smoke cut across me, burning my eyes and lungs. I rubbed my tearing eyes, coughing, searching out those screaming children.

Something large came at me. All I saw were the ragged remnants of clothes and a bloated white belly—but that was enough. I braced myself and fired the shotgun. The boom was thunderous, and I turned my face as hot blood sprayed across my body. Some got on my lips. I scrubbed my mouth with the back of my hand and skirted the writhing mass of white flesh bleeding out on the ground in front of me.

I found the children behind the farmhouse, near the open doors of the storm cellar. Doors, blocked by creatures with curving spines and odd joints that kept them low on the ground, bellies and knuckles dragging. Others drifted near, but these were upright, closer in appearance to the men they'd been. Pale, puffy, with holes for eyes. Feces covered their naked bodies. I could smell it, even with the smoke.

Rachel stood with her three little girls—sobbing, all of them—holding that ax in her shaking hands. Samuel lay in the dirt at her feet, bleeding from a head wound. He kept trying to stand, but his legs wouldn't work. He looked dazed, terrified.

But the creatures were not staring at them. Their focus was on Henry.

He stood so still, barefoot in the dirt. Firelight made his face shimmer golden, and the red in his eyes was more animal than man. More demon than animal.

"Come away," he said to them. "Kill me first."

"And me," I whispered, tightening my grip on the shotgun. "Don't lose your chance."

The creatures hesitated, swaying—until one of them, upright and shaped like a man—made a low, rasping moan and looked straight at me. I knew that pitted gaze. I had stared into it that afternoon, and years before: that heavy, hungry gaze and that hungry, searching mouth. I gritted my teeth, gripping the gun so tight my fingers hurt.

Finish what you started, I thought at the creature, and took a deliberate step back. *You know you want to.*

I stepped away again, lowering the shotgun. Playing bait. Cats pressed against my legs, growling. Henry slid toward me, his hands open at his sides. Neither of us looked away from the creatures—monsters, once men—still men, trapped in those bodies, with those instincts that continued to be murderous and hateful.

But I thought our distraction would work. I was certain of it. Until Rachel moved.

It should have been nothing. She lowered the ax, so slowly: but the blade flashed in the firelight, and one of the creatures at the cellar door snapped its jaws at her. She flinched, crying out—and her little girls' sobs broke into startled screams.

Everything shifted, twisted—monsters, turning inward, toward them—all those glittering teeth and long fingernails, those bloated, rippling faces with those tongues that protruded from stinking mouths to lick the rotting edges. I never saw Henry move, but he suddenly stood between his mother and a sharp hand—his teeth even sharper as he leaned in and ripped out the throat of the creature. I ran to help him, cats swarming ahead of me, leaping on those awful bodies to tear at them with their claws. I heard screams—not human—and jammed my shotgun against a shit-encrusted stomach. I pulled the trigger.

Blood drenched me, and guts. I didn't look. I moved on, reaching into the fanny pack for shells. My hands were hot, slippery.

I loaded the shotgun, glancing up in time to see Henry stand over his wounded father and punch his fist through a distended chest, his hand disappearing through broken ribs and emerging beside a curved spine. The creature screamed, flailing backward as blood poured from the wound. I heard a sucking sound as Henry yanked free. He stood there, so calm—and slowly, deliberately, licked his arm clean. I wondered if he knew what he was doing. His expression was monstrous—totally, utterly, merciless.

And I didn't care. I loved him for it.

I turned, shotgun jammed against my shoulder, ready to fire. But the monsters were retreating, staggering toward the front gate. I ran after them, skidding on gravel, and shot one in the back. I tried to shoot another, but missed.

Henry didn't seem to notice. He knelt beside his father. Samuel could barely hold up his head, and his eyes were dazed, wild. I wondered how he had gone years without acknowledging that anything was wrong beyond the borders of his land, even when others in his community had warned him to be careful at night. His only excuse was those monsters—those changed men—had never been consistent. Weeks would go by without seeing one.

I surveyed the yard. Nothing else seemed a threat. Cats sat in dirt, fur raised. Growls rumbled from their throats. Corpses everywhere, and the air stank. Rachel dragged her daughters close as she crouched beside Samuel, but she stared at Henry and not her husband.

"You're alive," she whispered to him, and I could not tell if it was fear or wonder in her voice.

He gave her a helpless look, marred by the blood around his mouth, on his clothing and his hands. "I'm not . . . ," he began, and then stopped, looking past his mother, at me. "I'm sorry I frightened you."

Rachel looked down. Samuel stirred, pushing weakly at Henry.

"Get away," he mumbled. "Oh, my God. Get away."

Henry stared at him and stood. I moved close, and when his hand sought mine, I gave it to him. Rachel saw, and looked at me, deep and long.

"Steven," I said. "Where is he?"

"Gone," Rachel replied softly, her face crumpled. "He's gone. They took him first. He tried to fight, and they dragged him away. And then . . . they came for us."

I knew that some of her despair had nothing to do with her missing son. "Rachel. It's not like before. It's over."

"Don't lie to me," she whispered harshly, clutching her belly, finally meeting my gaze. "I recognized him. He might have . . . changed . . . but I know him."

Him. I leaned back, unable to break her gaze, unable to stop remembering her face, years ago, ravaged with cuts and bruises. Same as mine. Mirrors should have disappeared with the rest of technology. I had buried two of them behind my barn, unable to stand seeing my eyes every time I walked down the hall or entered my bedroom.

"We'll find him," Henry said, tugging on my hand. "We'll bring him—"

He stopped before he said *home*, but Rachel gave him a sharp look. Samuel seemed barely conscious.

"No," said his mother, wrapping an arm around her daughters, all of whom clung to one another, weeping quietly. "No, don't bring him here if you find him."

Henry's jaw tightened. Rachel tore herself from her daughters and stood, staring up at her son, searching his eyes with cold resolve. "It doesn't matter that I love you. It doesn't matter that I would forgive you anything. There's no place for you here. Any of you." Rachel looked at me. "You won't be free if you stay."

I touched my throat. Felt like it was too tight to breathe. I wanted to protest, fight, argue—but I couldn't even speak. Rachel swayed, and turned away. Henry squeezed my hand. Stared at his mother.

We left them. I could hear distant shouts, the sound of horses. Help, coming. The fire would be visible for miles. Even the nighttime reputation of this stretch of road wouldn't be enough to stop the neighbors.

Henry and I stood at the front gate, staring at the trail of blood that led into the woods.

"He could be dead," Henry said. "You should stay here."

I reloaded the shotgun. It took all my concentration. I wanted to say something brave, but couldn't speak. So I looked at Henry, and he looked at me, and when I lifted my face to him, he kissed my cheek and then my mouth. Cats rubbed against our legs.

We entered the woods.

It had been three years. Maybe I expected snakes instead of vines, or razor blades in place of leaves, but everything that touched me was as it should be: a soft tickle of brush, the snag of thorns on my clothing and skin. I was almost blind in the darkness, and I was too loud. I crashed through the woods, clutching leaves and breaking branches, like a wounded creature, breath rasping. Henry moved in perfect silence, and only when he touched me did I know he was close.

"I can smell my brother," he whispered; and then: "I wish I'd had more time to explain."

"You had years." I touched trees to keep from tripping. "Time runs out. When I saw you tonight, I couldn't imagine how you had pretended for so long to be like everyone else. I don't know how they were so blind not to see that you had changed."

"Easier to believe," he said quietly. "Easier to pretend than face the truth. Even when I had you and Steven helping me adjust to my new . . . . instincts . . . I kept thinking I could be something else. If I prayed hard enough, if I stayed with the old way."

My fingernails scraped bark, and I felt heat travel through my skin in my blood, simmering into quiet fire—a sensation similar to knowledge, the same that guided me with blessing fences.

"The world is remaking itself," I found myself saying. "Men die, forests swallow the cities and bones. And what remains . . . changes. Life always changes."

"Not like this," Henry replied. "Not like us."

You're wrong, I wanted to tell him, but heard a low, distant cough. All the calm I had been fighting for disappeared. I reached down, nearly blind, and cats trailed under my shaking hand.

When we found the clearing, it didn't matter that I couldn't see well. I felt the open space, I looked up and saw stars, and my teeth began chattering. I gritted them together, trying to stop, but the chills that racked me were violent, sickening. Henry grabbed me around the waist and pressed his lips into my hair.

"I'm here," he murmured. "Think about what you told my mother. It's different this time."

I squeezed my eyes shut. "I didn't think I'd ever have to come back to this spot."

"It can't be the same one."

I pushed Henry away. "I shouldn't have visited you that night. I should have run and hid when I heard your mother screaming."

He froze. So did I. And then he moved again, reaching out, fingers grazing my arm. I staggered backward, clutching the shotgun to my chest.

"Amanda," he whispered.

"I'm sorry," I breathed, ashamed. "I'm so sorry I said that."

But even as I spoke, my throat burned, aching, and when I opened my mouth to draw in a breath, a sob cut free: soft, broken, cracking me open to the heart. I bent over, in such pain, shuddering so hard I could not breathe. Henry touched me. I squeezed my eyes, fighting for control. Not now. Not now.

But my mouth opened and words vomited out, whispers, my voice croaking. "When they saw me, when they chased me into the woods, you and Steven shouldn't have followed. You knew . . . you knew you were outnumbered, that they had weapons. If you had just stayed behind—"

"No," he said hoarsely, and then again, stronger: "No."

His hands wrapped around my waist, and then my chest, and he leaned over my body in a warm, unflinching embrace. His mouth pressed against my ear. "I couldn't protect my mother, and I couldn't protect you. But I had to try. Nothing else mattered."

I sensed movement on the other side of the clearing. Cats hissed. So did I, struggling to straighten. Henry let go, but stayed close.

Bodies detached from the dense shadows, some on two feet, others crawling along the ground, bellies tearing the undergrowth. I raised the shotgun, but did not fire. One of them separated from the others: tall, bloated head, those black eyes.

I knew him. Rachel had known him. She was right—there was something about the shape of his face, the lean of his body. Still the same. Still *him*. Leader of the pack.

The woods were so quiet around us. A dull silence, like a muted bell. I expected to see a flash of light, or feel the old fire in my veins, but nothing happened. I expected to feel fear, too, but an odd calm stole over me—like magic, all my uncertainty melting into my hands holding the shotgun, down my legs into the soles of my feet. I took a deep breath and tasted clean air.

I heard a muffled groan. Henry flinched. "Steven. Give him to us."

No one moved. I forced myself to take a step and then another, certain I would trip or freeze with fear. But I didn't. I made it across the clearing, Henry and the cats close by my side, those small, sleek bodies crowding into the clearing like swift ghosts.

I stopped in front of *him*. Just out of arm's reach. That lipless mouth opened and closed, and his black eyes never blinked. I did not question why I could suddenly see him so clearly, as though light shone upon his rotting face.

My finger tightened on the trigger. I let out my breath slowly. My heartbeat was loud. I could feel my pulse, my blood, bones beneath my skin. But I still did not fire, and the creature in front of me stared and stared, motionless. I tried to remember what he had looked like when he was still a man but that face was a blur. Dead now. All of us had died a little, and become something new.

I heard another groan. Henry strode past me. The creature in front of me never moved, though the others behind him swayed unsteadily.

"Amanda," Henry called out hoarsely.

I tightened my grip on the shotgun, and sidled sideways, never taking my gaze from the leader, the once-man. A rasping growl rose from his throat, but that was the only threat; and none of the others came near me.

Henry stood beside a massive tree, a giant with a girth that reminded me of a small mountain rising fat and rough from the earth. Roots curled, thick as my forearm—cradling a body.

Steven. He was so pale, wasted—and bleeding. So much blood, dripping down his skin into the soil, as though he was feeding the tree. Maybe he was. I heard a sucking sound in the roots, and when Henry bent to pick up his brother, I grabbed his shoulder, stopping him.

"Watch our backs," I murmured, all the hairs on my neck standing up as I knelt beside Steven and set down my shotgun. The boy's chest jerked with shallow rasping breaths, his fingers twitching in a similar rhythm. His wrist had been cut open, as had his chest and inner thigh. Cats sniffed his body, ears pressed flat.

My palms tingled. I almost touched him, but stopped at the last minute and laid my hand against the tree. I didn't know what I was doing, or why, but it felt right.

Or not. A shock cut through me, like static on wool—but with more pain, deep inside my skull. I tried to pull away, but my muscles froze. And when I attempted to call for Henry, my throat locked.

This is what you want, whispered a voice, reverberating from my brain to my bones. *This is what you need.*

A torrent of images flashed through my mind: open human mouths screaming, echoing over stone streets bordered by towers made of steel and glass; men and women staggering, falling, slumped in stiff, decaying piles as blood and rotting juices flowed between the cracks in the road, or in grass, upon the roots of trees that grew in shady patches. Bodies, watering the earth.

Heat exploded in my chest. I could move again. I grabbed awkwardly at Steven's clothes, hauling him off the roots. Henry helped. My muscles were weak. So was my stomach. I leaned sideways, gagging. Cats pressed close, dozens, surrounding me.

"Amanda," he said.

I shook my head. "Use your shirt to wrap his wounds. We need to stop the bleeding."

He did as I asked, but glanced over his shoulder at the pale, bloated bodies waiting in the shadows. "What about them?"

I hardly heard his question. I stared at the spot where Steven had been sprawled—a cradle made of roots—and suffered the weight of all those trees bearing down on me, as though full of watchful eyes, and watchful souls, and mouths that could speak. Steven's blood was invisible against the bark, but I could feel its presence.

Something changed us that night, I thought, and those once-men stirred as though they heard, coughs and quiet groans making me cold. They had laughed, before. Laughed and shouted and sung little ditties, and made hissing sounds between their teeth. Horror swelled inside me—mind-numbing, screaming horror that I was here, with them, again—but I fought it down, struggling to regain that spectral calm that had stolen over me.

Henry touched my shoulder. "We can go."

Steven hung over his shoulder like a dirty rag doll. I picked up the shotgun but did not stand. I held up my finger. "Give me blood."

He hesitated, glancing wildly at the monsters around us. I knew what he was thinking. Any minute now they would attack. Any minute, they would try to rip us to pieces and feed on our bodies: as in life, so now in this twilight death. I didn't understand why they waited—though I had a feeling.

"Please," I whispered.

Henry's jaw tightened, his gaze cold, hard—but he leaned forward and bit my finger. Blood welled. I touched the tree.

And went blind. Lost in total darkness. I could feel the sharp tangle of vines beneath me, and hear Henry breathing—listened, with a sharp chill, to wet, rasping coughs—but those sounds, sensations, might as well been part of another world.

Another world, whispered a voice. *We are more than we were.*

My finger throbbed. I bowed my head. Pressure built in my stomach, rising to my throat—nausea, but worse, like my guts were going to void through my mouth.

Instead of vomit, my vision returned. I saw all those dead bodies again, endless mountains of corpses sprawled on stone streets, and the sun—the sun rising between the towers, glowing with a crisp golden light. Beautiful morning, with clouds of flies buzzing over blood that was still not dry.

We were born from this, said the voice, which I now felt in my teeth, in my spine and ribs. *Blood that killed made us live.*

Time shifted. Again, I witnessed blood, and the fluids from those decaying bodies flow and settle, feeding the roots of grass and weeds, and the trees that grew from the stone inside the dead city. I felt a pulse sink beneath the street into the soil, and spread. I felt heat.

A rushing sensation surrounded me—as though I was being thrust forward, like a giant fist was grinding itself between my shoulder blades. Faster, faster, and all around me, inside me, I felt a surge of growth—my veins, bursting beyond my skin, branching like roots, bleeding blood into the darkness.

Blood, that became a forest.

A forest that swallowed a city.

Many forests, I thought. *Every city swallowed.*

And the blood spread, whispered the voice. *The blood changed us all.*

As it changed you.

I slammed down on my hands and knees, as though dropped from a great distance. Fire throbbed beneath my skin, a white light burning behind my eyes. I remembered that night, naked and bleeding, on the ground—Henry screaming my name, Steven sobbing, both of them beaten bloody—and I remembered, I remembered a terrible heat. I remember thinking the men had set me on fire, that I would look down and find my skin burning with flames.

We tasted all of your blood, whispered the voice. *We tasted a change that needed waking.*

So wake and feed us again.

I opened my eyes. I could not see at first, but the shadows coalesced, and became men and trees, and small, furred bodies, growling quietly. My hand still pressed to the blood-slicked roots of the tree, and something hummed in my ears. I felt . . . out of body. Drifting. When I looked at Henry, I saw blood—and when I looked at the monsters that had been monsters, too, while they were men, I also saw blood. Blood infected: blood changed by something I still didn't understand.

The trees are alive, I thought, and felt like a fool.

The leader of the pack shuffled forward and dragged his clawed fingers over his face with a gape-mouthed groan. He cut himself, so deeply that blood ran down his skin and dripped from his bloated cheek. I heard it hit the ground with a sound as loud as a bell. And I imagined, beneath my hand, a pleasurable warmth rise from the bark of the tree.

"Henry," I said raggedly, without breaking the gaze of the pack leader, the first and last man who held me down, so many years ago. "Henry, put Steven down. You're going to need your hands."

"Amanda," he whispered, but I ignored him, and picked up the shotgun. I settled it against my shoulder, my finger caressing the trigger, and looked deep into those black, lidless eyes.

Feed us again, I heard, rising through me as though from the earth itself. *All we want is to be fed again.*

I hated that voice. I hated it so badly, but I could not deny it. Like instinct, stronger than knowledge; like my blood on the fence or Henry burned by sunlight. We had changed in ways I would never understand, but could only follow.

"You know what you're doing," I said to the creature, which stood perfectly still, bleeding, staring, waiting. "You know what you want."

What it had wanted, all these years, I realized. Living half-dead, hungry for peace, listening to voices that wanted to be fed. Like me, but in a different way.

So I pulled the trigger and finished it.

I never did buy those pigs.

I found someone outside the Amish who would trade with me, and bargained for horses, good, strong Clydesdales, almost seventeen hands high. Four of them. I had to travel a week to reach the man who bred them, and all he wanted was four boxes of bullets.

We left at the end of summer. No one bothered us, but no one talked to us either. We were alone on the hill, though people watched from a distance as Steven and I took down the fence, board by board, and used each rail to build the walls of the two wagons. Real walls, real roofs, windows with solid shutters. I had seen abandoned RVs, and always admired the idea of a moveable home. Even if it was something I had never imagined needing. What we built was crude, but it would keep the sunlight out.

We left at the end of summer. I wrote a note and left it on the last post standing. My land, free for the taking.

I drove one wagon, while Steven handled the other. One of them was filled with food—everything we could store and pickle—and the other held Henry and our few belongings. The goats followed without much prodding. Cats were good at herding. When asked politely, anyway.

Henry rode in my wagon. He had a bed behind the wall at my back, and a hollow pipe he spoke through when he wanted to talk. After a day or two, I tied a long red ribbon to my wrist and trailed it through the pipe. Henry would tug on it when he wanted to imagine our hands touching.

"Do you dream of them?" he asked one day, his voice muffled as it travelled through sawed-off steel. It was sunny and warm, and birds trilled, tangled in sweet, wild music. Pasture-land surrounded us, but beyond the tall grass I saw a dark edge of a forest. I looked at it as I would a narrowed eye—with caution and an edge of fear.

We had travelled more than a hundred miles, which I knew because we followed old roads on my father's maps, and we calculated distances every evening around the fire. No destination, just far away, beyond where word could travel. I trusted my gut to tell me when to stop, and settle.

"I dream," I said. "Don't tell me you don't."

"I can't," he said quietly. "I still taste their blood, and it makes me afraid, because I feel nothing. No regret. No sorrow. I pray all the time to feel sorrow, but I don't. My heart is cold when I remember murdering them. And then I feel . . . hungry."

Sometimes, I felt hungry too, but in a different way. I hungered to be back inside the forest, bleeding for the trees, hoping that they would give me knowledge, again. More answers. Not just why we had been changed, but why we had been changed in so many different ways. I told myself that the virus that had caused the Big Death had affected more than humans. I told myself that maybe we had all been infected, but some had lived—lived, ripe for some new evolution. I told myself I was a fool, that it didn't matter, that I was alive, starting a new life. I told myself, too, that I was a killer.

I tugged on the ribbon and he tugged back. "Do you feel cold when you think of protecting Steven and your parents, or me?"

"No," he said. "Never."

"Then you're fine," I replied. "I love you."

Henry was silent for a long time. "Does that mean you forgive me?"

I closed my eyes and pulled the ribbon again.

From the second wagon behind us, I heard a shout. Steven. I pulled hard on the reins, untied the ribbon from my wrist, and jumped down. The cats sitting on the bench beside me followed. I took the shotgun.

Steven stood on the wagon bench, still holding the reins. Fading scars crisscrossed his face and throat, and his bared wrists were finally looking less savaged. Pale, gaunt, but alive. He still wore his plain clothes and straw hat. Unable to let go. If he was anything like his brother, it would be years, or maybe never. His gaze, as he stared over my head, was far-seeing.

"Someone will be coming soon," he said. "Someone important."

I stared down the road. All I saw was a black bird, winging overhead. A crow. I watched it, an odd, humming sound in my ears. Cats crowded the road, surrounding the bleating goats. I couldn't count their numbers—twenty or thirty, I thought. We seemed to pick up new ones every couple of days.

One of the windows in the wagon cracked open. Henry said, "Are we in trouble?"

"Not yet," I replied, but tightened my grip on the gun. "Steven?"

"We don't need to hide," Steven murmured, staring up at the crow: staring, though I wasn't entirely certain he saw the bird. "She's coming."

I didn't question him. Steven had become enigmatic since that night in the woods—that second, bloody night. Or maybe he had stopped fighting the change that had come over him all those years before.

It was a clear day, but after a while I heard thunder, a roar. Faint at first, and then stronger, ripping through the air. I couldn't place it at first, though finally I realized it reminded me of the military caravans. A gas engine.

A black object appeared at the end of the road, narrow and compact. Sunlight scattered on the chrome. It took me a moment to recognize the vehicle. I had seen only pictures. I couldn't remember its name, though I knew it had two wheels, like a bicycle. And that it was fast.

None of the cats scattered. I steadied myself as the machine slowed, stopped. Dug in my heels. It didn't matter that Steven seemed unafraid. I had no trust in the unknown.

A woman straddled the thing. Dark hair, wild eyes. Her jeans and shirt looked new, which was almost as odd as her gas-powered machine. I saw no weapons, though—and was comforted by the sharp look she gave me. As though she, too, had no trust.

"Your name is Amanda," she said.

I held steady. Made no reply. Watched, waited. The woman frowned, but only with her eyes; a faint smile quickened the corner of her mouth.

"I'm Maggie," she added, and tapped her forehead. "I saw you coming."

Steven jumped down from the wagon. I stepped in from of him, but he tried to push past me and choked out, "Are you like us?"

High in the sky, the crow cawed. Maggie glanced up at the bird, and her smile softened before she returned her gaze to me and the boy.

"No," she said. "You're new blood. I'm from something . . . older."

"I don't understand," I said.

She shook her head, rubbing her jaw. "It'll take time to explain, but there are others like you. Changed people. I've seen them in my dreams. I'm trying to find as many as I can, to bring them someplace safe."

"Safe," echoed Henry, from behind the wagon door. Maggie glanced sideways, but didn't seem surprised to hear someone speaking. The crow swooped close and landed on her shoulder. Cats made broken, chattering sounds. Golden eyes locked on the bird.

"Something is coming," Maggie said, reaching around to place a cautious hand on the crow's sleek back. "I don't know what. But we need to be together. As many of us as possible."

I stared, feeling the truth in her words. But I held my ground and said, "You're crazy."

"Amanda," Henry said, and I edged sideways to the back of the wagon. "Wife," he said again, more softly, for my ears only. "What did we run from before, and what are we running toward now?"

"Possibilities," I whispered, pressing my brow against the hammered fence rail, dotted with my blood. I touched the wooden heart hanging from a delicate chain around my neck. "All those frightening possibilities."

"I was never scared of loving you," he murmured. "But I was a coward with the rest. I don't want to be that man again."

And I didn't want to be that woman. I scratched my fingers against the wagon door and turned to look at Steven, who gave me a slow, solemn nod. I stared past him at the forest—silent and waiting, and full of power. Power it had given us—and maybe others. I leaned against the wagon, feeling Henry on the other side of the wall, strong in darkness.

My blood hummed.

It's fitting that "After the Blood" follows "Where the Heart Lives," as the latter is a prequel to my Dirk & Steele series, while the former exists as a possible future.

I wrote this as a sequel to another novella, "The Robber Bride," both set twenty years after a deadly pandemic sweeps through the world, taking out 80 percent of humanity. What's left is a fractured government, farming communities led by the Amish, abandoned cities overgrown by forests—and the rise of supernatural forces no longer contained by civilization. It's a somewhat peaceful future, actually—not entirely unpleasant, even if it's hard work. (And this is what happens when you live near Amish communities for an extended period of time—you write tales like this one.)

I felt somewhat queasy reading this story fresh, right now, in the middle of an actual pandemic. Amish vampires aside, the end of the world as we know it feels a little too close to home. And yet, and yet—life goes on, becomes something new—and we, for better or worse, become something new with it.

TANGLEROOT PALACE

CHAPTER ONE

WEEKS LATER, when she had a chance to put up her feet and savor a good, hot cup of tea, Sally remembered something the gardener said, right before the old king told her that she had been sold in marriage.

"Only the right kind of fool is ever going to want you."

Sally, who was elbow-deep in horse manure, blew a strand of red hair out of her eyes. "And?"

"Well," began the elderly woman, frowning—and then seemed to think better of what she was going to say, and crouched down beside her in the grass. "Here. Better let me."

They were both wearing leather gloves that were stiff as rawhide, sewn in tight patches to reach up past their elbows. Simple to clean if you let them sit in the sun until the manure turned to dry flakes, beat off with a stick. Sally, who did not particularly enjoy rooting through muck, was nonetheless pleased that the tannery had provided her with yet a new tool for her work in the garden.

"You know," Sally said, "when I told the stable boy to take care of my

182

new roses, burying them up to their blooms in excrement is not what I meant."

The gardener made a non-committal sound. "There were ravens in my dreams last night."

Sally finally felt hard stems and stubbly thorns beneath her fingers, and began clawing manure carefully away. "I thought we were talking about how only a fool would ever want me."

"All men are fools," replied the old woman absently, and then her frown deepened. "They were guarding a queen who wore a crown of horns."

It took Sally a moment to realize that she was speaking of the ravens in her dream again. "How odd."

"Not so odd if you know the right stories." The gardener shivered, and glanced over her shoulder—but not before her gaze lingered on Sally's hair. "Sabius is coming. Your father must want you."

Sally turned around, but the sun was in her eyes. All she could see was the blurry outline of a bow-legged man, stomping across the grass with his meaty fists swinging. She glanced down at herself, and then with a rueful little smile, continued clearing debris away from her roses.

"Princess," said Sabius, well before his shadow fell over her. "Your father requests your . . . Oh, dear God."

The gardener bit her bottom lip and kept her head down, long silver braids swinging from beneath her straw hat. Sally, gazing with regret at the one little leaf she'd managed to expose, leaned backward and tugged until her arms slid free of the rawhide gloves—left sticking from the manure like two hollow branches. Her skin was pink and sweaty, her work apron brown with stains.

"Oh, dear God," said her father's manservant, again, and turned his head, covering his mouth with a hairy, bare-knuckled hand better suited to brawling than to the delicately scripted letters he often sat composing for the king. He made a gagging sound, and squeezed shut his eyes.

"Er," said Sally, quite certain she didn't smell that bad. "What does my father want?"

Sabius, still indisposed, pointed toward the south tower. Sally considered arguing, but it was hardly worth the effort.

She shrugged off her apron and dropped it on the ground. Smoothing out her skirts—also rather stained, and patched with a quilt work of silk scrap from the seamstress' bin—she raised her brow at the gardener, who shook her head and returned to digging free the roses.

The king's study was on the southern side of the castle, directly below his bedchamber, accessible only through a hidden wall behind his desk that concealed a narrow stone staircase. Not that it was a secret. Everyone knew of its existence, what with the maids scurrying up and down in the mornings and evenings: cleaning, folding, dressing, doing all manner of maid-and-maidenly things, which Sally did not want to know about.

Her father was just coming down the stairs when she arrived at his study—even more slowly than she had intended, having been stopped outside the kitchen by two of the cook's young apprentices from the village, who, in different ways, could not help but try and clean her up. First, with scalding hot water and crushed lavender scrubbed into her face, loose hair tugged into a respectable braid, while the other girl fetched a fresh apron from the kitchen, which was not fine, and certainly not royal, but was clean and starched, and certainly in line with Sally's usual apparel. No use wasting fine gowns on long walks, or earth work, or even just reading in the library.

Her one concession to vanity was the amethyst pendant she wore against her skin, a teardrop long as her thumb, and held in a golden claw upon which half of a small wooden heart hung, broken jaggedly down the middle. Her mother's jewelry, and precious only for that reason.

"Salinda," said her father, and stopped, sniffing the air. "You smell as though you've been sleeping beneath a horse's ass."

"Do I?" she replied airily. "I hadn't noticed."

The old king frowned, looking over her clothing with a great deal more scrutiny than was usual. He was a barrel-chested man, tall and lean in most places, except for his gut and the wattle beneath his chin, which he tried vainly to hide with a coarse beard that was fading quickly from black to silver. He moved with a limp, due to an arrow shot recently into his hip.

Sally had been frightened for him—for as long as it had taken the old king to wake from the draught the doctor had poured down his throat in order to remove the bolt. His temper had been foul ever since. Everyone was avoiding him.

"Don't you have anything nicer to wear?" he asked, with a peculiar tenseness in the way he studied her that made Sally instantly uneasy. "I pay for seamstresses."

"And I have fine clothing," she replied cautiously, as her father had never commented on her appearance, not once in seventeen years. "These are for everyday."

The old king made a small, dissatisfied sound, and limped past her to his desk. "I suppose you heard about the skirmish at old Bog Hill? Men died. More good men every day. Little weasel bastard Bartin throwing gold at mercenaries to test our borders. But,"—and he smiled grimly—"I have a solution."

"Really," Sally said, suffering the most curious urge to run.

"Your darling mother, before we married, had a very dear friend who was given to one of those southern tribal types as part of a lucrative alliance. She bore a son. Who just so happens to be a very powerful man in need of a wife."

"Oh," Sally said.

Her father gave her a stern look. "And I suppose he's found one."

"Oh," Sally said again. "Oh, no."

"Fine man," replied the old king, but with a glittering unease in his eyes. "That Warlord fellow. You know. *Him.*"

Sally stared, quite certain that bumblebees had just committed suicide in her ears. "Him. The Warlord. Who commands all the land south of the mountains to the sea; who leads a barbarian horde of nomadic horsemen so fierce, so vicious, so perverse in their torments, that grown men piddle themselves at the thought of even breathing the same air? That Warlord?"

"He does sound rather intimidating," said her father.

"Indeed," Sally replied sharply. "Have you lost your mind?"

"Amazingly, no." The old king rubbed his hip, and winced. "I haven't felt this proud of myself in years."

Sally closed her eyes, grabbing fistfuls of her skirt and squeezing. "I think I'm losing *my* mind." She had heard about the man for as long as she could remember. Warlord of this-and-that: colorfully descriptive names that were usually associated with pain, death, and destruction. Sally had vague memories of her mother speaking of him, as well, but only in association with his mother. He would have been a small child at the time, she thought. Nice and innocent, probably skinning dogs and plucking the wings off butterflies while sucking suckling milk from his mother's teat.

"What in the world," she said slowly, fighting to control her temper and rising horror, "could a man like that possibly want from a woman like me? He could have anyone. He probably has had everyone, given his reputation." Sally leaned forward, poking her father in the chest. "I will not do it. Absolutely not. You are sending me to a short, hard, miserable life. I'm ashamed of you."

Her father folded his arms over his chest. "Your mother's best friend was sent to that short, hard, miserable life—and she thrived. Your dear, late, lovely mother would not have lied about that." He turned and fumbled through the papers on his desk. "Now, here. The Warlord sent a likeness of himself."

Sally frowned, but leaned in for a good long stare. "He looks like a dirty fingerprint."

"Of course he doesn't," replied her father, squinting at the portrait. "You can see his eyes, right there."

"I thought those were his nostrils."

"Well, you're not going to be picky, are you? At least he has a face."

"Yes," Sally replied dryly. "What a miracle."

The king scowled. "Spoiled. I let you run wild, allowed you teachers, books, a lifestyle unsuitable for any princess, and this is how you repay me. With sarcasm."

"You taught me how to think for myself. Which never seemed to bother you until now."

He slammed his fists onto the desk. "We are being overrun!"

His roar made her eardrums thrum. Sally shut her mouth, and fell backward into the soft cushions of a velvet armchair. Her knees were too weak to keep her upright. Terrible loneliness filled her heart, and sorrow—which she bottled up tight, refusing to let her father see.

The old king, as she stared at him, slumped with his arms braced against his desk, looking at maps, and embroidered family crests that had been torn off the clothing of the fallen soldiers, and that now were scattered before him, some crusty with dried blood.

"We are being overrun," he said again, more softly. "I know how it starts. First with border incursions, and petty theft of livestock. Then, villages ransacked, roads blocked. Blamed on vandals and simple thieves. Until one day you hear the thunder of footfall beyond the walls of your keep, and all that you were born to matters not at all."

He fixed her with a steely look. "I will not have that happen. Not for me, not for you. Not for any of the people who depend on us."

Sally swallowed hard. Perhaps she had been spoiled. Duty could not be denied. But when she looked at the small portrait of the man her father wanted her to marry, terrible, unbending disgust filled her—disgust and terror, and a gut-wrenching grief that made her want to howl with misery.

Married to that. Sent away from all she knew. Forced to give up her freedom. No matter how fondly her mother had spoken of her friend, that woman's son had a reputation that no sweet-talk could alter. He was a monster.

The old king saw her looking at the Warlord's likeness, and held it out to her with grim determination. She did not take it, but continued to stare, feeling as though she were going to jump out of her skin.

"I can't tell anything from that," she said faintly. "His artist did a terrible job."

"Probably because he never sits still," replied her father sarcastically.

"Or so I was told. I assume it's because he prefers to be out killing things."

Sally grimaced. "You're not seriously considering this?"

"Darling, sweet child, you golden lamb of my heart, my little chocolate knucklehead: I did consider, I have considered, and the deed is done. His envoy should be arriving within the week to inspect you for marriage, and sign the contracts."

"Oh, dear." Sally stared at her father, feeling as though she hardly knew him—quite certain that she did not.

And, since he was suddenly a stranger to her, she had no qualms in grabbing a nearby candle, and jamming it flame first into the tiny portrait he held in his hand. Hot wax sprayed. She nearly set his sleeve on fire. He howled in shock, dancing backward, and slammed his injured hip into the desk. He yelled even louder.

"And that," Sally said, shaken, "is how I feel about the matter."

She was sent to her room without supper, which was hardly a punishment, as the idea of food made her want to lean outside her window and add bile to the already bilious moat; which, briefly, she considered jumping into. Unfortunately, she had a healthy respect for her own life, and if the fall did not kill her, swallowing even a mouthful of that stinking cesspool probably would.

So she paced. Ran circles around her chamber, faster and faster, until she had to sit down in the middle of the floor and hold her head. No tears, though her eyes burned. Just a lump in her throat that grew larger and harder, and more sour—until she did bend over and gag, covering her mouth, trying to be quiet so that no one would hear her.

Her father, she thought, was not a bad man. But he was desperate, and had no son, and while that had not bothered him when she was young, now that he was getting on in years—hounded by insipid little squirts invading his borders—he had clearly lost his mind, and his heart, and if she did not control her temper, perhaps some other vital body parts.

Something had to be done.

Selfish, she thought. *You know he needs this alliance. He would not have gone to such extremes, otherwise.*

Of course not. But that did not mean that she had to put up with it. Being married to a warlord? And not just any warlord, but the Warlord of the South, with his endless army of barbarians, witches, and wolves? Even the horses were said to eat meat (an exaggeration, she knew that for a fact), and the Warlord himself lived in a tent so that he could up and move at the change of the wind, or if a good pillage was scented, or to evade all the assassins sent to take his head. That much was not an embellishment.

She wouldn't last a week. It was a death sentence.

So go, she thought. *Leave your father to his own devices.*

Leave the father whom she loved. Betray him to his enemies. Allow him to stand before an envoy of the most hated, villainous man to haunt the South, and say that his daughter had up and run—with apologies for having made the envoy make the trip for nothing. Yes, that would work perfectly.

Sally sighed, pounding her fists against her legs in frustration. She could not do that to her father. But she could not marry the Warlord, either. There had to be another way.

Except there was nothing.

Nothing, unless you turn to magic.

Simple, stupid, magic. Probably her imagination. Magic was something folks whispered about only when they were frightened, and then, if it was dark, only as ghouls and flesh-suckers, or men who transformed into wolves. Which wasn't even magic, in Sally's opinion. Just others kinds of people. Who probably didn't exist.

Magic was something else. Magic was power, and thought, and miracle. Magic could spin the threads of the world, and make something new. Magic could circumvent the future.

Sally's mother had dabbled in magic, or that was how Sally remembered it, anyway: small things that her father called eccentricities. Like singing prayers to roses, or speaking to the frogs in the pond as though they were human. Sketching signs over her chest when passing certain trees, or laying her hands upon others with a murmur and a smile. Cats had enjoyed her company, as did fawns from the wood (although, as the deer on her father's land were practically tame anyway, that was hardly evidence of the arcane), and sometimes, in a storm, with the lightning flickering around her, she would stand on the balcony in the rain and wind, staring into the darkness as though searching, waiting for something she thought would come.

Which was why she had died, some said. Being in the wind, chilled until a cough—and then a fever—had found her.

Many little things. Many memories. Her mother had been a witch, according to a very few, born in the heart of the Tangleroot Forest. But Sally knew that was a lie. Her mother had merely lived and died with far-seeing eyes, able to perceive what others could not. Sally wished she had those eyes. Her mother had said that she did, but that was cold comfort now.

If there was such a thing as magic, it was not going to save her. She'd have better luck asking blue birds or goldfish for salvation.

So Sally went for a walk.

Night had spun around, with stars glittering and the moon tipping over the edge of the horizon, glimpsed behind the trees. Sally strode down to the garden, led by habit and soothing scents: lavender and jasmine, roses full in bloom. She passed the kitchen plot, and plucked basil to rub against her fingers and nose, and a carrot to chew on, and listened to pots banging, cooks arguing, and to the wind that hissed, caressing her hair, while frogs sang from the lilies in the pond. Sally followed their croaks, lonely for them, and envious. She felt very small in the world—but not small enough.

Several ancient oaks grew near the water. Some said they had been transplanted as seedlings from what was now the Tangleroot Forest, though after three hundred years, Sally could hardly imagine how anyone could be so certain that was the truth. She had a favorite, though, a sleeping giant with fat, coiled roots that were too large for the earth to contain. She imagined, one day, that her gentleman tree would wake, believing he was an old man, and try hobbling away.

Her mother had often laid her hands upon this tree. Sally perched on the thick tangle of his once-and-future legs, bark worn smooth from years of her keeping company with his shadow, and leaned back against the trunk with a sigh.

"Well," she said. "This is a mess."

The oak's leaves hissed in the wind, and then, quite surprisingly, she heard a soft, female voice say, "Poor lass."

Sally flinched, turning—but it was only the gardener who peered around the other side of the massive oak. The old woman held a tankard in her wrinkled hands, her silver eyes glittering in the faint firelight cast by the sconces that had been pounded into the earth around the castle, lit each night and burning on pitch.

"I heard," said the gardener. "Thought you would come here."

Sally remembered the first time she had seen the old woman, who looked the same now as she had fifteen years before when Sally had first tottered into her domain, sticky with pear juice and holding the tail of a spotted hunting dog, her mother's finest companion besides her daughter and husband. The garden had been a place of wonderment, and the gardener had become one of Sally's most trusted confidants.

"You've always been a friend to me," she said. "What do you think I should do?"

The old woman pushed back her braids, and took a brief sip from the tankard before passing it on to Sally, who drank deeply and found cider, spicy and sweet on her tongue. "I think you should be useful to yourself."

"Useful to my father, you mean?"

"Don't be dense," she replied. "You know what you want."

Sally did. What she wanted was simple, and yet very complicated: freedom, simply to be herself. Not a princess. Just Sally.

Except that there was a cost to being free, and in the world beyond this castle and its land, she was useful for very little. She could garden, yes, and cook, or ride a bucking horse as well as a man could. But that was hardly enough to survive on. She was Sally, but also a princess—and that had never been clearer to her than now, when she thought of what she might be good for, out in the world.

"Useful," Sally said, after a moment's thought. "Useful to myself and others. That's a powerful thing."

"More than people realize," said the gardener. "Everyone has got something different to offer. Just a matter of finding out what that is."

She sipped her drink. "I was the youngest of seven children. A good, hardy farming family, but there wasn't enough for all of us to eat. So I left. Took to the road one day and had my adventures. Until I came to this place. They needed a person with a talent for growing things, and that I had aplenty. I was useful. So I stayed."

"I'm a princess. I have duties."

"That you do," said the old woman. "But following the duty to yourself, and the duty to others, doesn't have to be separate."

Sally narrowed her eyes. "You know something."

The gardener smiled to herself, but it was sad, and vaguely uneasy. "I dreamed of the queen and her crown of horns, sleeping in the forest by the silver lake. Guarded by ravens, who keep her dreams at bay."

She spoke the words almost as though she was singing them, and Sally found herself light-headed, leaning hard against the oak, which seemed to vibrate beneath her back. "But that's just a dream."

"No," whispered the gardener, fixing her with a look. "Those of us who ever lived in the shadow of the Tangleroot know of odd truths, and odder dreams that are truth, echoes of a past that slumbers, and of things that walk amongst us, fully awake. Stories that others have forgotten, because they are too strange."

Sally rubbed her arms, chilled. "The Tangleroot is only a forest."

"Is that why no one enters it?" The old woman's smile deepened, giving a particular glint to her eyes. "Or why no one cuts its trees, or stands long in its shadow? You know that much is true."

Sally did know. The Tangleroot was an ancient forest, rumored once to have been the site of a powerful kingdom. But a curse had fallen, and great battles had raged, and what was mighty had decayed, until the forest took root, with trees rising from the bodies of the dead. To cut a tree from the Tangleroot, some said, was to cut a soul—and bring down a curse upon your head.

Whether mere fancy or not, Sally had never met a man or woman who did not take heed of the old warnings. And it was true, too, that strange things seemed to happen around that forest. Lights, dancing in the shadows, and unearthly voices singing. Wolves who were said to walk as men, and men small as thimbles. Those who entered did not often come out, and the lucky few who walked free were always changed: insane or wild, or aged in unnatural ways.

Suddenly, Sally began to suffer the same uneasiness that had filled her just before the old king had announced his plan to marry her off. "Why are you telling me this?"

"Because there are answers in the Tangleroot, for those who have the courage to find them. Answers and questions, and possibilities."

"And dreams?" Sally asked.

"Dreams that walk," whispered the old woman, staring down into her tankard. "Your mother would have understood. She had been inside the forest. I could see it in her eyes."

Sally went still at the mention of her mother, and then placed her hand over her chest, feeling through her dress the pendant, warm against her skin, the wooden heart, especially. "If I go there, will I find something that can help me? And my father?"

"You'll find something," she replied ominously, and pointed at Sally. "The Tangleroot calls to some, and to others it merely answers the desire that it senses. You want that forest, and it'll bring you in, one way or another. It is a dangerous place, created by a dangerous woman who lived long ago. But there's danger in staying here, too. You can't stop a plant that wants to grow. You'll only crush it if you try."

Sally had felt crushed from the moment her father had mentioned marriage, but now a terrible restlessness rose within her, crazy anticipation feeding a burst of wildness. Her entire body twitched, as though it wanted to start walking, and for a moment she felt a strange energy between herself and the oak. Like something was waking.

Fool's errand, she told herself. *Magic, if it exists, won't save you.*

But she found herself saying, "And all I would do is enter the Tangleroot? There must be more than that. I wouldn't know what to look for, or how to start."

"Start by not making excuses. Go or stay." The gardener stood on unsteady legs, and handed Sally her tankard. "Princess or not, duty or no, you were born with a heart and head. Which, in my experience, is enough to make your own choices about how to live your life."

The old woman touched Sally's brow, and her fingertips were light and cool. "You have a week before the envoy arrives."

"That's not much," Sally said.

"It's a lifetime," the gardener replied. "Depending on how you use it."

CHAPTER TWO

Sally used it that night, when she slipped out of the castle and ran away.

She did not take much with her. Bread, cheese, dried salted beef; a sharp knife, and warm clothing that consisted of a down vest, a woolen cloak, and cashmere knitted leggings worn beneath her work dress, which still smelled faintly of manure. She took gold coins, and left behind her horse. If she was going to venture inside the Tangleroot—and that remained to be seen—she did not want to worry about leaving the animal behind. That, and it was harder to hide with a horse when one traveled the road.

The borders of the Tangleroot were everywhere, scattered and connected, twisting through the countryside across numerous kingdoms. The closest edge of the ancient forest was more than a day's walk to the south, a little farther if Sally stayed off the main road and traveled one of the lesser-used trails. Which she did, guided by the light of the moon, and the stars glimpsed through the leaves of the trees.

She moved quickly, almost running at times, afraid that she would hear the silver bells attached to her father's saddle, or the familiar call of his deep voice. Part of her wished that she *would* hear those things, not entirely certain she would keep on running.

She was terrified. This was a fool's journey. No direction, save faith in the unknowable, and the possibility of something miraculous.

But she did not stop. Not once. Afraid that if she did, even for a moment, she would turn around and return home. Like a coward, without even trying to fight for her freedom. The gardener was right: Sally had a week. One week to find an alternative, be it magic or simply inspiration—neither of which she was going to discover back home.

Near dawn, she found a small clearing behind a thicket of blackberry bushes that had lost their flowers. It was a cool night, and she curled deep inside her cloak to eat bread and cheese. Forest sounds filled the air: the hiss of the wind, and the crunch of a hoof in the leaves. Owls hooted. Sally was not frightened of the night, but sitting still made her think again of what she was doing, and that was far more terrifying. She shut her eyes and tried to sleep.

And dreamed of a queen.

Dawn, and though it is spring, there is ice on the lake, a sheen of frozen pearls smashed to dust, compacted into a shield against the undercurrent, dark water. A sleeping time: the fog has not yet burned away, and everywhere a glow, an otherworldly gleam.

It is not safe to walk on the ice. Ice belongs to the sleeping queen, the horned woman of the southern shore, who wears a crown to keep her dreams inside her head. Such dangerous things, her dreams. Like her voice, which makes thunder, raining words that drown.

She is silent now. Shackled, sleeping. Wearing the crown that binds her. A crown that has a lock. A lock that has a key.

A key that can be found.

Sally was still trying to find that key when something tugged her from the dream. She opened her eyes, and found herself staring into the face of a little girl.

It was an unexpected sight, and it took Sally several long moments to pull away from the dream, and convince herself that she was not yet still asleep. It should have been dawn, sun high, but the sky was dark with night. And yet the air was cool on her face, and there was a rock digging into her hip, and when she dug her own nails into her arm, she felt the pinch.

The little girl was naked, her dark hair long and matted with leaves, brambles, and feathers. Hard to see much of her, as the shadows loved her face, but she was a healthy, round little thing, not much older than five or seven, with sylph-like features and eyes that were huge and gray.

When Sally began to sit up, the little girl scuttled backward, half-crouching, each movement graceful and wild, but fraught with a startled energy that reminded her of a deer. She did not walk, but jolted; she did not crawl, but leapt; and the moon that dappled her skin with light seemed instead like the spots on a fawn, drifting sweetly across her smooth, soft flesh.

"Hello," Sally whispered.

The little girl flinched at the sound of her voice, swaying backward as though she wanted to run. Sally held her breath, afraid of moving, but, after a moment, let her hand creep slowly toward the satchel lying on the ground at her elbow.

"Are you hungry?" she asked the child. "Food?"

The little girl did not react, not even a blink. Sally fumbled inside the bag, and removed the half-eaten loaf of bread. The child showed no interest. Instead, she reached deep inside her matted hair, and pulled out a small, speckled egg. Sally stared, astonished, as the little girl placed it on her palm, and held it up at eye level, peering at Sally over the round, pale surface, like a small spirit, gazing over the curve of the moon.

And then, with hardly a wasted motion, the little girl popped the egg inside her mouth, crunched down hard—and ran.

Sally sat, stunned, watching as that fleet-footed little girl slipped into the night shadows like a ghost, so quick, so graceful, that for one brief second Sally wondered if she was not hallucinating, and that she had instead seen a deer, a wolf, some creature beyond human, beyond even life.

She struggled to her feet, sluggish, as though her limbs had been dipped in cobwebs and molasses, and when she finally stood, the world spun around her in waves of moonlight. She gathered up her belongings, and stumbled down the path that the little girl had taken.

It was down the same trail she had been traveling, but the moonlight made it feel as though she walked upon silver, and the shadows glistened as though edged in pearl dust, or stars. Ahead, a glimmer of movement, a flash like the tail of a rabbit, and then a breathless stillness. The little girl stood in the path, staring at her, tiny hands clutched into fists.

"Wait," Sally croaked, holding out her hand, but the child danced away. This time, though, she stopped after several long, leaping steps, and glanced back over her shoulder. Poised, lost in shadow, so that all Sally could see was the high bone of her cheek and the glint of a single eye.

I am sorry, whispered a low, sweet voice. *But she wants you.*

Sally tried to speak, but her throat closed and the only sound she could make was a low, strained croak. She managed to take a step, and then another, and it suddenly seemed like the most important thing in the world that Sally reach that little girl, as if night would crush them both if she did not.

But just before she could touch the child's shoulder, she sensed movement on her right, deep within the moonlit shadows of the forest. Sally froze, terrified to look, heart pounding. Finally, unable to help herself, she turned her head.

She saw children in the forest, boys and girls who wavered in her vision, wild and tangled as the roots they stood upon. Small hands faded and then reappeared, clutching at the trunks of trees, while mice poked their heads from nests of hair, and small birds fluttered free.

The little girl leapt out of reach, and stared at Sally with eyes so ancient, so haunted, her human body seemed little more than a fine shell, or a glove to slip on. Her small fingers traced patterns through the air, above her chest—as Sally remembered her mother doing.

Hurry and wake, whispered the little girl, just as Sally heard a thumping roar behind her, like the beating of a thousand wings. She could not turn—her feet were frozen in place—but the sound filled her with a cold, hard terror that wrapped around her throat in a choking, brutal grip.

The children covered their faces and vanished into the trees. The moon disappeared, and then the stars, and the trail she stood upon transformed into a ribbon of dark water. A raven cawed.

Sally found her voice, and screamed.

Later, far away, she heard men speaking. There was nothing she could do about it. Her arms were too heavy to move, and she could hardly feel her legs. Swallowing was difficult because her throat was sore, mouth dry, lips cracked and bleeding. Thirst burned through her, and she made a small sound: a croak, or whimper.

A strong, warm hand slid under her neck, and the cool rim of a tin cup touched her lips. Water flooded her mouth, and she choked on it, but she tried again, greedily, and managed to swallow every last drop. The effort exhausted her, though. Sally fell back against the rocky ground, eyes closed, too weak to care where she was, or who whom she was with. All she could see inside her mind were the children, and one in particular: the little girl, wild-eyed and inhuman, whispering, *Hurry*.

"Hurry," Sally heard a man say.

Strong arms slid beneath her body, lifting her off the ground. Her head lolled, and another set of hands, smelling of horse and ash, pushed under her neck, supporting her. She was carried a short distance, and her eyelids cracked open just enough to see sunlight filtering through the leaves, green and lush, whispering in the wind.

Sally was placed on another flat surface that was considerably softer than the ground, and felt as though it had been padded with blankets, bags of meal, hay, and several sharp objects that jutted uncomfortably into her side.

A man's face suddenly blocked the sun. Sally could see nothing of his features, but he held up her head again to drink from the same tin cup, and then wiped her mouth with the edge of his sleeve.

"Damn," said a gruff voice. "This is a strange place."

"Just drive," replied the man beside her, with a distinct weariness in his voice. Reins cracked, and the surface upon which Sally rested lurched with a groan. The leaves began moving overhead.

The man who had helped her drink water lay down beside her with a tired sigh. He did not touch her. Sally tried to look at him, but her eyes drifted shut, and her head felt too heavy to move. She heard the man humming softly to himself. His voice carried her into sleep, though she dreaded the darkness. She was afraid of her dreams.

But when she opened her eyes again, she remembered nothing of her sleep. The sun was still up. She stared at the branches of trees, and the wind was blowing. The wagon had stopped, and the man who had lain beside her was gone.

Sally smelled wood smoke. She rolled over on her side, and found that she still had her belongings, even the gold coins in her pouch. She checked her throat for her necklace, and pulled it out from beneath her neckline. Amethyst glittered, though her eyes were drawn to the tiny remains of the wooden heart, the grains of which suddenly seemed threaded with gold.

Sally tucked the necklace back inside her dress, and peered over the wagon wall. She saw a clearing surrounded by oaks and dotted with clumps of bluebells, and a man who was juggling stones.

Quite a lot of stones, all of them irregularly shaped as if he had just gathered them up from the ground and started juggling on the spot. His hands were a blur, and he was sitting in front of a small, crackling fire. Except for the juggling, he was utterly unassuming in appearance, neither tall nor short, big nor small, but of a medium build that was nonetheless lean, and healthy. His hair was brown, cut unfashionably short, and he wore simple clothing of a similar color, though edged in a remarkable shade of crimson. A silver chain disappeared beneath his collar.

Several horses grazed nearby. Sally saw no one else.

The man suddenly seemed to notice that she was watching him, and with extraordinary ease and grace, allowed each of the rocks flying through the air to fall into his hands. He hardly seemed to notice. His gaze never left hers, and Sally found herself thinking that his face was rather striking, after all—or maybe that was his eyes, which looked as though they had never stared at anything dull in his entire life.

His mouth quirked. "I wondered whether you would ever wake."

Sally was not entirely convinced that she had stopped dreaming. "How long was I asleep?"

He hesitated, still watching her as though she were a puzzle. "Since we found you yesterday. Just on the border of the Tangleroot. Another few steps and you would have been inside the forest."

Sally stared. "Impossible."

He tossed a rock in the air, and in an amazing show of agility, caught it on the bridge of his nose—swaying to hold it steady. "Which one?"

"Both," she said sharply, and tried to sit up. Dizziness made her waver, and she clung to the wagon wall, gritting her teeth. "When I stopped . . . when I stopped yesterday to rest, I was nowhere near that place."

"Well," said the man, letting the rock slide off his face as he stared at her again, thoughtfully. "Things happen."

And then he looked past her, beyond the wagon, and smiled. "What a surprise."

Sally frowned, and struggled to look over her shoulder. What she saw was indeed a surprise—but not, she thought, any cause for smiles.

Men stood on the edge of the clearing, which she realized now was beside a narrow track, hardly used, by the length of the grass growing between the shallow wagon tracks. The men were dressed in rags and leather, with swords belted at their waists and battered packs slung over lean shoulders. Some wore bent metal helms on their heads, and their boots seemed ill-fitting, several with the toes cut out.

Mercenaries, thought Sally, reaching for the knife belted at her hip. A small scouting party, from the looks of them. Only four in total, no horses, little to carry except for what they could scavenge. Sally had no idea how far she had come from home, but she knew without a doubt that she was still well within the borders of the kingdom. Her father had been right: one day soon there would be the sound of hard footfall outside the castle, and then it would be over.

The mercenaries walked closer, touching weapons as their hard, suspicious eyes surveyed the clearing. The man by the fire started juggling again, but with only two rocks, a slow, easy motion that was utterly relaxed, even cheerful. But something about his smile, no matter how genuine, felt too much like the grin of a wolf.

And wolves, Sally thought, usually traveled in packs.

"You've come for entertainment," he said to the mercenaries, and suddenly there was a red ball in the air, among the rocks. Sally could not guess how it had gotten there. The mercenaries paused, staring, and then began smiling. Not pleasantly.

"You could say that," said one of them, a straw-haired, sinewy man who stood slightly bent, as though his stomach hurt. He gave Sally an appraising look. She refused to look away, and he laughed, taking a step toward her.

By the fire, the juggler stood and kicked at the burning wood, scattering sparks and ashes at the mercenaries. They shouted, jumping back, but the juggler kept his rocks and red ball in the air, and added something small and glittering that moved too quickly to be seen clearly. He began to sing and stood on one leg, and then the other, hopping in one place, and finally, just as the mercenaries were beginning to chuckle coarsely and stare at him as if he was insane, the juggler threw everything high into the air, twirled, and flicked his wrist.

Sally almost didn't see him do it. She was crawling from the wagon, taking advantage of the obvious distraction—but she happened to look at the juggler just at that moment as the rocks and red ball went up—taking with them the mercenaries' attention—and caught the glint of silver that remained in his hand.

The straw-haired man staggered backward into his companions and fell down, twitching, eyes open and staring. A disk smaller than the mouth of a teacup jutted from his forehead, deeply embedded with edges that were jagged and sharp, as irregularly shaped as the points on a snowflake. His companions stared at him for one stunned moment, and then turned to face the juggler. He was tossing rocks in the air again, but was no longer smiling.

"Accidents," he said. "Such a pity."

The mercenaries pulled their swords free. Sally scrambled from the wagon, but did not run. Her dagger was in her hand, and there was a man in front of her with his back exposed. She could do this. She had to do this. It was she or they, them or the juggler—even though everything inside her felt small and ugly, and terrified of taking a life.

But just before she forced her leaden feet into a wild, headlong lunge, a strong hand grabbed her shoulder. She yelped, turning, and found herself staring into hooded brown eyes, almost entirely obscured by coarse, bushy hair and a long-braided beard shot through with silver.

A human bear, she thought, with a grip like one. He held a crossbow. Beside him stood another man, the tallest Sally had ever seen, whose long blond hair and strong, chiseled features belonged more to the ice lands than the green spring hills of the mid-South. His hands also held a bow, one that was almost as tall as him.

Startled, sickening fear hammered Sally's heart, but the bearded man gave her a brief, beaming smile, and fixed his gaze on the mercenaries—who had stopped advancing on the juggler, and were staring back with sudden uncertainty.

"Eh," said the bearded man. "Only three little ones."

"I'm going back for the deer," replied the giant, sounding bored. He glanced down at Sally. "Congratulations on not being dead. We took bets."

He turned and walked away toward the woods. Sally stared after him, and then turned back in time to see a rock slam into a mercenary's brow with bone-crushing force. She flinched, covering her mouth as the man reeled to the ground with a bloodless dent in his head that was the size of her fist.

Pure silence filled the air. Sally was afraid to breathe. The juggler was now tossing the red ball into the air with his left hand, holding his last rock in the other. He stood very still, staring with cold, hard eyes at the two remaining mercenaries—both men obviously rattled, trying to split their attention between him and the bearded man, who patted Sally's shoulder and pointed his crossbow at their chests.

"I think," said the juggler, "that you should consider your options very carefully. My hands are prone to wild fits, as you've seen—which I have most humbly come to suspect are possessed occasionally by various deities in lieu of hurling thunderbolts."

"In other words," said the bearded man, "you should drop your weapons and strip. Before he kills you."

"But not in front of the lady," added the juggler.

"Don't mind me," replied Sally weakly.

The mercenaries looked at each other, and then at their dead companions on the ground, both of whom had finally stopped twitching.

Slowly, carefully, they put down their swords, unbuckled their knives, dropped their helmets and then their trousers (at which point Sally had to look away, because a nude man was not nearly as startling as one that appeared to have never washed), and pulled off the rest of their raggedy clothing, which gave off a remarkable odor that would have been funny if Sally had not still been so shaken by everything she had just witnessed.

"Run along," said the juggler, when they were finally disarmed and disrobed. "I hope you meet some lovesick bears. 'Tis the season, and you would make excellent fathers."

The mercenaries ran. Sally watched them go, but only until she was convinced they would not be returning. Humans, she thought, were far more attractive with clothes than without.

She sagged against the wagon's edge, unpeeling her fingers from the knife hilt. Her knees felt shaky, and she was breathless. She glanced at the dead, who were being searched by the bearded man, and had to look away.

A water skin was shoved in front of her face. It was the juggler, peering down at her with a peculiar compassion that was utterly at odds with the coldness she had seen in his face, or the wolf's smile, or the cheerful, even madcap glint that had filled his eyes while distracting those mercenaries with his tricks.

"You've been ill," he said. "I'm sorry you had to see that."

"I would be sorrier if I hadn't," she replied. "Who are you?"

"Oh," he said, with a grin. "We're just actors."

CHAPTER THREE

They were the Traveling Troupe of Twister Riddle, which was a name that Sally told them made no sense, but that (when they prodded her for additional commentary) was rather catchy, in a crazed sort of way. The juggler was supposed to be Lord Twister Riddle himself, though his real name (or as real as Sally could only assume it to be) was Mickel Thorn.

The small bear of a bearded man was called Rumble, and the giant— when he returned from the forest with a deer slung over his shoulders— introduced himself as Patric. Neither seemed capable of performing anything more complicated than a good beating, but Sally knew better than to judge.

"There used to be more of us—" began Mickel.

"But there's no such thing as loyalty anymore," interrupted Rumble. "One little whiff of gold—"

"And the years mean nothing," said Patric, who folded himself down upon on a fallen tree to begin skinning the dead animal. "They left us for another troupe. Without a word, in the night. I nearly drowned in tears."

He said it with a straight face. Sally frowned, unsure what to make of them. They were most certainly dangerous, but not rough or coarse, which was a contradiction—and created an odd atmosphere among them all. She had always considered herself to be a good judge of character, but that had been at home—and she had never, not once in seventeen years, been on her own beyond the protection of her father's lands. Sally was not entirely certain she could trust her judgment. And yet she thought— she was quite sure—that she was safe with these men.

For now. She thought of her dream, her dream that had felt so real: that little girl with her ancient eyes, and the children in the trees. A shiver ripped through her, and she gritted her teeth as she glanced behind at the woods—feeling as though someone was watching her. The hairs on her neck prickled. It was not quite the afternoon, and the weather was chilly, though clear. If she could backtrack to the Tangleroot . . .

"I should go," Sally said reluctantly. "But thank you for your help."

Patric's hands paused. Rumble gave her a quick look of surprise. Mickel, however, reached inside his coat for a small metal spoon, which he waved his hand over. It appeared to bend. "Are you running from something?"

"Of course not." Sally peered at the spoon, trying to get a closer look. Mickel hid it in his fist, and when he opened his hand, it had vanished.

"You're a trickster," she said. "Sleight of hand, games of illusion."

"Not magic?" Mickel placed a hand over his heart. "I'm shocked. Most people think I have unnatural powers."

Sally tried not to smile. "You have an unnatural gift for words. Anything else is suspect."

Rumble grunted, picking at his teeth. "Won't be safe with mercenaries still out there. Not for you, lass."

"Too many of them," Patric said absently. "More than I imagined."

Chilly words. Her father was losing control over his land. For a moment Sally considered returning home, but stopped that thought. She would have to make a choice soon—but not yet. Not until she stepped into the Tangleroot and discovered whether a power was there that could make a difference.

Sally forced herself to stand. Her legs were still unsteady. Mickel stood as well, and kicked dirt over the fire. "We were also leaving." Rumble and Patric stared, and he gave them a hard look. "What direction are you headed?"

Sally folded her arms over her chest. "South."

"Remarkable. Fate has conspired. We're also headed that way."

Rumble coughed, shaking his head. Patric sawed at the deer a bit harder. Glancing at them, Sally said, "Really."

"And tomorrow we'll begin ambling north." Mickel tilted his head, his gaze turning thoughtful. "Where are you from?"

"I don't think it matters," she replied curtly. "If I asked you the same question, I suspect you would feel the same."

"Home is just a place?" he replied, smiling. "You're jaded."

"And you smell," Rumble said, peering up at her.

"Like manure," Patric added. "Very alluring."

Sally frowned. "You three . . . saved my life. I think. And I appreciate that. But—"

"But nothing. No harm will come to you. If you travel with us, you are one of us." Mickel held her gaze, as if he wanted her to understand. When she finally nodded, he turned away to nudge Rumble with his boot. "Come on, then. We'll go to Gatis. It's not far."

No, not far at all. Only two days' ride from home. She could be recognized, or her father might find her there—assuming he had begun looking.

But it was also close to the Tangleroot.

Sally held out her hand to Mickel, who stared for one long moment before taking it with solemn dignity. His grip was warm and strong, and a tingle rode up her arm. From the way he flinched, she thought he felt it, too.

"My name is Sally," she told him.

"Sally," he said quietly. "Welcome to the family."

She began seeing ravens in the trees as they drew close to Gatis. Hardly noticeable at first, until one of them launched off a branch in a burst of black feathers, cawing in a voice so piercing the sound seemed to run straight down into her heart. Images flashed through her mind—ravens and horns, and silver, frozen water—making Sally sway with dizziness. She leaned hard against the edge of the rickety wagon, holding her head.

Mickel rode close on a swift black mare that was surprisingly fine-boned and sleek: a lovely creature, and a surprise. She had seen such horses only once before, those from a trader who had come from south of the mountains. The Warlord's territory.

She would not have guessed a mere performer would have such a horse, nor Patric nor Rumble. Rumble's mount was tied to the back of the wagon. He sat up front, holding the reins of the mules.

Sally caught Mickel's eye. "You said you found me near the Tangleroot."

"Yes," he said, drawing out the word as though it made him uncomfortable. "You were unwell."

"Unconscious, you mean."

Mickel rubbed the back of his neck. "Not quite."

"You were screaming," Rumble said, turning to look at her. "It's how we found you. Just standing as you please in front of the border of that cursed forest, making the most bloodcurdling sound I've ever heard. And I've heard plenty," he added, a moment later.

Sally stared at him. "I was . . . screaming."

"Quite a fighter, too," Patric said, guiding his horse past the wagon.

She blinked, startled. "And I fought?"

"You were delirious," Mickel told her. "Simple as that."

"You were trying to enter the Tangleroot," Rumble said. "Almost did. Took all three of us to hold you down."

"Stop," Patric called back, over his shoulder. "You'll scare her."

"No," Mickel said slowly, watching her carefully. "No, I don't think you will."

Sally, who had no idea what her expression looked like, had nonetheless been thinking that it would have been a great deal easier if they had just let her go. Perhaps more terrifying, too, given what she remembered of her dream. If it had been a dream.

But she did not like having her thoughts written so clearly upon her face. She studied her hands, noting the dirt under her nails, and then looked back up at Mickel. He was still watching her. She studied him in turn, and suffered a slow rush of heat from the boldness of his gaze— and her own.

Gatis was a rambling village built into the high hills of a river valley, a place that had belonged to shepherds for hundreds of years, and still belonged to them; only now they lived in comfortable cottages with fine large gardens bordered by stone, and fruit orchards growing on the terraced hills that dipped down to the Ris, its winding waters blue and sparkling in the late-afternoon sun.

Sally had been to Gatis years before with her family—while her mother was still alive. The villagers were known for the quality of their yarn and dyes, and the fine craftsmanship of their weaving. Her cloak and vest were Gatis-made, and likely the cloth of her dress, as well. She pulled up her hood as they neared the village, hoping that none would remember her face. She had only been only ten at the time. Surely she looked different.

The road sloped upward around a grassy hill covered in boulders, and at the crest of it, Sally saw the border of the Tangleroot. It was far away, but there was no mistaking those woods, however distant. The border was black as pitch, a curving wall of trees that looked so thick and impenetrable, Sally wondered how it would even be possible to squeeze one arm through, let alone travel through it.

Seeing the forest was like a slap in the face. She had known that one of the borders to the Tangleroot was near this village, but looking at it in broad daylight twisted in her gut like a knife. Sally felt afraid when she saw the far-away trees; she felt fear and hunger. She closed her eyes, hoping the sensation would fade, but all she saw was the little girl, running fleet-footed down the moonlit path.

It made Sally wonder, briefly, about her mother—if it was true that she had been inside those ancient woods, and if so, what she had seen. The young woman wondered, too, if coming to Gatis had bothered her mother, what with the Tangleroot so close. She had died soon after that trip, though until now, Sally had never thought to associate the two. Perhaps there was still no reason to.

A hand touched her shoulder, and she flinched. It was Mickel, riding close beside the wagon. He looked away from her at the distant forest, sunlight glinting along the sharp angles of his face, and highlighting his brown hair with dark auburn strands.

"Not all trees are the same," he murmured. "Something I heard, growing up. Some trees are bark and root, and some trees have soul and teeth. If you are ever foolish enough to encounter the latter, then you'll know you've gone too far. And you'll be gone for good."

Sally had heard similar words, growing up. "It seems silly to give a forest so much power."

He shook his head. "No, it seems just right. We are infants in the shadows of trees. And those trees . . . are something else."

"Some say they used to be human."

"Souls stolen by the forest of a powerful queen. Roots that grew from bones and blood, and imprisoned the spirits of an entire people." Mickel smiled. "I've heard it said that red hair was a common trait among them, and that descendants of those few who escaped the curse, who battled the queen herself, still bear that mark."

Sally brushed a strand of red hair self-consciously from her eyes. "You and your stories. How could something like that be true?"

"Maybe it's not. But either way, something about you is affected by that place, even by looking at it."

She began to deny it. He touched a finger to her lips. The contact startled her, and perhaps him. His hand flew away as though burned, and something unsettled, even pained, passed through his gaze. Sally suddenly found it hard to breathe.

"You think too much in your eyes," he said quietly. "I can practically read your thoughts."

"How terrifying," she replied, trying to be flippant, though hearing herself was quite different: she sounded serious as the grave.

A rueful smile touched his mouth, and he stroked the neck of his horse. He hardly used a saddle, just a soft pad and a molded piece of pebbled leather. He held the reins so lightly that Sally thought he must be guiding the horse with his legs. "Yes, it is frightening."

Sally fought the urge to touch her warm cheeks. "Why do you do this?"

"Perform? Create masks for a living? Haven't you ever wanted to be someone else?" Mickel's smile deepened. "No, don't answer that. I can see it in your eyes."

Sally thought she should start wearing a blindfold. But before she could ask him more, he said, "So what are you useful for? Are you good for anything?"

"I can read," she said, stung. "Garden, cook, ride a horse—"

"All of which are admirable," he replied, far more gently. "But I was referring to skills that would be useful in a . . . performance setting."

"Performance," she echoed, eyes narrowing; she recalled overheard discussions between her father's men about "performances" involving women. "What kinds of skills do you think I might have?"

Rumble, who had been silent, began to laugh. Mickel shook his head. "Reading, I suppose, would be enough. Precious few can do that. If you know your letters, you might earn your keep writing messages that we can carry along the way."

"Earn my keep? You expect that I'll be traveling with you for much longer?"

Rumble glanced over his shoulder and gave the man a long, steady look. As did Patric, who was suddenly much closer to the wagon than Sally had realized. Both men had messages in their eyes, but Sally was no good at reading them. Mickel, however, looked uncomfortable. And, for a brief moment, defiant.

It's all right, she wanted to say. *I'll be gone by tonight.*

Ahead, a small boy stood in the road with several sheep and a dog. He stared at them as they passed, and Mickel's hands were suddenly full of small, colorful balls that flew through the air with dazzling speed. He did not juggle long, though, before catching the balls in one large hand—and with the other, tossing the boy something that glittered in the sun. A silver mark, though the cut of it was unfamiliar. The child stared at it with huge eyes. Sally was also impressed, and puzzled. The coin, though foreign, would buy the boy's family at least a dozen fine sheep, or whatever else they needed.

"You run ahead," Mickel said, in a voice far deeper, and more arrogant, than the one he had just been speaking with. "Let your village know that the Traveling Troupe of Twister Riddle has arrived for their pleasure, and that tonight they will be dazzled, astonished, and mystified."

The boy gulped. "Magic?"

"Loads of it," Mickel replied. "Cats chasing kittens will be coming out of your ears by the end of the night."

"Or more silver!" he called, when the boy began running down the road, halting only long enough to come back for his sheep, which had scattered up the hill behind him, herded by the much more diligent dog.

Patric chuckled quietly to himself, while Mickel gave Sally an arch look. "Warming up the crowd is never a bad thing."

"That was an expensive message you just purchased."

"Ah," he said, rubbing the back of his neck. "We've performed for many important people."

"I'm surprised, then, that the rest of your troupe left you behind, even for the promise of yet more riches." Sally frowned. "I also thought actors were supposed to be poor."

"We're immensely talented."

"Is that how you afford such lovely horses?"

Rumble coughed. "These were a gift."

"A gift," she echoed. "You've been south of the mountains, then."

Mickel gave her a sidelong look, followed by a grim smile. "You have a keen eye, lady."

"I have a good memory," she corrected him. "And I've seen the breed."

"Have you?" he replied, with a sudden sharpness in his gaze that made her uncomfortable. "So go ahead. Ask what's really on your mind."

She frowned at him. "The Warlord. Did you see him?"

Rumble started to chuckle. Mickel gave him a hard look. "We performed for him."

Heat filled her, fear and anger and curiosity. Sally leaned forward. "I hear he sleeps with wolves in his bed and eats his meals off the stomachs of virgins."

Patric laughed out loud. Rumble choked. Even Mickel chuckled, though he sounded incredulous, and his nose wrinkled. "Where did you hear such nonsense?"

"I made it up," she said tartly. "But given how other men speak of him, he might as well do all those things. Such colorful descriptions I've heard. 'Master of Murder.' 'Fiend of Fire'—"

"Sex addict?" Rumble said, his eyes twinkling. "Ravisher of women? Entire villages of them, lined up for his . . . whatever?"

Mickel shot him a venomous look. Patric could hardly speak, he was laughing so hard. Her face warm, Sally asked, "You disagree?"

"Not at all," he said, glancing at Mickel with amusement.

Sally drummed her fingers along her thigh. "So? Was he truly as awful as they say?"

"He was ordinary," Mickel said, with a great deal less humor than his companions seemed to be displaying. "Terribly, disgustingly, ordinary."

"Or as ordinary as one can be while eating off the stomachs of virgins," Rumble added.

"This is true," Mickel replied, his eyes finally glinting with mischief. "I can't imagine where he gets all of them. He must have them grown from special virgin soil, and watered with virgin rain, and fed only with lovely virgin berries."

"Now you're making fun of me," Sally said, but she was laughing.

Mickel grinned. Ahead, there was a shout. Children appeared from around a bend in the road and raced toward them. The boy who had been given the silver mark was in the lead. Sally thought they resembled little sheep, stampeding.

"Damn," Rumble said, slowing the mules as Patric whirled his horse around, and galloped back to the wagon. "You and your bright ideas."

"Brace yourself," Mickel said.

But Sally hardly heard him. She had looked up into the sky, and found ravens flying overhead: a handful, soaring close. She swayed, overcome with unease, and touched her throat and the golden chain that disappeared beneath the neck of her dress.

Two of the birds dove, but Sally only saw where one of them went— which was straight toward her head. She raised her hands to protect herself, but it was too little, too late. Sharp claws knocked aside her hood and pierced her scalp, ripping away a tiny chunk of hair. Sally cried out in pain and fear.

Her vision flickered. Inside her head, she glimpsed images from her dream, which swallowed the wagon, and Mickel, and the sun with all the steadiness of something real: a silver, frozen lake, and a woman sleeping within a cocoon of stone, her head dressed in a crown of horns. An unearthly beauty, pale as snow.

But the woman did not stay asleep. Sally saw her again, standing awake within a dark, tangled, heaving wood, gazing from between the writhing trees to a castle shining in the sun, an impossibly delicate structure that seemed made of spires and shell, built upon the lush, green ground. But in the grass, warm and still, were the fresh bodies of fallen soldiers, so recently dead that not even the flies had begun buzzing. Among them stood women, strong and red-haired and bloody, staring back with defiance and fury at the pale queen of the wood.

Sally felt a pain in her arm, a sharp tug, and the vision dissolved. She fell back into herself with a stomach-wrenching lurch, though she could not at first say where she was. The sun seemed too bright, the sky too blue. Her heart was pounding too fast.

Mickel's fingers were wrapped around her arm. She peered at him, rubbing her watery eyes, and was dimly aware of the other men watching her, very still and stunned, and the children below, also staring.

"I wasn't screaming, was I?" Her voice sounded thick and clumsy, and it was hard to pronounce the words.

Mickel shook his head, but he was looking at her as no one ever had, with surprise and compassion, and an odd wonder that was faintly baffled. Blood trickled down the side of his face. He looked as though he had been pecked above the eye.

"You're hurt," she said.

"I got in the way," he replied, and reached out to graze her brow with his fingers—which came away bloody. Sally touched the spot on her head and felt warm liquid heat where part of her scalp had been torn off. Pain throbbed, and she swallowed hard, nauseous.

"You are a curious woman," Mickel said quietly. "Such a story in your eyes."

"Magic," Rumble muttered. "When a raven sets its sights . . ."

But Patric shook his head, and the older man did not finish was what he was going to say. Mickel murmured, "The raven who attacked you spit out your hair. I could almost swear he simply wanted to taste it . . . or your blood."

The children scattered, melting away from the wagon. Perhaps afraid. Sally did not want to look too closely to know for certain. She shut her eyes, feeling by touch for the hem of her skirt. She tore off a strip of cloth, and bundled it against the wound in her head.

"I should go," she mumbled.

"Rest," Mickel replied. "Dream."

No, she thought. *You don't understand my dreams.*

But she lay down in the wagon bed, thinking of ravens and her father, and her mother, and little girls with wild hair and wilder eyes, and slept.

CHAPTER FOUR

Sally danced that night. It was not the first time she had ever danced, but it was the first beyond the watchful eye of home, in a place where she was not known as the eccentric tatterdemalion princess—but as Sally, who was still a mystery, and unknown, without the aura of expectation and distance that so many placed on her. If anyone recognized her face—and there were several older women who gave her and her clothing sharp looks—no one said a word.

And no one seemed to be aware of the encounter with the ravens, nor commented on the wound in her head. She thought the children must have talked, but the people of Gatis were either too polite—or too used to strange occurrences—to make much of it.

Instead, she was treated as another Twisting Riddle, a woman of letters, who held children in her lap while she transcribed messages on the backs of flat rocks, smooth bark, and pale, tanned hide, listening with solemn patience to heartbreak, tearful confessions, stories that would be amusing only to family and friends; news about births, livestock, weather; and the growing mercenary presence with pleas attached to be safe, be at ease, stay out of the hills.

I love you, people said. *Write that down*, they would tell her. *I love you.*

And all the while, Mickel juggled and sang, and juggled and danced, and juggled some more: no object was too large or small, not even fire.

The other two men were also gifted, in surprising ways. Rumble dragged a stool into the heart of the gathered crowd, where he slouched with his elbows on his knees and began reciting, half-heartedly, a well-known fable that also happened to be utterly boring. But at the end of the first verse, his hand suddenly twitched, and the ground before him exploded with sparks and fire and smoke.

215

The crowd gasped, jumping back, but Rumble never faltered in his story, his voice only growing stronger, richer, more vibrant. More explosions, and he began striding forcefully across the ground, punctuating words and moments with clever sleights of hand: cloth roses pulled from thin air, along with scarves, and coins, small hard candies, and once a rabbit that looked wild and startled, as though it couldn't quite believe how it had gotten there.

Patric was a marksman: daggers, arrows, any kind of target. Sally was convinced to stand very still against a tree with a small, soft ball on her head—holding her breath as the blond giant took one look at her, and threw his blade. She felt the thunk, listened to the gasps and cheers, but it was only when she walked away that she was finally convinced she'd survived.

The men had other acts that impressed—shows of horsemanship, riddles, recitations of famous ballads (during which Sally beat a drum)—indeed, several hours of solid entertainment that no one in Gatis would likely forget for a long time to come. Nor would Sally. And, when the show was over, it only seemed natural that the village treat the little troupe to dinner (at which Patric's catch of venison was sold), and to a performance of their own—as all the local musicians took up a corner of the square, and began playing to their heart's content.

It was night, and the air was lit with fire. Sally danced with strange, smiling men, and then Rumble and Patric, but she danced with Mickel the longest, and he was light on his feet, his hands large and warm on her arms and waist. She felt an odd weight in her heart when she was close to him, a growing obsession with his thoughts and the shape of his face, and it frightened her, even though she could not stop what she felt. She thought he might feel the same, which was an even graver complication. His eyes were too warm when he looked at her—cut with moments of flickering hesitation.

But neither of them stopped, and when the music slowed, Mickel twirled her gently to a halt, as Sally spun with all the careful grace she possessed and had been taught.

"Well," he said hoarsely, standing close.

"Yes," Sally agreed, hardly able to speak past the lump in her throat.

The people of Gatis offered them beds in their homes that night. The men politely refused. Sally helped them pack the wagon, including fine gifts of cloth and wine, and then the troupe followed the night road out of the village, toward the north. Sally kept meaning to jump out and head in the opposite direction, but her heart seemed to be heavier than her body, and refused to move from the wagon bed.

"Why did you leave?" she asked Mickel.

"It's never good to overstay," he replied, sounding quiet and tired. "What feels like magic one night becomes something cheap the next, if you don't take care to preserve the memory. Familiarity always steals the mystery."

"Always?"

"Well," he said, smiling. "I believe you could be the exception."

Sally smiled, too, glad the night hid her warm face. "Who taught you all these things?"

"We learned on our own, in different places," Rumble said, the bench creaking under him as he turned to look at her. "All of us a little strange, filled with a little too much wild in our blood. Got the wanderlust? Nothing to do but wander. Now, Mickel there, he comes from a long line of those types. Knows how to recognize them. He put us all together."

"And how long have you been at this?"

Patric flashed white teeth in the dark. "How long have you? You were quite good tonight."

"I read. I held children and beat a drum, and stood while you threw a knife at my face."

"But you did it easily," Mickel said. "You made people feel at ease. Which is not as simple as it sounds. I know what Patric means. You have it in you."

"No," she replied. "I was just being . . . me."

"As were we."

"Mostly," Rumble added. "I don't usually keep chickadees in my pants, I'll have you know."

"That," Sally said, "was a remarkably disgusting trick."

"It only gets better," Patric replied dryly.

They set up camp near the road, beside a thick grove of trees that was not the Tangleroot, but nonetheless made her think of the ancient forest. It was somewhere close, but if she kept going north with these men, she would lose her chance, lose what precious time she had left.

Perhaps it was for nothing, anyway. Despite her strange dreams and the behavior of the raven (her head still ached, and she could not imagine her appearance), the longer she was away from the gardener and her words, the less faith she had in her chance of finding something, anything, that could help her in the Tangleroot. It might be a magical forest, filled with strange and uncanny things, but none of that was an answer. Perhaps just another death sentence.

You think too much, she told herself. *Sometimes you just have to feel.*

But her feelings were not making anything easier, either.

Rumble and Patric rolled themselves into their blankets as soon as the troupe stopped, and were snoring within minutes. Mickel stayed up to keep watch, and Sally sat beside him. No fire, just moonlight. He wrapped himself in one of the new cloaks the villagers had given them, and fingered the fine, heavy cloth with a great deal of thoughtfulness.

"This is a good land," he said. "Despite the mercenaries."

Sally raised her brow. "You say that as though you've never been here."

He shrugged. "It's been a long time. I hardly remember."

"So why did you come back?"

"Unfinished business." He met her gaze. "Why are you running? More specifically, why are you running to the Tangleroot?"

"My own unfinished business," she replied. "I have questions."

"Most people, when they have questions, ask other people. They do not go running headfirst into a place of night terrors and magic."

Sally closed her fists around her skirts. "I suppose you're lucky enough to have people who can help you when you're in trouble. I'm not. Not this time."

"Apparently." Mickel did not sound happy about that. "Perhaps I could help?"

I wish, she thought. "I doubt that."

"I have two ears, two hands, and I have seen enough for two lifetimes. Maybe three, but I was very drunk at the time. Certainly, I could at least lend some advice."

Sally hesitated, studying him and finding a great deal of sincerity in his eyes. It almost broke her heart.

"You don't understand," she began to say, and then stopped as he held up his hand, looking sharply away, toward the road. Sally held her breath, listening hard. At first she heard only the quiet hiss of the wind—and then, a moment later, the faint ringing of bells.

Sally knew those bells.

She stood quickly, weighing her options—but there were none. She turned and began running toward the woods. Mickel leapt to his feet, and chased her. "Where are you going?"

"Horses," she muttered. "Deaf man, there are horses coming."

"And?"

She could hardly look at him. "My father. My father is coming to find me, and when he does, he will drag me home, stuff me in a white dress like a sack of potatoes, and thrust me into the arms of the barbarian warlord he has arranged to marry me."

Mickel, who had been reaching for her, stopped. "Barbarian warlord?"

"Oh!" Sally stood on her toes, and kissed him hard on the mouth. Or tried to. It was the first time she had ever done such a thing, and she was rushed. Her lips ended up somewhere around his cheek, left of his nose. Mickel made an odd choking sound.

"I do like you," she said breathlessly. "But I have to go now. If my father finds me with you and your men, he'll assume you all have dispossessed me of my virtue, in various unseemly ways. And then he'll kill you."

Mickel still stared at her as though he had been hit over the head with one of the rocks he was so fond of juggling. "I have a strange question."

"I probably have a strange answer," she replied. "But unless you want to see your man parts dangling around your neck while my father saws off your legs to feed his pet wolves, I best be going. Now."

He followed her, running his fingers through his hair and pulling so hard she thought his scalp would peel away. "Why would your father need to make an alliance with a warlord? He sounds perfectly ghastly enough to handle his enemies on his own."

"Oh, no," she assured him, walking backward toward the woods. "That's me. I have a much better imagination than he does."

A pebble was thrown at them, and hit Mickel in the thigh. Rumble poked his head out from beneath the covers. "Eh! Shut up, shut up! I'm trying to sleep! Can't a man have a decent night's—"

Mickel found something considerably larger than a pebble, and threw it back at him. Sally heard a thump, and Rumble shut his mouth, grumbling.

"You can't go," Mickel said.

"Oh, really." Sally marched backward, pointing toward the forest. "Well, here I am, going. And you should be thanking me."

Mickel stalked after her. "You are the craziest woman I have ever met. You make *me* crazy. Now come back here. Before I . . ."

"Do something crazy," Rumble supplied helpfully.

"Dear man," she said quickly, "I don't think that would be prudent."

And she turned and ran.

Mickel shouted, but Sally did not look back. She wanted to, quite badly, with all the broken pieces of her grieving heart.

But her father would find her if she stayed with him, and she liked Mickel too much to subject him to the harm that the old king most certainly would inflict. He might not be an imaginative man, but he was thorough. And a princess did not travel with common performers, not unless she wanted to become a . . . tawdry woman.

Which, she thought, sounded rather charming.

The forest was very dark, and swallowed her up the moment she stepped past its rambling boundary, suffocating her in a darkness so complete that all she could do was throw up her hands, and take small, careful steps that did not keep her safe from thorns, or the sharp branches that seemed intent on plucking out her eyes. She had to stop, frequently—not for weariness, but because she was afraid, and each step forward was a struggle not to take another step back.

Or to simply hide, and wait for dawn, until her father passed by.

But that would not do, either. Returning to Mickel and his men would endanger them, and she could not tell them who she was. No man—no common, good, men—would want to deal with a princess on the run. All kinds of trouble in that, especially for one who was betrothed to the Warlord of the Southern Blood Wastes, Keeper of the Armored Hellhounds, Black Knight of the Poisoned Cookies—or whatever other nefarious title was attached to his name.

Sally could depend only on herself. She had been foolish to imagine otherwise, even for a short time.

And, like the gardener enjoyed saying, life never fell backward, just forward—growing, turning, spinning, burning through the world day after day, like the sun. One step. One step forward.

Until, quite unexpectedly, the forest became something different. And Sally found herself in the Tangleroot.

She did not realize at first. The change was subtle. But as she walked, she found herself remembering, *Some trees are bark and root, and some trees have soul and teeth*, and she suddenly felt the difference as though it was she herself who was changing, transforming from a human woman into something that floated on rivers of shadows. It became easier to move, as though vines were silk against her skin, and she listened as words riddled through the twisting hisses of the leaves, a sibilant music that slid into her bones and up her throat: in every breath a song. Sweet starlight from the night sky disappeared. The world outside might as well have been gone.

Sally had journeyed too far. The Tangleroot, she had thought, lay farther away—but the ancient had reached into the new, becoming one.

She was here. She had been drawn inside. Nor could she stop walking, not to rest, not even to simply prove to herself that she could, that her body still listened to her. Because it did not. Her limbs seemed bound by strings as ephemeral as cobwebs, tugging her forward, and though she glimpsed odd trickling lights flickering at the corners of her eyes, and felt the tease of tiny, invisible fingers stroking her cheeks and ankles, she could not turn her head to look. All she could see was the darkness in front of her.

And finally, the children. Tumbling from the trunks of trees like ghosts, staring at her with sad eyes. Tiny birds fluttered around their shoulders, while lizards and mice raced down their limbs, and though there was no moon or stars to be seen through the canopy, their bodies nonetheless seemed slippery with light: glimpses and shadows of silver were etched upon their skin.

The little girl from her dream appeared, dropping from the branches above to land softly in front of Sally. She was different from the others, less a spirit, fuller in the flesh. More present in her actions. Her matted hair nearly obscured the silver of her eyes. She crouched very still, staring. Sally could not breathe in her presence, as if it was too dangerous to take in the same air as this child.

The girl held out her hand to Sally. Behind her, deep in the woods, branches snapped, leaves crunching as though something large and heavy was sloughing its way toward her. She did not look, but the children did, silently, their eyes moving in eerie unison to stare at something behind her shoulder.

The girl closed her hand into a fist, and then opened it urgently. Swallowing hard, Sally grabbed her tiny wrist—suffering a rapid pulse of heat between their skin—and allowed herself to be drawn close, down on her knees.

The girl reached out with her other hand, and hovered her palm over Sally's chest. Warmth seeped against her skin, into her bones and lungs. She became aware of the necklace she wore, and began to pull it out. The girl shook her head.

Better if you never had the desire to find this place, came the soft voice, drifting on the wind. *She would not have heard your heart.*

"Who are you?" Sally whispered. "What are you?"

The child glanced to the left and right, at the watching, waiting children. *I am something different from them. I was born as I am, but they were made. Forced into the forms you see. They were human and dead, but the trees rose through them, around them, and trapped their souls in this tangled palace, from which they can never leave.*

"The queen," Sally said.

She sleeps, and yet she dreams, and though the crown that shackles her mind weakens her dreams, her power is still great through the green vein of the Tangleroot. You have entered her palace, you red-headed daughter, and you will escape only through her will.

Sally leaned back on her heels, feeling very small and afraid. "Why are you telling me this?"

The child made an odd motion over her chest, as though sketching a sign. *Because you have lain in my roots from babe to woman, and it is my fault the queen heard your desire. I could not hide your heart from her mind, though I tried. As I try even now, though I cannot disobey her for long.*

Sally's breath caught. "You are no tree."

But I am the soul of one, replied the little girl, and tugged Sally to her feet. *Beware. She will try to take you, and what you love. And we will have no choice but to aid her.*

"No," Sally said, stricken. "How can this be? I came here for help."

There is no help in the Tangleroot. Do not trust her bargains. All she wants is to be free.

And the child forced Sally to run.

She lost track of how long they traveled, but it was swift as a bird's flight, and silent as death. The girl led her down narrow corridors where the walls were trees and vines, and the air was so dark, so cold, she felt as though she was running on air, that beneath her was the mouth of a void from this world to another, and that if she fell, if the child let go, she might fall forever.

Beyond them, in the tangle of the forest, she glimpsed clearings shaped like rooms, replete with mushrooms large as chairs, and steaming pools of water within which immense, scaled bodies swam. She glimpsed other runners, down other corridors, ghosting silver and slender, limbs bent at impossible angles that startled her with fear. Voices would cry out, some in pain or pleasure, and then fade to an owl's hoot. And once, when a wolf howled, its voice transformed into slow, sly laughter, accompanied by the whine of a violin: clever music that women danced to, glimpsed beyond a wall of vines, their breasts bare, with nipples red as berries, their faces sharp and furred like foxes, and eyes golden as a hawk's.

Sally saw all these things, and more, but none seemed to see her. It was as though all the strange creatures within the Tangleroot abided in separate worlds, lost in the maze that was the queen's dreaming palace. It was haunting, and terrifying. Sally was afraid of becoming one of those lost, living dreams, sequestered and imprisoned in a room made of vines and roots, and ancient trees.

But the little girl never faltered, though she looked back once at Sally with sadness.

Finally, they slowed. Ever so delicately, Sally was pulled through a wall of trees so twisted they seemed to writhe in pain. Even touching them made her skin crawl, and she imagined their leaves weeping with soft, delicate sobs. And then Sally and the girl broke free, and stood upon the edge of a lake.

It felt like dawn. A dim silver light filled the air, though none had trickled into the forest. She had thought it was night until now—and perhaps it was still, on the other side of the Tangleroot.

No birds sang, no sounds of life. The water was frozen, and the air was so cold that Sally could see each breath, and her face turned numb. When she looked up, examining the rocky shore, she thought that the trees still carried leaves, black and glossy, but then those leaves moved—watching her with glittering eyes—and she realized that the branches were full of ravens. Hundreds of them, perhaps thousands, sitting still.

It made her feel small and naked. Fear had been her constant companion for the last several days—but now a deeper, colder terror settled in her stomach. Not of death or pain, but something worse that she could not name, worse even than those rooms in the forest filled with strange beings. It had not seemed such a bad thing before, to enter a place and come back changed—but she had been a fool. Sally felt as though she sat on the edge of a blade, teetering toward sanity or madness. One wrong slip inside her heart would be the end of her.

The little girl pointed at the ice. Sally looked into her silver eyes, uncertain.

Only through her, whispered words on the wind, though the child's mouth did not move. *She has you now.*

Sally gazed out at the frozen lake, which shone with a spectral glow. Far away, though, the mists parted—and Sally glimpsed a long, dark shape on the ice.

She found herself stepping onto the ice. The little girl did not follow, nor did the ravens move. She walked, sliding and awkward, terror fluttering in her throat until her heart pounded so hard she thought it might burst. And yet she could not stop. Not until she reached the coffin. Which, when she arrived, was not a coffin at all, but a cusp of stone jutting from the water, dark with age and carved to resemble the bud of a frozen flower. It seemed to Sally that the stone might have been part of a tower—the last part—reaching through the ice like a broken gasp.

Sally peered inside. Found a woman nestled within. She knew her face from dreams: pale, glowing, with a beauty so unearthly it was both breathtaking and terrifying. There was nothing soft about that face, not even in sleep, as though time had refined it to express nothing but truth: inhumanly cruel, arrogant, and cold.

She wore a crown of horns upon her head, though they seemed closer to branches than antlers, thick with lush moss covered in a frost that enveloped much of her body, painting her dark brow and hair silver, and her red dress white, except for glimpses of crimson. The crown seemed very tight upon her head, and there was a small, heart-shaped groove at the front of it, set in wood.

The lock for a key.

Sally could hardly breathe. She started to look behind at the shore to see if the little girl was still there, but a whispering hiss drew her attention back to the sleeping queen. Her eyes were closed, her mouth shut, but Sally heard another hiss, and realized it was inside her head.

I know your face, whispered the sleeping queen. *I know your eyes.*

Sally stared at that still, pale face, startled and terrified. "No. I have never been here."

I know your blood. I know your scent. You bear the red hair of the witches who imprisoned me. So, we are very close, you and I. I know what you are.

A chill beyond ice swept over Sally. "Is that why you brought me here?"

You wanted to come, murmured the queen. *So you have. And now you stand upon the drowned ruins of the old kingdom, among the souls of the long dead. You, who share the blood of the dead. You, whose ancestors escaped the dead. And left me, cursed me, bound me.*

Sally trembled. "I know nothing of that. I came for answers."

Release me, and I will give you answers.

Her hand tightened, and she realized that she was holding her mother's necklace, squeezing it so forcefully the chain was digging into her hand. She was almost too afraid to move, and glanced back at the shore—glimpsing movement among the trees. Children. The little girl. Ravens fluttering their wings. She did not know how it all pieced together. It was too strange, like a dream.

Someone else stumbled from the woods, down to the edge of the lake.

Mickel. He had followed her into the wood.

CHAPTER FIVE

Mickel saw her, and tensed. He did not appear hurt, but even from a distance she could see the wildness of his eyes, and the determined slant of his mouth.

I am the Tangleroot, whispered the queen, frozen as the ice within her tomb. *This forest is my dream. All who touch it belong to me. My trees who were human, who became my children. My trees, whose roots reach for me, though ice confines them.*

Release me, she breathed. *Or I will make him mine.*

"Why do you think I can release you?" Sally forced herself to look at the queen, feeling as though her feet were growing roots in the ice—afraid to see if that was her imagination, or truth. "I am no one."

My ravens tasted your blood. You are born of a witch, and I feel the key. Sweet little girl. Release me.

Mickel stepped on the ice and fell to his knees, sliding with a quiet grunt. Sally tried to move toward him, but her feet refused to budge.

He, too, whispered the queen. *His blood is also sweet.*

"And if you were free?" Sally asked hollowly, still staring at Mickel.

A great hiss rose from the ice, a terrible, vicious sound that might have belonged to a snake or the last breath of the dead. On shore, children swayed within the shadow of the wood, covering their hearts.

Little hearts. Sally looked down at her necklace, and the broken remnants of the wooden heart dangling from the precious amethyst. A heart the size of the indent in the queen's crown.

Mickel rose to his feet, half-crouched. His eyes were dark and hard, cold as the ice. Silver glimmered in his hands.

"Sally," he said.

"Stay there," she said hoarsely. "Run, if you can."

But he did not. Simply walked toward her, his unsteadiness disappearing until it seemed that he glided upon the ice, graceful as a dancer. He never took his gaze from her, not once, until he was close to the tomb. And then he looked down at the queen, and flinched.

"Whatever she wants," Mickel said, gazing down at the sleeping woman with both horror and resolve, "don't give it to her."

"She wants her freedom," Sally whispered, almost too frightened to speak. "She thinks I can give it to her."

I came searching for freedom, she thought, and realized with grim, bitter irony that whatever happened here would be a far worse, and more irreversible, loss than any she might have faced outside the wood.

The ice rumbled beneath their feet. Sally fell forward against the stone tomb. She gripped its dark, cold edge with both hands, and the necklace swung free. Mickel made a small sound, but she could not look at him. The queen commanded every ounce of her attention, as though the roots she had felt in her feet were growing through her neck, up into her eyes—forcing her to stare, unblinking, at that frozen, chiseled face.

The key, whispered the queen. *It has been broken.*

Sally gritted her teeth, sensing on the periphery of her vision the split, jagged remains of the heart swinging from the chain. "Then it is no use to you. Let us go. Let him go and keep me, if you must. But stop this."

"Sally," Mickel said brokenly, but he, too, seemed frozen to his spot.

Another terrible hiss rose from the ice, vibrating beneath her feet. *Half is better than none at all. Perhaps I will find enough power to break free. Place it in my crown, witch. Do this, and I will let him go free.*

Sally hesitated. Mickel whispered, "No."

A terrible cracking sound filled the air, as though the world was breaking all around them. But it was not the world. Mickel cried out, and Sally watched from the corner of her eye—suffocating with horror—as the ice broke beneath his feet, and he plunged into the dark water.

Swallowed. His head did not reappear.

A scream clawed up Sally's throat, and she gripped the edge of the stone tomb so tightly her nails broke.

Give me the key and I will save him, whispered the queen in a deadly voice. *I will save him.*

"No," Sally snapped, anger burning through her blood with such purity and heat that she felt blinded with it. Her hands released the stone. Her feet moved. Her head turned, and then her body. She could move again.

Sally jumped into the icy water.

It was dark beneath the ice. Pressure gathered instantly against her lungs, immense and terrible, but she did not swim back to the hole of light above her head. She kicked her legs, fighting the painful cold, and searched the drowning void for Mickel. Desperation filled her, and despair; there was nothing of him. He was gone.

Until, quite suddenly, a ghost of light glimmered beneath her. Just a gasp, perhaps a trick. But Sally dove, feet kicking off the ice above her, and swam with all her strength toward that spot where she had seen the light. Her lungs burned. Her eyes felt as though they were popping from her skull. She was going to do this and die, but that would be another kind of freedom, and no doubt better than what the queen had in store for her.

She saw the light again, just in front of her, and then her hands closed around cloth, and she pulled Mickel tight against her body. He moved against her, his hands weakly gripping her waist—which surprised her— though not nearly as much as the light that glowed from a pendant that floated free from a chain around his neck.

A tear drop jewel, like her own—which she realized was also glowing. She stared, stunned, discovering the jagged half of a heart that was linked to his pendant.

She tore her gaze away to stare at Mickel's face, and found him ghastly. Alive, though, barely. More lights danced in her vision, but that was death, suffocation. Sally kicked upward, and after a moment, Mickel joined her. His movements were awkward, almost as if his strength and grace had been sapped away even before he'd plunged into the water and lost air.

The queen had her hold on him.

The light in the ice was very far away, but the light around their necks, much closer. Sally heard voices whispering deep in the darkness, almost as if the water was speaking, or the palace that had drowned and whose last spire entombed the queen. Visions flickered, and Sally saw her mother's face, soft with youth, and another at her side—two girls, little enough for dolls, holding hands and standing on the ice. Red hair blazing. Jaws set with stubbornness, though their eyes were frightened.

She is strong in her tangled palace, even in dreams, murmured a soft voice, *but this is also where she fell, and where her greatest weakness lies. She was bound by a crown made from her own flesh, bound in the blood of those who captured her.*

She cannot touch you, said another voice, sweeter than the other. *She cannot touch either of you, if you do not bend. Your blood makes you safe to all but the fear and lies that she puts into your heart. What flows through your blood made her crown.*

Choose, whispered yet another. *Choose what you want, and not even she can deny you.*

I want to live, Sally thought with all her strength, as darkness fluttered through her mind, and her body burned for lack of air. *I want him to live.*

Light surrounded her, then. Cold air, which felt so foreign that Sally almost forgot to breathe. But her jaw unlocked, and she gasped with a burning need that filled her lungs with fire. She dragged Mickel up through the hole in the ice, and he sucked down a deep breath, coughing so violently she thought he might die just from choking on air, rather than water. His skin was blue. So was hers.

Somehow, though, they dragged themselves from the water onto the ice, and when they were free, collapsed against one another, chests heaving, limp with exhaustion. Cold seeped into her bones, so profound and deadly she was almost beyond shivering.

"Sally," Mickel breathed.

"Come on," she whispered. "We have to move."

But neither did, and all around them the ice shook, vibrating as though a giant hand was pounding the surface in rage.

Free me, snapped the queen, *and I will give you anything. Deny me and I will kill you.*

"No," Sally murmured, her eyes fluttering shut. "We'll be going now."

A howl split the air, a heartrending cry jagged as a broken razor. Sally closed her eyes, pouring all of her remaining strength into holding Mickel's hand. His fingers closed around her wrist as well, tight and close as her own skin. A rumble filled the air.

And suddenly they were moving. Rolled and rippled, and shrugged along the ice, until rocks bit through their clothing, and their bodies were lifted into the air. Sally tried to hold fast to Mickel's hand as they were carried through the wood, flung hard and thrown to sharp hands that pinched her body and dragged claws against her skin. She heard voices in her head, screams, and then something quieter, softer, feminine: her mother, or a voice close enough to be the same, whispering.

Her bonds are renewed as though she is winter lost to spring. You have bound her again. You have raised the borders that had begun to fall.

She was already bound, Sally told that voice. *Nothing had fallen.*

Nothing yet, came the ominous reply. *Her strength is limited only by belief.*

But Sally had no chance to question those strange words. She heard nothing more after that. Nor could she see Mickel, though she caught glimpses of those who touched her—golden, raging eyes and silver faces—and felt the heat and deep hiss of many mouths breathing. Mickel's hand was hard and hot around her own, but Sally was dying—she thought she must be dying—and her strength bled away like the air had in her lungs, beneath the crushing weight of water. Her heart beat more slowly, as though her blood was heavy as honey, and warm inside her veins, full of distant fading light.

Mickel's hand slipped away. She lost him. Imagined his broken gasp and shout, felt her own rise up her throat, but it was too late. He disappeared from her into the heaving shadows, and no matter how hard she tried, she could not see him.

And then, nothing. Sally landed hard on her back within tall grass, and remained in that spot. Small voices wept nearby, and another said: *You found your answer, I think.*

But the souls, the children, thought Sally. *Mickel.*

Rest, whispered the little girl. *Someone is coming for you.*

"Mickel," breathed Sally, needing to hear his name.

But she heard bells in the night, and hooves thundering, and she could not move or raise her voice to call out. Nothing in her worked. Her heart hurt worse than her body, and made everything dull.

Sally tried to open her eyes and glimpsed stars. A shout filled the air. Warmth touched her skin. Strong hands.

"Salinda," whispered a familiar voice, broken and hushed. "My dear girl."

Her father gathered her up. Sally, unable to protest, fell into darkness.

She came back to life in fits and gasps, but when her eyes were closed, she did not dream of tangled forests and queens, but of men with dark eyes and fierce grins, who juggled fire and stone, and riddles. She grieved when she dreamed, and her eyes burned when she awakened, briefly, but there was nothing to do but rest under heavy covers, and recover. She was suffering from cold poisoning, said her father's physician—something the old man could not reconcile, as it was spring, and the waters had melted months before.

But it was cold that had damaged her, and the prescription was heat. Hot water, hot bricks, hot soup poured down her throat, along with hot spirits. Sally grew so hot she broke into a sweat, but that did not stop the shivers that wracked her, or the ache in her chest when she breathed.

A cough took her, which made the old king flinch every time he heard it, and would cause him to roar for the physician and the maids, and anyone else who cared to listen, including the birds and stars, and the moon. He did not leave her side, not much, but once after a brief absence, she heard him whisper to Sabius, "Not one person can explain it. Mercenaries were crawling past the border only days ago, but now not a sign of them. Some of the locals say they found swords and horses near the Tangleroot."

"Pardon me saying so, sire, but it used to be that way when your queen still lived. It seemed that nothing wicked could touch this kingdom."

But her father only grunted, and Sally glimpsed from beneath her lashes his thoughtful glance in her direction.

She received preoccupied looks from the gardener, as well, who would slip into the king's chair while he was away, and hold Sally's hand in her dry, leathery grip.

"You knew," Sally whispered, days later when she could finally speak without coughing. "You knew what would happen."

"I knew a little," confessed the old woman. "Your mother told me some. She said . . . she said if anything ever happened to her, that I was to point you in the right direction, when it was time. That I would know it. That it would be necessary for you; necessary for the kingdom."

She leaned close, silver braids brushing against the bedcovers. "I had red hair once, too, you know. Many who live along the Tangleroot do. It is our legacy. And for some, there is more."

More. Warmth crept into Sally's heart, a different heat than soup or hot bricks, or the fire burning near her bed. There was honey in her slow-moving blood, or sap, or lava rich from a burning plain, felt in brief moments since her rejection from the Tangleroot, as though something fundamental had changed within her.

"Tell me what you mean," Sally said, though she already knew the truth.

The gardener held her gaze. "Magic. Something your mother possessed in greater strength than anyone believed."

Sally looked away, remembering her vision of two little girls facing the queen of the Tangleroot. Seeing herself, for a moment, in that same place—but holding hands with a strong young man.

Some days later, Sally was declared fit enough to walk, though the king refused to hear of it. He had a chair fashioned, and made his men carry the princess to her favorite oak by the pond, where she was placed gently upon some blankets that had been arranged neatly for her. Wine and pastries were in a basket, along with pillows that the gardener stuffed behind her back. It was a warm afternoon, and the frogs were singing. Sally asked to be left alone.

And when finally, after an interminable time, everyone did leave her— she tapped the oak on its root. "I know you're in there."

There was no wind, but the leaves seemed to shiver. Sally felt a pulse between her hand and the root. And then soft fingers grazed her brow. She closed her eyes.

"What happened in that place?" Sally whispered. "What happened, really?"

I think you know.

She could still feel those hands on her body, carrying her from the forest.

"Her strength is limited only by belief."

You wear a key, whispered the little girl. *Or so the queen believes. But there is no such thing. No key. Just lies. What binds the queen is only in her mind, and the greatest trick of all. The witches who bound her used magic . . . but only enough to convince her that she had been caught. The queen gave up.*

Sally opened her eyes, but saw only green leaves and the dark water of the pond. When the frogs sang, however, she imagined words in their voices, words she almost understood. "You mean that she could be free if she wanted to be?"

If she believed that she was. When she is denied her freedom, as you denied her, she gives up again. And so binds herself tighter to the lie. There is a duty to confront the queen, once a generation. To strengthen the bonds that hold her. You fulfilled that duty as the women of your line must.

"What of them?" Sally whispered. "Those souls imprisoned in the Tangleroot?"

Time answers all things, said the little girl. *They are tragic creatures, as are all who become imprisoned in the palace of the queen. But nothing lasts. Not even the queen. One day, perhaps a day I will see—though surely you will not—she will fall. But the Tangleroot will outlast her. She has dreamed too well. Magic has bled into the bones of that forest, into the earth it grows from. Magic that is almost beyond her.*

But not beyond you, she added. *You are your mother's daughter. You are a daughter of the Tangleroot.*

Sally stared down at her hands. "Did my mother know you?"

But the little girl who was the soul of the oak did not answer. Nearby, though, Sally heard a shout. Her father. Sounding desperate and angry. She tried to sit up, concerned for him, and saw the old man limping quickly down the path to the pond. She heard low cries of outrage behind him—gasps from the maids, and more low shouts.

Her father's face was pale and grim. "Salinda, I am sorry. I have been a fool, and I pray you will forgive me. When you left, when I almost lost you, I realized . . . oh, God." He stopped, his expression utterly tragic, even heartbreaking. "I will do everything . . . everything in my power to keep you safe from that man. I should not have agreed to such a foolish thing, but I was desperate, I was—"

Sally held up her hand, swallowing hard. "The Warlord's envoy is here?"

"The Warlord himself," hissed the old king, rubbing his face. "I looked into his eyes and could not imagine what I was thinking. But your mother . . . your mother before she died spoke so fondly of her friend and her son, and I thought . . . I was certain all would be right. It was her idea that the two of you should meet one day. Her idea. She could not have known what he would become."

Sally held herself very still. "I would like to meet him."

"Salinda—"

"Please," she said. "Alone, if you would."

Her father stared at her as though she had lost her mind—and perhaps she had—but she heard footsteps along the stone path, and her vision blurred around a man wrapped in darkness, flanked by a giant and a bear. Sally covered her mouth.

The old king stepped in front of the Warlord and held out his hand. "Now, you listen—"

"Father," Sally interrupted firmly. "Let him pass. I'm sure you don't want to test those homicidal tendencies that the man is known for. What is he called again? Warlord of Death's Door? Or maybe that was Death's Donkey."

"Close enough," rumbled the Warlord, a glint in his eye as the old king turned to give his daughter a sharp, startled look. "Your Majesty, I believe I have an appointment with young Salinda. I will not be denied."

"You," began the king, and then glanced at Sally's face and closed his mouth. Suspicion flickered in his gaze, and he gave the Warlord a sharp look. "If you hurt her, I will kill you. No matter your reputation."

"I assure you," replied the Warlord calmly, "my reputation is not nearly as fierce as a father's rage."

The old king blinked. "Well, then."

"Yes," said the Warlord.

"Father," replied Sally, twitching. "Please."

She felt sorry for him. He looked so baffled. He had tried to marry her off to the man, and now he wanted to save her. Except, Sally no longer wanted to be saved. Or rather, she was certain she could save herself, quite well on her own.

The old king limped away, escorted by the bear and giant, both of whom waved cheerily and blew kisses once his back was turned. Sally waved back, but half-heartedly. Her attention was on the man in front of her, who dropped to his knees the moment they were gone, and laid his large, strong hand upon her ankle.

"Sally," he said.

"Mickel," she replied, unable to hide the smile that was burning through her throat and eyes. "I thought you might be dead."

He laughed, but his own eyes were suddenly too bright, and he folded himself down to press his lips, and then the side of his face, upon her hand. A shudder raced through him, and she leaned over as well, kissing his cheek, his hair, his ear; spilling a tear or two before she wiped at her eyes.

"You're not surprised," he said.

"The pendant." Sally fingered the chain around his neck with a great deal of tenderness and wonderment. "I had time to think about it, though I wasn't sure until I saw you just now. I couldn't believe. Why? Why the illusions?"

He rolled over with a sigh, resting his head in her lap. "When people hear there is a warlord passing through, they tend to get rather defensive. Pitchforks, cannons, poison in the ale—"

"They hide their daughters."

He smiled, reaching up to brush his thumb over her mouth. "That, too. But you find the most interesting people when you're a nobody."

Sally kissed his thumb. "And the names? The reputation?"

Mickel closed his eyes. "My people are decent fighters. Really very good. You couldn't find better archers or horsemen anywhere. But that doesn't mean we want to fight, or should have to. So we lie when we can. Dress men and women in rabbit's blood and torn clothes, and then send them off into the night blubbering senselessly about this magnificent warlord who rode in on a fire-breathing black steed and set about ravaging, pillaging, murdering, and so forth, until everyone is so worked up and piddling themselves that all it takes to win the battle is the distant beating of some drums, and the bloodcurdling cries of my barbarian horde."

He opened his eyes. "You should hear Rumble scream. It gives me nightmares."

"That can't work all the time."

"But it works enough. Enough for peace." Mickel hesitated, giving her an uncertain look. "You ran from the man you thought I was. You were so desperate not to marry me, you were willing to enter the Tangleroot."

"And you agreed to marry a woman sight unseen." Sally frowned. "You seem like too much a free spirit for that."

"Our mothers were best friends. Growing up, all I ever heard about was Melisande and how brave she was, how good, how kind. How, when there was trouble, she was always the fighter, protecting my mother. And vice versa." He reached beneath his leather armor and pulled out a pendant that was an exact mirror of her own. "I never knew. I never imagined. She was devastated when she learned of Melisande's death. I think it hastened her own."

"I'm sorry," Sally said.

He tilted his shoulder in a faint shrug. "She told me that Melisande had borne a daughter, and that one day . . . one day she would like for us to meet. And so when your father advertised the fact that he was looking for a husband for his daughter—"

"Advertised," she interrupted.

"Oh, yes. Far and wide. Princess. Beautiful. Nubile. Available to big, strong man, with even bigger sword." Mickel thumped his chest. "I was intrigued. I was mortified. I thought I would save the daughter of my mother's best friend from a fate worse than death."

"And if I had been a loud-mouthed harridan with a taste for garlic and a fear of bathing?"

"I would have been the Warlord everyone thinks I am, tossed her aside like a sack of potatoes in a white wedding dress, and asked for the hand of a peculiar redheaded woman I met on the road."

Sally smiled. "And if she said no?"

"Well," Mickel said, kissing her hand. "I may not be the Warlord of the Savage Bellyache, but I am exceptionally brave. I would fight for her. I would battle magic forests and sleeping queens for her. I would plunge into icy waters—"

"—and be rescued by her?"

"Oh, yes," he whispered, no longer smiling. "I would love to be rescued by such a fair and lovely lady. Every day, every morning, every moment of my life."

Sally's breath caught, and Mickel touched the back of her neck and pulled her close. "You, Princess, are far more dangerous than any Warlord of Raven's Teeth, or Ravisher of Dandelions." Again, uncertainty filled his eyes. "But do you still want me, knowing all this?"

"I never wanted a warlord," Sally said. "But you . . . I think you'll do just fine. If you don't mind having a witch as your bride."

238

"Queen Magic and Warlord Illusion," he whispered, and leaned in to kiss her.

Sally placed her hand over his mouth. "But I want another name."

Mickel blinked. "Another?"

She removed her hand and grinned against his mouth. "Well, the Warlord must have a wife who is equal to his charms, yes?"

Mickel laughed quietly. "And what will I call you? War Lady? My Princess of Pain?"

"Just call me yours," she whispered. "The rest will take care of itself."

And it did.

Never After was the name of the anthology, and we were charged with telling stories about "fairy-tale weddings"—but from a feminist standpoint. Well, I don't know anything about weddings, but I sure could imagine escaping from one.

This also happens to be the third story in a row (seriously, I looked at the dates) where I was writing about magical forests with terrible, powerful secrets sleeping within. I don't know what was working through my unconscious during that time, but you, reader, are bearing witness to an imagination that was haunted by the spirits of trees.

MARJORIE LIU is an attorney and *New York Times* bestselling novelist and comic book writer. Her work at Marvel includes *X-23*, *Black Widow*, *Han Solo*, *Dark Wolverine*, and *Astonishing X-Men*, for which she was nominated for a GLAAD Media Award for outstanding media images of the LGBTQ community. She is also the co-creator of *Monstress* from Image Comics, which has won multiple Hugo Awards, British Fantasy Awards, the Harvey Award, and five Eisner Awards, making Liu the first-ever woman (and woman of color) to win an Eisner in the Best Writer category.

Liu has written more than seventeen novels, including both the award-nominated Dirk & Steele paranormal romance and Hunter Kiss urban fantasy series. Liu has also appeared on MSNBC, CNN, and MTV, and has been profiled on *NPR*'s All Things Considered, *The New Yorker Radio Hour*, *The Atlantic*, and *The Hollywood Reporter*. She teaches a course on comic book writing at MIT.